# Tales from the Magitech Lounge

*Saje Williams*

A Samhain Publishing, Ltd. publication.

Samhain Publishing, Ltd.
577 Mulberry Street, Suite 1520
Macon, GA 31201
www.samhainpublishing.com

Tales from the Magitech Lounge
Copyright © 2008 by Saje Williams
Print ISBN: 1-59998-749-X
Digital ISBN: 1-59998-467-9

Editing by Sarah Palmero
Cover by Dawn Seewer

First Samhain Publishing, Ltd. electronic publication: May 2007
First Samhain Publishing, Ltd. print publication: March 2008

# Dedication

To those who have meant the most to me, and given me the most support through all my adventures. Shay, Charlie, Kevin, the Best Dave, The Glennertainment Center, and to so many others who've made an impression on who I am and the words I craft.

This one is for everyone.

# Act I

# The Future

# Episode I:
# A Woman Walks into a Bar...

Call me Jack. Most people do.

I started out as a time traveler, but I had to give it up. Not only is it illegal, but it's dangerous to the continuum. One cannot go around creating new universes willy-nilly, and that's the most probable result of time travel.

I became a time traveler completely by accident, stumbling across what I assumed to be a unique device while exploring some ancient ruins in South America. The device had apparently been left there by another time traveler, whom, I'm sure, wasn't thrilled when I accidentally hijacked it.

Unlike many such devices, this particular gadget, which looked a lot like a small pyramid crafted out of blue glass, could cross both time and space with equal efficiency. It dumped me in the American West in the year 1884.

That was the first of many stops and it's possible I'll share them with you at a later date. But this particular story is not so much about my travels as it is about how my travels ended, and how I ended up where I am today.

The year is 2260. The place, San Francisco, California, in the former United States. The exact locale is on Haight Street, less than three blocks from the legendary Golden Gate Park.

I'm probably lucky to be alive, considering that no one told me that time travel was illegal until I ran into a group who took it upon themselves to police the activity. I'd skipped back to a time just around the second year BC in an attempt to meet Jesus Christ.

Apparently that's not an uncommon thing for time travelers to do, so this aforementioned agency keeps a monitor in place to watch for our arrival. I was snatched off the dusty road within minutes of setting out to find the guy.

Two people seemed to pop out of nowhere, each grasping one of my arms, and frog-marched me into an alley between two mud huts. One, a remarkably tall fellow (he must've been seven feet if he was an inch), shoved me against a wall as the other, a short, elfin-faced woman, went through my pockets and frisked me in a so professional a manner that I didn't even consider making a lewd comment about it. That should tell you how freaked out I was.

"He's clean," she said finally, glancing up at her companion. "Where's your time machine?" she asked me.

Shocked to my core, I saw no option but to answer honestly. I'd been running around in the thing for nearly a year by this time and hadn't ever run across anyone like these two. I had the feeling that if I jerked them around, I'd live to regret it.

"You take care of him, I'll go get the machine," the woman told her partner.

The big guy nodded.

"What's all this about?" I asked him as the woman dashed away.

"It's about you being in big trouble," he told me soberly. "Time travel is illegal, dangerous, and really, really stupid."

"Okay," I said. "When was it made illegal?"

This took him by surprise and he gave me an odd look. I noticed then that the whites of his eyes were literally silver in color, the iris an extremely pale green. I couldn't quite tell, but there was something weird about the pupil as well.

He never did answer me, but I found out on my own later. Time travel was made illegal in 2236, years before I ever found my time machine. I'd been breaking the law the whole time and had no idea.

Yeah, I know. Ignorance is no excuse. I have discovered, however, that stupidity makes a *great* excuse. Sometimes.

As it turned out, he was a lycanthrope. A were-tiger, to be exact. He and the elfin woman, who was indeed an elf, were agents of an agency called Hex which had taken over monitoring time travel from another agency known as TAU.

None of this was known to me at the time, nor would it have mattered. I'd rarely been as scared as I was at this precise moment. Not even when I'd been hunted by a posse in the old west for a train robbery I hadn't had anything to do with. All I needed to do then was make it back to my machine and escape—which was apparently no longer an option.

I wasn't sure what the punishment would be for unauthorized time travel, or who'd decide my fate.

As it turned out, I had very little to worry about. Hex's first mission was to eliminate the time machine and return me to my own time. Rather than facing punishment, I discovered that my adventures had impressed someone important, namely the legendary Jasmine Tashae.

Now keep in mind that the people of my time *know* about other universes, and are at least aware of rumors surrounding the interworld agencies. Not much, I'll admit. And most of us don't spend time thinking about it. The "monsters" that appeared just before the Cen War back in the early part of the twenty-first had pretty much been acclimated into our society. Vampires, lycanthropes, mages, and the various kinds of "supers" had become part of the landscape. Jasmine Tashae— known by most only as "Jaz", or, alternately, "The Lady of Blades",—had been a major player in that war. Her name was in the history books along with such luminaries as Deryk Shea, Nemesis Breed, and the vampire Raven.

After the Cen War, most of the old national boundaries dissolved, or new unions were formed. This precluded the eventual formation of a single world government, but not before the most intractable were assisted off the planet. They went on to colonize other star systems. Some had wanted to escape through the worldgates into other universes, but the newly formed interworld agencies didn't want malcontents from Earth Prime flooding the metaverse. They made it abundantly clear they were willing to back up that preference with force, if need be. So with the help of Deryk Shea, now the richest man on Earth, a fleet of colony ships was constructed and launched into space, aiming for potential homelands spread out amongst the stars.

I'll admit it. Earth is a strange place these days. But it's still my home. I didn't flee through time to escape this world, but to discover new ones. And discover them I did.

My rather unique method of self-education caught the interest of the near-mythical Jaz, and she approached me with an astounding offer. In the place the interworld agencies call home, on Starhaven, there exists a watering hole called the Magitech Lounge, known as a refuge for all manner of sentient beings.

As Jaz told me, Earth could use a place like that. Even with all the preternaturals, parahumans and metahumans here, it's still a melting pot that hasn't been stirred real well. Normal folk are fascinated by the strange and unusual, but they're also still afraid of it and no amount of book learning will change that. They needed something a little more...immediate.

I took her offer. It wasn't as though I had anything better to do.

Earth's Magitech Lounge is in an old converted warehouse half a block off Haight Street in San Francisco, above which we set aside a few rooms for rent and my own living quarters and office.

San Francisco, as you can imagine, has become quite the Mecca for the preternatural and paranormal. Not as much as Tacoma, which is where it all began, but San Fran always did have an open-door policy for society's misfits.

*June 18th, 2267*

*San Francisco*

*Another Earth*

The doors opened at noon and even then there was a line forming. I stood just inside, staring out through the one-way glass that forms one side of the entry-way. That gives me the option of excluding anyone I think might end up being a bigger problem than my security staff can handle.

On a positive note, most of those in line seemed pretty normal today. Ordinary humans mixed in with possible paras and metas. It's hard to recognize some of them on sight.

Mostly tourists, I figured, which definitely wasn't a bad thing. The night before we'd had a rather rough customer—a visiting troll—try to start a fight with one of our vampire patrons. I was looking forward to an easier time of it tonight.

I should have known better. Peace and quiet will never be my lot in life.

It was the three-hundredth anniversary of the Summer of Love here in the Bay City, and that fact alone had drawn the tourists in droves from the far reaches of the galaxy. Not sure why anyone even cared, but there was something about the old counter-culture and its mystique that touched a chord deep within far too many people.

I'd been there—the original Summer of Love, that is—and I knew full well it wasn't quite all peace, love and cosmic hippy shit. The 1960s had been a turbulent time, and the historians never really did it justice. They liked to emphasize the good stuff and ignore the rough edges.

Of course, that's pretty much what historians have always done.

This meant, of course, that there were an awful lot of tie-dyed shirts in the crowd, with a lot of long hair, flowers and John Lennon glasses. Everyone wanted to be a Beatle, it seemed. I made a mental note to make sure there were a lot of Beatles tunes on the rotation tonight.

I spotted someone at the back of the line and found myself scowling. "Boneyard?" I murmured into the transceiver implanted in my jawbone.

"Yeah, boss?" his deep bass voice rumbled back.

Boneyard was my head of security, a six-foot-eight were-panther with skin as black as pitch and a huge, bullet-shaped head. Despite his fearsome appearance and name, Bone was the very soul of discretion and temperance. When you're a six-foot-eight were-panther, you can afford to be. "See that blonde woman at the back of the line? The one with the mirrored sunglasses perched on top of her head? Don't let her in."

"Okay, boss." I caught a note of curiosity in his voice, but he was too much of a professional to ask.

Bone is from New Orleans, originally, but left before the rising sea claimed that once proud city. Global warming was a reality and, while mages and scientists were working feverishly to reverse its effects, the long-term consequences of ignoring it had become sickeningly apparent, and far too many people paid the price for their folly. Half of Golden Gate Park was now underwater. Quick action on the part of San Francisco's mage community had saved the rest.

Thankfully the mages were also able to rescue most of those who would have died as a result of global flooding, but a lot of people lost everything they owned, and were displaced not only around the globe, but even out to some of Earth's colonies. Whole islands ceased to exist as livable space. Suffice it to say the only way to get a Caribbean vacation these days is to do it the way I did.

Good luck with that.

I sighed. One of the problems with being a former time traveler is that it changes one's whole image of the world. I had more of a personal connection to history than most folks. Sometimes I found it distracting as hell.

I nodded welcomingly to the patrons as they filed through the door, greeting each with a smile. They seemed an ordinary mix of folks, probably tourists interested in checking out the newest hotspot in San Francisco with nothing else in mind, but my suspicion had gone into overdrive when I'd spotted Lilith at the back of the crowd.

She hadn't changed all that much from high school, and I couldn't help but wonder what she was doing here. Had she heard I ran this place, or was it just a coincidence? I don't trust coincidence. Particularly wise of me, I think.

Sure, she was the woman who'd yanked out my heart and danced on it back then, but why was I expecting trouble from her now? We were both twelve years older and, presumably, much, much wiser. Well, at least *I* was.

She'd made it to the front of the line, I noticed, and she was arguing with Bone. She didn't look happy, and the big were-panther took her venom with his usual stoic indifference. Insults bounce off him as easily as bullets, which is why he makes a great security chief.

She'd always had a particularly sharp tongue, and less of a tendency to curb it than most folks. She had been accustomed to getting her way. She'd been the captain of the soccer team and the Queen of the May at our prom, as well as student body president our senior year. Lack of ambition had never been one of her faults.

I had to admit that she still looked as good as ever. I'd long harbored suspicions that she was a parahuman, but, if she was, she didn't broadcast it. She hadn't pulled anything obvious on the field, and hadn't beaten up the local bullies with anything approaching regularity, but somehow I knew there was much more to her than met the eye.

Now, of course, was my opportunity to discover more. Or so I told myself. In all actuality, the sight of her standing there, her long, wavy strawberry blonde hair stirring in the breeze, her jaw tensed and her pale blue eyes flashing, hit me below the belt. I felt the stirrings of feelings I hadn't allowed myself since the day she'd thrown my promise ring in the dirt at my feet and damn near broke my jaw with a wicked left hook that came out of nowhere.

I glanced over my shoulder at the painted portrait hanging in the foyer, a unique little piece I'd happened to stumble on while touring New York not long after I got out of high school. The long, lanky fellow stared back at me, a wry grin across his face, and I reminded myself of what I'd had in mind when I took the job here. WWSD. What-Would-Spider-Do?

I knew the answer without asking. He'd be a bigger man and invite her inside. It didn't do any good to offer every other weird denizen of San Francisco and beyond a safe haven if one kept someone else out because of petty personal differences that should have been swallowed by the intervening years.

I sighed again. "It's okay, Bone. Let her in."

"All right, boss. Whatever you say."

Lilith entered and almost missed me, standing as I was under the Spider Robinson portrait in the dark hole next to the ramp leading onto the main floor. She's always been pretty sharp-eyed, so, as soon as her eyes adjusted to the gloom, she swiveled around and pinned me with her gaze.

She drew up short. "Jack?"

I nodded, lips twisting into a half smile. "Yeah. How are you doing, Lilith?"

"Buy me a drink and I'll tell you about it," she said, returning my half-hearted smile with a giga-watt grin. "I was hoping I'd run into you here. You the one who told the bruiser outside to keep me out?"

I nodded sheepishly. "I'm afraid I wasn't feeling particularly welcoming when I saw you standing out there."

"What changed?" she asked, as I led her up the ramp and out onto the upper level. I took a sharp right, cut past the dance floor, and pressed my hand to the reader plate next to the VIP lounge. The door slid open and I ushered her inside. "Lights, fifty percent."

The lights came on obligingly, revealing a couple of low-slung chairs against one wall, separated by a small table just the right size for a couple of drinks. A long couch filled another wall, and a self-serve bar took up the one remaining. "Have a seat," I told her, walking over to the bar. "What's your poison?"

"Mai-Tai," she said, slipping into the chair and crossing her legs. She was wearing a pair of beige Capri pants and a loose-fitting white peasant top that bared the very tops of her creamy white breasts. I resolved not to spend any more time staring at them than I absolutely had to.

I yanked my eyes away and concentrated on mixing the drinks. A Mai-Tai for her, a Kung Fu Monkey for me. I carried them over to the table and set them down gently before sliding into the chair beside her. "It's good to see you," I said and, to my surprise, I actually meant it.

To her surprise too, it seemed. She gave me an odd look and a smile just short of a smirk. "I'm glad to hear that, Jack. You have no idea how glad."

I really didn't like the sound of that. I returned her look through suddenly narrowed eyes. "What does *that* mean?"

"I'm in trouble."

"No, really?" I grunted irritably. "What kind of trouble?"

"I've pissed off some dangerous people and needed somewhere safe to hide."

"So you came *here?*"

"The Magitech Lounge has a reputation for being a sanctuary. I thought I'd test that out."

"So this has nothing to do with me, does it?" I felt like a complete idiot for hoping, even at the deepest level, that something would be different this time around. Apparently with all my hopping through time, I didn't gain any damned sense when it came to women.

"The fact that I heard you were running the place had something to do with it, sure."

"Lilith, if you don't tell me the whole story, I'm going have you thrown out so fast you'll bounce half a block down the street."

"You've turned hard, Jack."

If only. I smiled grimly and leaned back in the chair. "Start talking."

She took a long sip from her Mai-Tai and grimaced. "A little strong, don't you think?"

"No," I replied tersely, giving her my best evil eye. Not that it does anything but evoke amusement in most people. I'm pretty sure that no one considers me scary.

She sighed. "Fine. You know about the Conclave, right?"

"No," I said sarcastically, "I've been living under a rock." The Conclave was the vampire union—a way for that particular preternatural type to lobby the Confed government as a bloc rather than as individuals. The inception of the Conclave went back to before the Cen War, and had probably prevented untold amounts of bloodshed. "Don't tell me you pissed off the Conclave."

She shook her head. "I didn't. I pissed off the clans."

I goggled at that. The Conclave was a democratic group, while the clans were arranged in a pseudo-feudal system, each clan gaining a foothold and owing allegiance to the strongest among them in any given city. Most of the violence that arose from the vampire culture came from the clans, and no one in their right mind would do anything to offend them unless they had someone very powerful to back them up. Like the Confed Adjuster himself hiding in their back pocket. For example.

I smiled at her, feeling a little sick to my stomach. "How in the hell did you manage that?"

"You don't pay a lot of attention to the news, do you?"

I shrugged. "Most of the corporate services are full of shit," I told her. "Been like that since before the Cen War."

She didn't like that, but she let it pass. "I have a column in the *West Coast Alliance-Herald.* We're a real service—we actually pay our own journalists to collect the news, unlike most of the wire outfits these days. One of our street reporters ran into something of a hassle with the Master of Portland last week and damn near got himself killed. So I wrote an editorial on the whole clan system. I'm afraid I was a little harsh."

I closed my eyes and groaned aloud. She'd always been a talented writer. When she pointed her pen at someone in particular, they obligingly caught fire. I could only imagine what she'd chosen to write in this case. "And now they're after you?"

"I think so. I received a call this morning, right after my column hit the stands. The voice on the other end of the transmission wasn't normal. It resonated weirdly. You know what vampire voices sound like. He told me that I'd better watch my back or I'd end up *wishing* I were dead."

That didn't sound too bad to me, and I told her as much. She gave me a look like I had a mound of gravel instead of a brain rattling around inside my skull.

"What can *you* think of that's worse than death, Jack? How about being turned into a vamp and made a blood-slave to a clan master?"

I shuddered. She was right. That was a pretty damn scary notion. "Writing that editorial was a damn silly thing to do, but I understand why you did it. C'mon. We need to figure out what kind of backup we can drum up for you here."

"You surprise me, Jack. I figured you'd just throw me out anyway."

"Why? You didn't do anything wrong, Lilith. A bit stupid, maybe, but I wouldn't say it was wrong."

"Gee, thanks." She picked up her drink again and climbed to her feet. "So...you plan to announce my problem to all those *tourists* out there?"

I shook my head. "Nope. We're going to tell my security crew and wait for the tourists to clear out this evening. Then I'm going to tell my regulars. And, yes, we have regulars. When they get here the tourists will make themselves scarce. The average Joe and Jill can only stand so much rubbing elbows with the terminally weird."

She chuckled at that, a deep throaty sound that made my stomach clench. I'd missed that laugh more than I'd realized.

I led her out into the common room and motioned for Kevin to join us. He gave me a quick nod, said something to the pretty young lady he was schmoozing and trotted across the dance floor toward us.

Kevin's so pale his skin is almost translucent. A lot of people mistake him for a vampire at first. He's a lithe, almost androgynous being with dark eyes that contrast completely with his colorless complexion and the shock of blonde hair perched upon his skull.

Kevin's a mage, and a pretty good one by all reports. He's also a powerful empath and one of the nicest people I've ever known. He's got a good word for everyone, and just his presence tends to defuse tense situations. He's in his early twenties and rumor has it he was one of those amazing prodigies who graduated from high school when he was thirteen and, allegedly, completed medical school by the age of twenty. I seriously doubted that last part. What would a doctor be doing working security in a club, even one as unique as the Magitech Lounge? I thought it very unlikely.

"What's up, boss?"

I resisted the urge to roll my eyes. Bone had started that nonsense and it had taken off as if wearing rocket skates. Being called "boss" made me feel like a mobster. Bugged the crap out of me.

Kevin knew it too. He didn't miss much. He did it just to be a pain. "Kevin, this is Lilith. She's in trouble with the clans and I'm offering her sanctuary."

"Lilith? You're the one that writes that column in the *West Coaster?*"

She beamed at him, plainly pleased that he recognized her. "That's me."

"Wow. I was just thinking this morning that you were either stupid or incredibly brave." He paused a moment. "Now that I've met you, I'm leaning more toward brave."

She wasn't quite sure how to take that. Or so I imagined by the expression on her face. Which, I assumed, had been his intent.

Did I mention that Kevin has a quirky sense of humor? "Do we have any clan members in our regular crowd?" I asked him.

He thought about it, then shook his head. "I don't think so. We've got a few Conclavers, but the clans have their own clubs. They wouldn't be comfortable with all the warm fuzzies here at the Lounge."

I grinned at that. He had a point. The clan vamps thrived on the dark and forbidding aura they carried with them like the stench of the grave. Most sentient folk preferred the company of Conclave vamps, with good reason. They tended to be decent people who just happened to be dead.

"You hungry?" I asked Lilith.

"Famished," she replied. "I haven't been able to eat since I got that call."

"What would you like?"

She shrugged. "I don't care. Food."

I laughed. "Fine. I take it you're not allergic to anything?"

"Nope. What kind of menu do you have here?"

"Pretty eclectic," I answered. "Kevin—do me a favor and let the rest of the crew know we might have some problems later. It's a good bet that the clans will be able to track her here."

He nodded. "Not a problem, boss." He smiled at Lilith. "Pleasure to meet you."

"Same here," she replied, sounding sincere enough. I walked her through the tables and to the bar, where I leaned across and told Jeremy, the day bartender, to have Fisk, our cook, make up a couple of burger baskets when he had the chance.

When night fell, Lilith was upstairs in my suite getting cleaned up. I'd managed to convince her to take a nap.

I'd come down in time to watch the exodus of the day crowd when my freaks began to arrive. As usual, the first of them was Hydra, a massive gray-skinned troll who can barely fit through the door. One look at him as he trundled up the ramp sent most of the day-timers fumbling for their jackets and racing for the exit. The ramp creaked warningly as he shambled up its length.

I wanted to laugh but didn't dare. Hydra looked like an unholy cross between an elephant and a human being, but he was a gentle giant if there ever was one. I'd seen him go out of his way to rescue one of our giant wharf rats from a feral cat. The rat, panicked beyond reason, had tried to bite him, but Hydra's skin was too thick for its teeth to pierce. He'd gently reached up and placed it on the roof of a nearby building. It would hurt his feelings if I laughed, so I didn't. Even though I would have been laughing at the stampede of folks *leaving* the place, I was afraid he'd take it wrong. I wouldn't hurt Hydra's feelings for anything in the world.

Behind Hydra came Hammad, a bearded Muslim street busker who carried his guitar everywhere he went. On Tuesday nights he plays a couple sets for the crowd and always refuses payment. "I play all day for people who aren't really interested. I'm not going to charge my friends," he said once. Though he'd never confirmed it, I had a suspicion Hammad was also a mage.

A few minutes later the door opened and Steph entered, walking up the ramp so smoothly it looked as if she were floating. Steph's a vampire and she plays the neo-goth to the hilt. Everything on her is black, including hair and lipstick, and she wears enough eyeliner to be mistaken for a slumming Egyptian queen. Kevin's got a thing for her but she pretends not to notice. I haven't stuck my nose into it because, for one, it's none of my business, and for another, they seem to be good friends. Sometimes that works out, sometimes it doesn't. For the two of them, it seemed to work just fine.

Steph's a Conclave vamp, and something gives me the impression she's pretty high up in their hierarchy, though she's never quite come out and said as much. I was hoping she'd show up that night. She's a regular, but not nearly as regular as Hydra or Hammad.

Some time later Seth strolled in, dressed as usual in a five hundred cred silk suit. The man's a clotheshorse and just about as vain as they come. I have to admit he has reason to be. The man has the looks and bearing of a movie star and, despite being entirely too concerned about his appearance, he's a lot of fun to be around. He's witty, urbane, and unfailingly polite, even when he's annoyed by something. In fact, he's even *more* polite when annoyed.

I was one of the few people who knew he was a meta, though how all of the others avoided making the connection between our buddy Seth and the super who calls himself "Captain Glorious", I'll never know. The first time I saw him on the view—what those in other universes might call a television, if I remember right—with his sparkling silver suit and neatly pressed cape flapping in the breeze as he tried to talk a jumper down from the Golden Gate Bridge, I just *knew* it was Seth.

I'm still a bit shaky on what his meta power is, since I'm pretty sure he uses magical devices to fly and enhance his strength. At least that's what Kevin said about Captain Glorious, and I have no reason to doubt his word on the subject. He would know, after all.

And I'd forgotten that it was the third Thursday of the month. For some reason that particular day brought in a couple of our most unusual patrons—the retired rock god Stormchild and his paramour, the dark and mysterious lady vampire, Rio. They'd been coming in since the first day we opened, which just happened to be a third Thursday.

After Stormchild and his lady love came the Twining Twins. They're not really twins, we just call them that. They're actually the same person from two different universes who happened to meet up and form a business partnership. They have a kind of telepathy with one another and it can get downright creepy at times.

It wasn't a full crowd, but by ten it was pretty clear that no one else was going to show. So I climbed up on the stage, grabbed the mic we occasionally used for karaoke, and gave everyone the rundown on Lilith's problem.

"Do you think she's really in danger?" Seth asked, visibly puffing up just a little. I could almost read his mind—he was imagining riding to the rescue as Captain Glorious in his sparkling clean, and exquisitely tailored, superhero gear. The big goofball.

"Why doesn't she just go to the Adjuster's Office?" rumbled Hydra.

"Because that would spark a war," Lilith replied, from the landing at the top of the first flight of stairs. "Deryk Shea would *love* to take on the clans, but we all know how bad that could get."

"You know how the clans came to be, don't you?" Rio said suddenly, surprising everyone. Rio wasn't the most talkative of our regulars. In fact, I'm not sure when last I actually heard her address the group. Or if she ever had. Nice lady, but quiet.

She continued after a pregnant pause. "A vampire named Jason Keening talked a powerful wizard into crafting a spell to throw him back in time, to a point long before his kind existed. This, of course, spawned a whole new universe, and he began creating his own minions to spread through the human population. His goal was to recreate the background of some stupid role-playing-game he and his friends played as teenagers, where vampires lived in the shadows of the human world, ruled by powerful feudal lords and a covenant of secrecy.

"He succeeded there, but that wasn't enough for him. One of the founders of the Conclave was his mother, who'd also been turned, and he wanted revenge on her and the other vamps who supported her as well.

"It took them a while to manage it, but they found a way to jump between the universes. This small contingent of those vamps who didn't want to join the conclave has since become a force to reckon with. They don't want to live in peace with mortals—they want to dominate them like they do on their own world."

That was a bit of history I *didn't* know. "So do you have *all* the clans pissed off at you, or just the ones in Portland?"

Lilith shook her head. "I have no idea. The voice wasn't exactly specific about that."

"So what are the chances we'll have to deal with this Keening character?" Bone asked Rio.

She shrugged. "I don't know if he's even here on this Earth. He's under a sentence of death—there are any number of people who'd love to get their hands on him. He's probably terribly powerful now though, which means your average bounty hunter or Adjuster's agent wouldn't stand a chance."

I didn't like the slow grin that crawled across the were-panther's face. "What kind of reward are we talking here?"

"Last I heard it was up to five million creds."

Stormchild glanced at her, an unreadable expression on his countenance. Maybe he was wondering why *she'd* never tried to collect the reward. Legend had it that she was considerably more powerful than most vamps herself. I'd be willing to bet she'd be able to give Keening a run for his money.

Then again it was certainly possible I was reading him wrong. Stormchild was an immortal, and could be as inscrutable as they come. When you've been around for over twenty-five thousand years, ordinary human motivations don't make a lot of sense to you anymore.

Or so I would imagine. I'll probably never know for sure.


At about midnight I heard a cry from outside and tensed. I glanced at Kevin, who'd taken up a position near the bar. He nodded at me, squinted for a moment, then held up five fingers. He made a motion and Bone materialized in our midst, looking a little disheveled, but none the worse for wear. He did, however, look angry. "What the hell did you do that for?" he spat at Kevin. "I was thumping some vamps and doing a damn good job at it until—"

"I told him to," I interrupted. "You're not going to fight these guys alone, Boneyard. Not if I have anything to say about it."

He nodded; a little sullenly, I thought.

The door exploded inward and a handful of vampires floated in. Not literally, but that's what it looked like. I scowled and gave them my best laser glare. "It wasn't locked," I told them. "I hope someone plans on paying for that."

Their leader, a golden-skinned fellow with hip-long dreadlocks and eyes like pits of fire, met my gaze squarely and smiled grimly. "Where's the bitch?"

"If you're looking for a female dog," said Rio icily, "I suggest you visit the Humane Society."

He ignored her, which I didn't think was particularly wise.

About then I spotted Seth creeping up the stairs to my suite and suppressed a grin. Captain Glorious was about to make an appearance. He'd probably leave via my window and come in through the front door behind the vamps. I gave him even odds on getting past Lilith without being noticed.

Dreadlocks took a single step onto the ramp and Stormchild stepped forward. "I wouldn't suggest coming any farther," he drawled, lightning crackling between his outstretched fingers. "It might not kill you, but it ain't gonna feel too good either."

The vamp leader froze in place. "Who the hell are you?" he asked in a snarl.

The immortal smiled. "Some people call me Thor...but my name is Stormchild."

For a brief second, the dark-skinned vamp actually looked like one. He visibly blanched. You didn't move up in the preternatural community if you didn't know who the immortals were. Storm was one of the big bads, and this vamp knew it all too well. "You can't back us off," he hissed. "She deserves to pay for what she said."

"Or get paid for it," I heard Kevin mutter. "Hey, asshole! Haven't you ever heard of freedom of the press?"

It was pretty clear that these were just lackeys—either ordered to make an example of Lilith, or taking it upon themselves to do so. They'd be a threat to her if she were alone, but they weren't going to gain any ground against the Lounge regulars.

And something told me they knew it. Hydra ambled forward, cracking his massive knuckles. "You guys *sure* you wanna brawl?" he asked. "I've been itchin' for a fight."

They all gave him the once-over and winced. Tangling with the gray-skinned troll would be a lot like going toe-to-toe with a bulldozer. They'd be faster, but one good hit on his part would be enough to crush a skull. And damage to the brain or spinal column was a vamp's one weakness. Other than sunlight, of course.

We all jumped when another human figure came flying through the door, bowling over a couple of the vamps who were taken by surprise, and landing in a heap on the ramp. Shining like a thousand-watt halogen lamp, Captain Glorious stepped across the threshold, expression hidden behind the full face mask he wore.

I bet he just *hates* having to cover his face.

"Found this creep lurking outside," the superhero announced loudly. "I think he's in charge of these losers."

The vamp in question slowly rose, glaring back down at Captain Glorious, nearly quivering with suppressed rage. "I wouldn't," Glorious warned him. "That wasn't even my *best* punch."

"I can't get over how familiar that Captain Glorious guy seems," Kevin murmured in my ear. I nodded distractedly. Things were about to get very interesting. I didn't know who this last vampire was, but I had a feeling he was considerably more powerful than the minions we'd been staring at for the past few minutes.

He turned to face us and I was initially struck by his unearthly beauty. This was a very old vamp, I realized. Not Jason Keening, I thought, but possibly one of the first of his bloodline. Not a good sign. "We want the woman."

"Tough," said Rio, pushing past Stormchild and folding her arms over her breasts. "You can't have her. You have no authority here. Go crawl back under your gravestone," she growled menacingly.

Their eyes met and he frowned just slightly, barely enough to notice. Did he recognize her? Or was he just surprised to find another vampire standing up for Lilith? "We're not leaving until we get what we came for."

Stormchild groaned. "Boy, was *that* the wrong thing to say."

Shaking her head as if disgusted by the whole proceeding, Rio reached down and snatched something from the charm bracelet she wore at her wrist. She flung out her hand and suddenly three short, slightly curved swords were streaking toward the vampire lord.

He tried to dodge, his movements little more than a blur, but it took less than a second for him to realize he couldn't evade the razor death coming down on him. One sword plunged into each eye, respectively, and the third simply separated his head from the rest of him.

The head tumbled to the floor as the body crumpled. The blades reversed course and flew back to Rio. She plucked them out of the air and they subsequently vanished. "Spread the word," she told the lackeys calmly. "This woman is under *my* protection. If *anything* happens to her, I'm going to make it the whole focus of my existence to find every single clan vampire and cut you down like the rabid dogs you are. Do I make myself clear?"

They stared at her for a second, then down at their leader's body, which had already started to dissolve. Some vampires did that for some reason, especially the older ones. In less than an hour it would be a pile of ash on the floor.

Made for easy cleanup, at least.

Dreadlocks nodded thoughtfully and the others followed suit.

I couldn't see Rio's face, but something told me she was smiling, showing plenty of fang. "I'm going to count to sixty. When I'm done, any vampire within a mile of this place is going to get the same treatment *he* did," she told them. "One. Two. Three..."

They vaporized. Well, not literally. At least I don't think they did. They just moved faster than I could see, blowing by ol' Captain Glorious without even ruffling his cape.

"Think the threat will work?" I asked Rio, once they were gone.

She turned to look at me and shrugged. "It had better. It wasn't a bluff. If I have to track down and destroy Keening himself, I will. I'd suggest either keeping your lady friend around, or sending someone with her as a bodyguard for a while—at least until we know for sure if they're going to leave her be."

I chewed at my upper lip as I considered that. I wasn't sure I wanted to keep her around. She wasn't really any more trustworthy than she'd ever been, and she still did things to my hormones that left me more dazed than I liked. But I also didn't want anything to happen to her.

"Did you say bodyguard?" Glorious asked. "I'd be honored to provide protection for the lady," he said. Behind that mask I knew he was grinning at me. I think he suspected I knew his secret. It still shocked me that no one else did. He isn't exactly subtlety incarnate.

I glanced up at the landing and Lilith, who looked shaken, but determined. "I can't stay here," she said. "For a number of reasons. I accept your offer, Captain Glorious. With pleasure."

He strutted up the ramp and peered up at her through the gold orbs that formed the eyes for his mask. "We can leave any time you're ready, Milady."

"Milady?" I muttered. "Laying it on a little thick, aren't you?"

His face was, of course, unreadable as he turned to regard me. "You have your way, I have mine."

I rolled my eyes. Damned drama king. "Kevin—you want to get rid of the body for us? I'd lock the doors, but I don't think that's an option for the time being."

"I can fix the doors, boss," Bone told me. "Take me a couple hours but they'll be as good as new."

"Go to it, then. I'd like to be able to lock the place up come closing time."

"You got it."

Kevin gestured and the dead vampire disappeared. I didn't ask him what he did with the body. I wasn't sure I wanted to know.

Lilith's voice cut through the din. "Jack? I'd like a couple minutes to talk to you before I leave."

I glanced at Glorious. "Give her a few, okay?"

He saluted. Since I wasn't sure if it were meant in mockery or sincerity, I decided to ignore it. I walked up the stairs and followed Lilith back into my suite.

She stopped just inside the door and closed it behind me as I entered. I turned to her, frowning, then stumbled back into the door as she put her hand on my chest and shoved. The knob grazed my hip and sent a spear of pain down my leg. She then leaned forward and kissed me, her lips soft as they brushed against mine. "Thank you."

"For what?" I asked. "I didn't do anything. Glorious, Stormchild, and Rio did. Especially Rio," I added hastily, not wanting to give Seth any more credit than he deserved.

"You don't get it, do you? This is an amazing place and it suits you. Very few people could accomplish what you've managed here. You do know that, don't you? Those people down there stood up for me because you asked them to. You've got something very special, and what's really remarkable is that you don't even know it."

She kissed me again, pulled me away from the door, and opened it. "I'll be back, Jack. You can bet on that. Now that I've gotten to know this place, I don't think I can stay away."

She walked out the door and shut it behind her. I stayed where I was until I was sure she'd gone, then rejoined the crowd for a round of drinks on the house. They'd earned it. And more.

Lilith wrote a wonderful column about the Lounge in the next day's edition of the *West Coaster*. I didn't read it, but Kevin did. He said it was very complimentary. I was thankful for that, but found myself wishing she hadn't gone to the trouble.

In the end, Lilith didn't quite get it. The regulars didn't stand up for her because I asked them to. They did it because it needed doing. Because they care about people—freaks and normals alike—and don't like to see anyone being pushed around by those more powerful than they are.

It wasn't about me at all. It was about a bunch of people who know what's important in life. It was about my friends and *why* they're my friends.

It's about a place called the Magitech Lounge.

# Episode II:
# The Girl in the Mirror

Another wild and crazy night at the Magitech Lounge. Hydra was regaling us with his seemingly endless supply of off-color jokes and most of the regulars were trying to take swigs from their drinks between punch lines to prevent themselves from choking and spraying everyone else in the process.

"And so the dolphin says to the fisherman— 'mermaid my left fin...that's a manatee!'"

I shook my head and leaned back against one of the support columns, folding my arms over my chest as I glanced around the room. I was rather sure I'd heard that one before, but it was still pretty funny. Something caught my eye and I shot a glance at the bar mirror and froze. Someone was staring *out* of the mirror at us. At first glance it looked like just a reflection of one of the patrons, but everyone present was a regular. The kid in the mirror stood out.

She was pretty, I thought, in a pale, fragile kind of way. Her big brown eyes hinted at a great depth of sorrow and something within me tore wide open as I met her gaze. I switched to magesight and looked again, seeing nothing remarkably different than I had a moment before.

Magesight is weird. It allows us to see and manipulate the strands of mana that float through the world, long threads of silver gossamer webbing visible only to those with the right genetics to be mages in the first place, but created as a natural by-product of all sentient life.

Mana glows slightly and casts an eerie illumination as it swims through the air. This is the secret of why mages can see in the dark. We don't, actually, but it seems like we do. We just have access to illumination not available to the average person.

Other than several mana threads currently passing through the Lounge, magesight revealed nothing worthy of mention. The girl still stared out of the mirror, and the rest of the patrons still roared with laughter as Hydra delivered another punch line.

I was no longer listening.

My boss, Jack, apparently noticed my distracted air, and walked over to see if everything was all right. Jack's like that. He's the best boss one could hope for, soft-spoken and empathetic. He treats us all like family, staff and regulars alike.

Jack's a rather non-descript individual in appearance, being barely over six feet tall, with a nice but easily forgettable face. He wears his long brown hair in a ponytail, usually, and his quick hazel eyes are always on the move. This week he wore a goatee and mustache, but that could change without notice. He was prone to sudden bouts of facial renovation.

"Everything okay, Kevin?" he asked as he approached, wearing a concerned frown.

I nodded. "Pretty much. Except we have company."

"What?"

I nodded toward the bar mirror and he turned to look, eyes widening as his gaze fell upon the image in the mirror. "Okay," he said slowly. "That's just a little creepy."

"Thinking that myself, boss."

He winced. He hates being called boss, but we all do it anyway. One of these days he's going to get used to it and it won't be any fun anymore. "What do you suggest we do about it?"

"Not sure there's anything we *can* do," I told him. "She's there and we're here."

He lanced me with a hard stare. "That's not helpful, Kevin."

I smiled and shrugged. "The Dimension of Mirrors isn't exactly my realm of expertise, boss."

I'm a mage, and a good one. But the D of M is Jasmine Tashae's demesne, and not for the likes of me. If she was some mortal who'd been trapped there, it would be Jaz who'd have to get her out.

"What the hell are you two whispering about?" asked Steph, appearing by our side as if she'd popped out of the floor. Steph's a vampire, and, as such, is very good at sneaking up on people. She doesn't make any sound unless she wants to, so she's always appearing unexpectedly. We're all more or less used to it.

Steph does the whole neo-goth thing. To her, black is the *only* primary color.

She spotted the figure in the mirror and joined us in gaping at it.

"You should try out for a gig doing stand-up!" someone shouted to Hydra.

"Are you kidding?" he responded in his basso rumble. "I'd bring the house down. Literally."

Everyone laughed at that, but this time it was tinged with a hint of sadness. Trolls weren't a common kind of freak, but they existed in large enough numbers that everyone knew how much fear and hatred they drew from "normal" folk. There wasn't a regular at the Lounge who didn't empathize with Hydra's plight.

And before you ask—no, he can't be fixed with magic. Most trolls are highly resistant to even beneficial magic. There is no way to fix them by mystical means.

More's the pity.

I glanced over and spotted Seth, our resident fashionista, looking our way and frowning. He climbed down off his bar stool and ambled over—though describing his motion as ambling might be an abuse of understatement. Seth doesn't really amble as much as strut. The guy thinks a lot of himself, and dresses the part. His wardrobe alone probably costs as much as I'll make throughout my lifetime, and mages tend to live a *long* time.

That night he wore a gray pin-stripe silk suit with a thin, baby blue tie. "What are you—my gods! What's *that?*"

"It's called a girl, Seth," Steph said dryly, not even casting her gaze his direction.

Jack snorted.

"I can tell that much," Seth replied irritably, "but what's she doing in there?"

"That's a very good question," Jack asked. "We're wondering the same thing ourselves."

"We need to get her out of there!" Seth exclaimed.

"Okay. How do you recommend we do that?" I asked him pointedly. "Somehow I don't think breaking the mirror will do the job."

"You're the magic man," he said unnecessarily. "Can't *you* do something?"

"I'm thinking," I answered, honestly enough. Actually, I was thinking that I didn't have the faintest idea what to do, but I wasn't going to tell him that.

"Maybe we should give Captain Glorious a call," Jack said, a sly note in his voice. He was referring to one of San Francisco's most notable superheroes, a costumed vigilante known for his outlandishly ornate outfit and over-dramatic bearing.

The way he said it made me think it wasn't just an idle comment, but I'll be damned if I know what he meant by it. Captain Glorious is a constant source of amusement for most of us here, especially since he'd arrived to help us deal with an errant bunch of vampires who'd been harassing Jack's ex-girlfriend and subsequently ended up playing bodyguard for the lady for several weeks.

Most people didn't know it, but Glorious was magically enhanced. He also had some meta power I hadn't been able to identify, but there were runes hidden in his cape and costume that gave him the ability to fly and greatly enhanced strength. I did not, however, get the impression he himself was a mage.

He probably had a mage in the family, I'd decided.

"I fail to see what good *that* would do," Seth muttered. Probably jealous of all the attention Glorious got when he was here. When the meta was around, people didn't even notice Seth.

The floor shook beneath our feet and we looked up to find Hydra staring down at us. "There I am, making a spectacle of myself for your amusement, and I find you all standing over here pretending I'm NOT the elephant in the room."

In all fairness, Hydra does have a lot of elephant-like qualities. He's huge, covered in wrinkled gray skin, and has a miniature trunk in place of a nose. Despite this, or perhaps for this reason specifically, his elephant references rarely generate any laughter.

This time was no exception. Steph silently lifted her arm and pointed at the mirror.

"Mary, Mother of God," the troll exclaimed. "Who is *she?*"

"We don't know," Jack answered. "We didn't mean to ignore you, Hydra, but, as you can imagine, we found her a bit of a distraction."

"No kidding. Huh. Hey, you all. Come get a load of *this!*"

So that's how it was the whole damn bar ended up standing in front of the mirror staring at the girl staring back out at us.

"She looks sad," murmured one of the Twining Twins. I have no idea which one. I honestly can't tell them apart. They're not really twins, but doppelgangers. The same person from two different universes. They met entirely by accident and now they're business partners and best friends. With the disconcerting habit of communicating telepathically with one another, which adds a whole new dimension of strangeness to it all.

"I wish Rio were here," I heard Jack say, and I nearly fell over. Not to say he doesn't *like* Rio, but I know he doesn't completely trust her. Not an easy thing for him to admit, considering that the Lounge has become a pretty close-knit community over the past several months. Rio and her guy, the immortal rock god Stormchild, had a habit of showing up only on the third Thursday of the month, and this was a Tuesday, so, unless the girl in the mirror stuck around for another week and a half, Rio wasn't going to be any help whatsoever.

Rio's a very powerful vampire mage, and she travels in circles I can only dream about. She probably knows all about the Dimension of Mirrors, which puts her way ahead of me.

"Poor thing," chimed in Merry, our resident Wiccan Priestess and another mage. She leaned against me and looked as though she was about to cry. I put my arm around her and pulled her close.

"Ja be wit' her," murmured Timothy Moggan, the Rastafarian meta who'd wandered in for the first time a couple of months ago. The diminutive reggae singer had an amazing voice packed in that little body of his. And when I say 'amazing,' I mean powerful enough to pulverize granite.

He and our other resident busker, Hammad, occasionally engaged in jam sessions for our entertainment. I'd been hoping for such a show tonight, but, unfortunately, Hammad hadn't made it in. The girl in the mirror pretty much postponed that sort of thing anyway. I'm sure Timothy didn't feel much like singing tonight.

"We can't just stand here and stare at her," Steph said into the well of silence we'd fallen into.

Jack grunted and we broke apart, most returning to where they'd been before they'd realized we had been standing there for a reason. A more or less normal buzz of conversation resumed, but Hydra didn't return to telling his jokes. Somehow humor seemed completely out of place now.

I trailed behind Jack, who wandered back toward his corner booth. "Can you get in touch with Jaz?"

He shook his head as he slid into the booth. I took the seat opposite him. "She said she'd know if we needed help and would show up right away."

"It's not *us* who needs help," I said, unnecessarily.

He replied with a glower. "We don't even know if she *needs* help." He took a long pause as he swallowed half his beer in one gulp. "She sure looks like she does, though," he added somberly.

Some twenty minutes later Hydra announced to the lot of us that the girl had vanished. We were left wondering what her appearance had actually meant. Had it been some sort of group delusion? The Twining Twins actually put forth that theory, to the universal disgust of the rest of us.

Steph calculated when she'd appeared—eleven on the dot, apparently—and how long she'd remained there in the mirror. Thirty-seven full agonizing minutes.

I wondered if that meant something.

For the next week the apparition appeared at eleven and remained until eleven thirty-seven, much like clockwork. After a while we grew accustomed to her appearance, and went about our business as usual, but we remained slightly subdued while she was visible. It was hard to enjoy ourselves while her sad eyes followed us around the room.

It also tended to put a damper on the rest of the evening. Most of the regulars stuck it out, but the spirit of the place seemed somehow diminished once she'd shown and then vanished again.

Jack was growing desperate. It wasn't about money—he made enough from the daytime business to make up for the lack of custom at night in normal circumstances, and few of the regulars were loathe to pay for their drinks anyway, but the Lounge was about the community, which was suffering in sympathy with the girl in the mirror. We were all frustrated and wanted answers we had no way to get.

Jack most of all.

Come Wednesday night we were crouched over our drinks, the mood in the bar heavy and somber, when the door burst open and a stranger appeared. It was 10:59 and the girl had yet to appear, though all of us were waiting expectantly for her arrival.

Boneyard, who usually stood guard at the door, had entered only a moment before, anguish plain on his square face as he stared at the mirror.

When the door opened, all our eyes were drawn there, a collective gasp escaping our throats as we took in the man standing just inside the threshold. He was not a particularly large man—particularly here at the Lounge, where several members of the clientele and staff were near seven feet or better—but he was certainly striking in appearance.

His skin was black. Not the black of a dark human of African or similar descent, but an almost unearthly black. Hair the same hue as his skin flowed back from a widow's peak and fell across his shoulders like a torrent of liquid midnight. Eyes of pale blue scraped across the interior and the bright tattoos across his bare arms seemed to writhe against his skin. "I have heard that one might find absolution here," he said, his voice a loud purr in the sudden silence.

"Depends on your sin," Jack replied from behind the bar without missing a beat.

"My sins are many," the stranger—it was bothering me that I couldn't put a name to him, though I had the feeling I should have been able to—replied coolly.

I caught a hint of movement in the mirror behind Jack. He was tending bar tonight, a rare occasion indeed, but Callie, the regular 'tender, had called in sick. Jack preferred to be out with the customers, but *someone* had to pour drinks.

The girl had appeared, right on schedule. The stranger didn't seem to notice.

Jack slapped the top of the bar. "Why don't you come have a seat and we'll discuss it in length," he said. "But first I think we should know your name."

The way he said it led me to believe he already did. Which meant he was ahead of me. I recognized the dark stranger for a mage instantly, and, what's worse, he was a completely distinctive figure. Yet I couldn't put a name to him.

"I am Hades," he said, and the silence in the room grew even more profound. There wasn't one among us who didn't know that name. Hades. The immortal who'd stolen human children and turned them into goblins. The one who'd used the last of the Sidhe bloodline to create a whole new race he dubbed Abyssian. *That* Hades.

The man made Hitler look like a schoolyard bully and he had the nerve to come in here and ask for absolution? Like we even had the power to grant it in the first place.

Hades scanned the barroom, dark face impassive. "You don't believe in redemption? I've heard otherwise."

"Some people are beyond redemption," Jack said slowly, meeting the immortal's gaze without any sign of hesitation. There was an edge to his voice I'd never heard from him before.

Hades's face tensed in anger. "I'm not so sure about that. How about the rest of you? Is there a crime so evil that you can never come back from it?"

"You tell *us*," someone said. The voice was strangled enough I wasn't able to identify the speaker. "Can you actually make restitution for your crimes, Hades? Is there anything out there significant enough to balance the scales?" The crowd parted and Hydra stepped forward, his huge eyes filled with a simmering rage that would have sent *me* fleeing in the opposite direction at full speed.

I imagine immortals are made of sterner stuff than I am, but that anger wasn't something anyone would choose to confront, or so I'd imagine.

Hades nodded at the troll. "And I suppose you do not curse Loki's name every time you look in the mirror? It was *his* crime that set the metavirus loose among the human population that has made you what you are," he reminded him.

"The difference is intent, Hades. Loki's intent was not to harm, but to save. Your only intent was to enhance your own power and standing."

"So they say."

Jack was on his feet so swiftly that I didn't see him rise. "One cannot ask for absolution and, in the next breath, deny one's crimes—or attempt to rationalize them away." A muscle in his jaw jumped, the only outward sign of his anger. "What the fuck are you doing here, Hades? What do you expect of us?"

The immortal shook his head, seemingly suddenly uncertain. "I expect you to listen to me," he snapped. "I have things I need to say."

"Then say them," Jack growled in response. "Stop banging about the shrubbery and get to the goddam point."

"I was wrong, damn it! Wrong from the beginning. Some of it was jealousy. Loki was a crappy scientist, but he got all the accolades, all the recognition I thought should have come to me. Then our world ended and we fled here. I nursed my hatred of him all that time, and when I was caught working against the other immortals, Deryk Shea had me exiled! Yet he tolerated Loki's meddling. He did nothing to punish *him*.

"Maybe Deryk saw something I didn't. Loki may go off half-cocked most of the time, but he has good instincts. Somehow the harm he does is vastly outweighed by the good he accomplishes. Damned if I know how. His methodology is shit. Always has been. He's a genius, but he's no kind of scientist. What kind of scientist works from the gut, for god's sake? What kind of scientist doesn't examine and re-examine his theories before acting upon them?" He snorted derisively. "I hated him so bad it consumed me.

"I was swallowed up by envy, hatred, and my hunger for revenge. I wanted all of them to pay for what they'd done to me. For tolerating Loki's excesses and refusing to tolerate mine. I took the children, sure. I took them and changed them. I caused irreparable harm to countless families—tore parents apart from the inside out. I realize this. And I know how wrong it was. When it became apparent that the goblins would be useless to me, I just threw them out...I abandoned them and turned my ambitions in other directions.

"Maybe I was simply mad. Looking back at it, I can't even say why I did all these things. I did evil things...unspeakable things...for no other reason that I can see but hubris."

We listened in stunned amazement to an immortal, a former god, a true dark genius, pouring his heart out onto the barroom floor in front of us. By the time he was finished, tears streaked his ebon features and he leaned against one of the support columns as if he'd fall down if he didn't.

"Fine," said Jack into the stillness. "What are you going to do about it?"

"What *can* I do about it? I cannot restore the goblins to their humanity, to their families now long dead. I cannot take back all the things I did in the name of my own pride and ego."

"How long ago did you turn your back on the self who did all these things?" asked Boneyard, out of the blue.

Hades turned to look at him and shrugged. "Sometime before the Cen War," he told him. "In the end I could not betray humanity to those monsters."

That struck a false note, but no one commented on it. There was more to it than that, but none of us had any idea what it might have been. "So what have you done since?" Jack asked him.

"What do you mean?"

"It's one thing to repudiate the evil you've done in the past. But have you once thought of what you could do to redeem your crimes? To begin to pay back the debt you owe? To try to make up for all your sins?"

Hades shook his head. "I wouldn't know where to start."

"You're in luck," Jack said. "I have an idea." He glanced up at the clock above the bar and nodded as if to himself, then strode over to a spot directly across from where the girl stood, gazing out at us all.

He lifted his arm and pointed at her. "You want to make the first symbolic gesture toward redemption, Hades? Free *her.*"

Hades turned his attention to where Jack was pointing and stared in astonishment. "Who...what...how...what's she doing in there?" he asked.

"We'd all dearly love to know the answer to those questions," Jack replied. "If you can free her, you realize, it's just a tiny step in the right direction."

Hades nodded thoughtfully, not taking his eyes off the girl for a second. "What I don't understand is why none of the mages around here have already freed her."

"We don't know how," I said in a low growl. "I take that to mean *you* do?"

"Yes. It's not all that difficult, really. Jasmine Tashae was the one who discovered the route to enter the Dimension of Mirrors. I suggest you mages watch how I do this."

That was an unmistakable suggestion to switch to magesight, which I did. Hades snatched a passing thread and hurled one end at the mirror while holding the other end firmly in his hand. A second later, he tossed the thread out of his hand and the girl stumbled out of the open end. She stumbled, and would have fallen, but Steph, moving like only a vampire can, caught her before she hit the floor. The girl smiled faintly and passed out in her arms.

Time passed.

"She's coming around," I said. I'd already done a scan of the girl and she checked out okay. There was nothing noticeably wrong with her. All her vital systems came back healthy, which was something I'd been concerned about the whole time. There was no telling how long she'd been in there, and what effect it might have on the human body.

"How did she eat in there?" Boneyard asked, leaning over me as I knelt by her side.

"I don't think she had to," I responded. A glance at Hades affirmed this suspicion. He was nodding.

"The Dimension of Mirrors is completely outside of time— even farther out than Starhaven, if that makes any sense at all. People *do* need to eat on Starhaven, though they do not age significantly while they're there. The Dimension of Mirrors is almost like a place of stasis...time crawls by so slowly, if at all, that such things as food and liquid become, at best, an afterthought.

"I would imagine she's hungry now."

She blinked up at me. "Where am I?" She spoke with a slight accent—Eastern European, I thought, but I couldn't be sure.

"Safe," I responded, feeling silly for replying with such a non-answer. But it seemed like the best bet. "How do you feel?"

"Hungry," she answered. This prompted a chuckle from the room.

Now that she was out of the mirror and plainly visible, I estimated her age to be about twelve or thirteen. Just a kid, slightly taller than average, a little bit gangly. As I said before, pretty in a pale, undernourished sort of way. "I'm Kevin. What's your name?"

I helped her sit up and she looked around the room. "Am I in a bar?" she asked.

"Yes. But don't worry about it. No one is going to come in and cause trouble. Not here."

She looked dubious. "My name's Anya," she said, answering my earlier question.

"Nice to meet you, Anya. What would you like to eat?"

"A hamburger?"

"Coming right up. Hey, boss, you want to order her up a burger?"

"I'm on it," Jack replied. "Take her to my booth, will you? She doesn't need to be sitting there on the floor."

I helped her to her feet and guided her to his corner table. "How did you get in there?" I asked, then cursed myself for broaching the subject so quickly. I should have given her time to adjust to the change before interrogating her.

She didn't seem to mind. "I don't know. I just wanted out of where I was so bad I looked in a mirror and zap, I was looking out of it."

"When did this happen?" I asked her.

"What do you mean, when?" She glanced over and smiled as Boneyard approached carrying what looked suspiciously like a strawberry milkshake.

He set it down in front of her. "This should tide you over until your burger's done," he said with a smile.

From out of the corner of my eye I spotted Hades standing alone, momentarily forgotten in the excitement of the girl's rescue. Everyone wanted to say hello to her, to introduce themselves, but hung back for fear of overwhelming her. They left her care to Jack and myself.

I watched unobtrusively as Timothy walked straight up to Hades and passed him a mug of beer. "Ya did a good t'ing, mon. Ya should be feelin' a better mon already." He laughed and clapped him gently on the shoulder of the arm not holding the beer. "Ja is a bein' of infinite forgiveness."

Timothy's voice was powerful enough that it carried over the background murmur of the Lounge with little trouble, whether he wanted it to or not.

"Time passes very oddly where you were," I explained to the girl. "I was wondering what year it was when it happened to you."

"I think it was in May of 2006," she said. "What do you mean, 'passes very oddly'?"

Jack met my gaze and gave a nearly imperceptible shake of his head. I shifted gears rapidly. "What did you do while you were in there? The last few days you watched us, but what did you do before that?"

"I...I'm not sure. I avoided the gray ghost," she said, "and the people who traveled with it sometimes. But I don't remember seeing anything that I wanted to be a part of until I ran into this place. You all seemed so bright and cheery and I wanted to be a part of that."

I wanted to ask about this "gray ghost", but her hamburger arrived at that very moment, so we left her to eat in peace and found a spot to talk away from the others for a moment. "You don't want to tell her how long she's been gone, do you?" I asked Jack.

"Not yet I don't," he answered. "Can you imagine the shock? This world is completely different than the one she left. I'm not sure any of *us* know enough about her world to help her adjust."

"But there are those who do," I reminded him. "Steph might."

He shook his head. "She's only about a hundred years old," he said. "She was born after the Cen War, and grew up knowing about vamps and 'thropes and all kinds of freaks. This girl knows about none of those things except maybe from movies made back in the day.

"I'm wondering how she got into the mirror in the first place."

"I have a theory about that," I told him. "What if she's a meta?"

He frowned. "But that would mean..." He let his voice trail off, face twisting as he realized the implications. "The only way those viruses were transmitted back then were through sexual contact."

I nodded. "It would explain her needing to escape bad enough to activate the meta ability without realizing what she was doing."

"Oh, god. I don't think we're qualified to deal with this, Kevin. Not in the least."

He was right, as far as it went. My training had covered dealing with physiological damage to the brain as well as the body, but here we were talking about something that went a damn sight deeper. If my theory was correct, she'd been traumatized *before* she'd found the means to escape, and then suffered through what must have seemed like an eternity of being alone, before being cast back into a world it might take her decades to understand. "So what do you suggest?"

"I've got to ask you something first. Rumor has it you're a doctor. Are you?"

I'd been expecting him to ask this question for quite some time. I was actually surprised it had taken this long. "Yes," I told him. More or less true, at least.

"So what are you doing here? Why aren't you practicing medicine professionally?"

Becoming a doctor at the ripe age of twenty was heady enough, I wanted to tell him, but being a mage on top of it was akin to challenging the very gods themselves. I'd been too willing to experiment with both disciplines, too willing to try things no one had even considered before, and it was inevitable that someone would pay for my arrogance.

I'd practiced a long way from Earth, which was the only reason Jack didn't already know the story of my fall from grace. I'd done something unforgivable in my profession: I'd used my knowledge to destroy a man. Consciously, willfully and arrogantly.

There are some who would argue that he deserved what I'd done to him. I could even make that argument myself. He was a petty tyrant, the son of a powerful political figure, and he liked using his position to force women into compromising positions. To either have sex with him or be financially or socially destroyed.

He tried to do it to my sister. Rather than bowing to his will, she'd taken her own life. It was a coward's way out, but it was truly the only escape she could see. He'd threatened to use his position to make her life hell, and to take me down with her.

I don't know if he could have done either of these things, but the only thing that mattered was that *she* believed he could. I'd probably never know all the details.

When she was found dead of an overdose of sleeping aids, I was the one who sought answers. There wasn't anyone else, considering our parents had died in an accident when we were both teenagers. I was the only one that questioned the apparent suicide. Suicide isn't illegal, after all. Not anymore. But I couldn't understand why she'd done it.

My investigation had turned up the reason, and, in what might have been the ultimate act of foolishness, I made the bastard pay for what he did to her. I used my knowledge of the human brain to destroy the neural pathways in his head that made him an adult. I systematically eliminated memories, connections, and the bio-chemical responses that made him what he was. I turned him back into a child and froze him there. He will never again see the world other than through the eyes of a five year old.

I was nearly warlocked for the crime, locked away from my magic for the rest of my life. To be honest, I'm not sure why I hadn't been. But I'd been stripped of my license to practice medicine, and sent back to the Earth my parents had fled before I was even born.

"Bad choices," was all I said to Jack. What more could I say? He could take that any way he wanted.

He seemed willing to do just that, responding with a nod. "Would you be willing to take the girl under your wing, to give her a place to stay until we can find somewhere suitable for her to go?" he asked suddenly.

I froze, a rabbit nailed to the highway in front of an oncoming freight-mover. "What? Shit, Jack...I wish I could. I just don't have the room."

He frowned, not quite realizing what was wrong with that statement. Thankfully his grasp of the mechanics of magecraft was rather limited. No mage worth a damn couldn't create space—or the illusion of space—as needed.

And my house wasn't particularly tiny to begin with. Cluttered and filled with all sorts of junk I didn't need, but hardly too small to take in a young boarder.

My reasons were simpler, and more selfish, than that. I didn't want the disruption. Judge me for it if you want. I've been judged before and survived the experience. And as far as sins go, it was nothing compared to the sins of the dark god in the room.

"It doesn't leave me with many choices," Jack sighed. "I can make room for her upstairs if I have to, but I'm not sure a tavern is the best place for a kid. Even this one."

Great. The guilt card. And what's worst of all was that he didn't know he was playing it. He'd taken my words at face value and his only concern was the well-being of the kid. "Maybe we should take a minute to ask her what she would like," I said.

He considered this for a moment, then nodded. "You're right. We should ask her." He walked over and slid back into the seat opposite her, waiting for her to finish chewing and swallow before asking, "So your name is Anya? It's a pretty name."

I hung back, curious to see how he handled this. She set the burger down and lifted her gaze to his. "Thank you," she said shyly.

"Hi, Anya, my name is Jack. That a good burger?"

She nodded.

"Well, we were wondering what to do with you until we find somewhere for you to go. You can stay in one of my extra rooms upstairs, if you like."

"Can't I just go home?"

Jack winced visibly. That, of course, was impossible. Even if the house or apartment in which she'd lived still existed, her family was most likely long dead.

Jack's mouth moved silently as he tried to think of an appropriate response, but before he could, she raised her eyes back to his. "They're dead, aren't they?"

"Probably," he answered. "It's been a long time."

"How long?" As I watched her face transform, I realized the shyness was fading quickly, replacing itself with a sense of calm maturity that looked positively alien on her small, thin body. I began to think we may have underestimated the girl. There was no way to tell what she witnessed while trapped in the Dimension of Mirrors, or the effect it had on her. In a very real way, she wasn't the child she appeared.

"Almost three hundred years," Jack told her.

She nodded and took another bite of her burger. "So my parents—"

"Are probably gone."

She snorted mid-swallow and looked pained. She coughed twice to clear her throat. "Probably?"

"It's a different world," he explained. "Some people live hundreds of years or longer now. There are some who were alive then who are still alive now. But the chance of your parents being among them is pretty small."

"You say that as if it's a bad thing," she said, watching him unblinkingly. "My father was a sick bastard and my mother as useless as they come. The only good thing about going into the mirror was that I no longer had to live with them."

I'd seen that kind of anger, that kind of pain before. I wished I could raise the dead just so I could bring them back and kill them again. I knew what she meant without even asking. I knew it from the sudden throb in my temple and the taste of something vile at the back of my throat. I was a doctor, and even in these enlightened times there were those who preyed on children. Even their own children, and those who stood back and did nothing about it.

We already knew she'd been infected by one of the viruses. My first guess was the primary metavirus. It easily explained her sudden shift into the Dimension of Mirrors. That she got it from her bastard father seemed a foregone conclusion. Of course, it might also have been the first and only manifestation of the Arcane virus. There was little or no mana in the Dimension of Mirrors, from what I understood, and, even had she the knowledge of how to use it, she wouldn't have known what to do to escape.

I wished I could tell just by looking at her, but that only worked with trained mages who set their spells in orbit around themselves.

This led me to another thought. If her father *was* a mage, he might still be alive. Mages lived longer than ordinary folks, longer even than metas, paras, and many 'thropes.

Anya was shaking her head in amazement. "I was in there for three hundred years?"

"Two-hundred and fifty four, give or take," Jack replied. "So what do you want to do?"

"You say the world has changed. Is there still a Social Services office?"

"Of a sort, yes. We can take you there, if you want, but, if you'd rather, you can just stay with one of us. We can file a writ with the courts and they'll send a case worker out to investigate, make sure you're who you say you are. Then you'll be registered as a citizen and be allowed to make up your own mind where you go from there."

She blinked at him. "I'm only twelve," she said. "They're not going to let me decide for myself..." Her voice trailed off as she saw a look of mild amusement flick across his face. "What?"

"I told you it was a different world. You're not twelve years old anymore. You're well over two hundred. You're legally an adult. If you understood the world as it is today, you could go out tomorrow and get a job and an apartment, and start living whatever life you chose to live."

"A job? Really? Doing what? I have no skills. I never got past sixth grade."

"Well, then, I'd say you'd best stick with one of us until you get some skills," he answered smoothly.

I felt a hand on my shoulder and turned, to find Hades looking down at me. I hadn't realized he was that much taller than I was until that moment. He topped me by at least four inches, if not more. "She's a mage," he told me. "I can see it in her."

"How?" I asked, hating to admit my ignorance to him.

He shrugged. "I don't know, exactly. I can just tell. I'd like to offer my services as a tutor." He raised his hand to forestall my reflexive objection. "Not to say I don't think you're competent, or that there aren't many good mage schools out there. But I have several thousand years of practice to lean upon...far more than anyone you know. And I would like to do something good for a change."

It may sound strange, but I believed him. "I'll tell you what. Once we get Anya settled in, we'll all sit down and talk about it. That's the best I can do."

"That's the most I can ask of you," he replied with a tight smile. He walked up to the bar and laid something down. "I

55

must be going," he said, "but I wanted to thank you all for being here. It's been good for me, and, I dare say, good for your other unexpected guest as well. This is a five hundred credit chit. Everyone here should be able to drink for free tonight with some left over. Put the rest toward getting young Anya some new clothes and whatever else she needs."

With that, he cast a smile around the room and walked out the door. The regulars watched in silent amazement as he left, then looked at each other in puzzlement. I went and ordered another drink, then returned to the table where Jack and Anya remained deep in conversation.

She smiled up at me as I approached. "Hi, Kevin." She slid over and patted the seat next to her. "Go ahead and sit down. We were just talking about you."

Somehow I wasn't surprised. "Hades said something strange before he left," I told Jack. "He said that Anya's a mage and he wanted to volunteer to tutor her."

Jack chewed his lower lip thoughtfully. "What do you think of that?" he asked me.

"What does he mean, mage?" Anya asked with a frown.

So I explained how the Cen had come to Earth a thousand years ago and spread several viruses around, to kill as many of us as possible, and damage our DNA so we'd lose the ability to sense or touch mana—the very stuff of magic. And how the immortal Loki, not long before she'd gone into the mirror, had sent out several counter-viruses, one of which repaired the genetic damage. And how she'd most likely contracted one of those viruses and unknowingly used magic to escape into the Dimension of Mirrors.

"And who's this Hades guy? The one who got me out, right?"

"Yeah," Jack said. "He's an immortal, and one bad guy. Or, rather, he *was* a bad guy. Now...we're not so sure."

"And he wants to teach me? Why?"

I shrugged. "We don't really know. He says it's to make up for some of the shitty things he's done."

"And do you believe him?"

"I want to. I believe it's possible to change. I know he took himself out of the equation before the war. He could have fought on the side of the Cen and done a lot of damage, but he disappeared instead."

She nodded. "Fine. So say I want to learn. Can I take lessons from him with one of you there?"

"Of course," Jack said quickly. "Kevin is a mage too. I'm sure he'd be willing to keep an eye on your lessons."

I didn't really appreciate him speaking for me, but he was right. "I'd be glad to," I said.

She smiled sweetly and finished off the last of her milkshake. "I'm tired," she told Jack. "Can you take me to my room now?"

"Sure." He stood as I slid out of the booth. "Things are going to get very interesting around here for a while," he said, grinning at me.

"As if they weren't always interesting around here," I responded. "Go. Get her set up and I'll see you when you get finished. If you're not back by closing time, we'll take care of it."

"I know you will."

I watched the two of them head upstairs and motioned for the rest of the crowd to join me near the bar. "There's a good chance she's going to be around for a while," I told them. "We all need to look out for her."

En masse, they gave me a look as if the dumbest words ever spoken had just fallen out of my mouth. I shrugged and pointed to the credit chit on the bar. "Who wants a free drink?"

Boneyard, who'd taken Jack's place behind the bar, sighed dramatically and began lining shots along its length.

I spent the rest of the night immersed in the easy camaraderie of the Lounge, deliberately blocking out any thoughts of what tomorrow might bring. It's a rare occasion when I manage it, but sometimes you have to live in the moment. And this moment was better than most.

# Episode III:
# Judgment

I hadn't quite gotten used to the enthusiastic greeting I received when I strode through the door into the Magitech Lounge. It wasn't all that long ago, as I measure time, that I was one of the greatest villains Earth had ever known.

An ironic fate for a man who'd originally turned to science to help people. Then death had come to my world and only a few of us survived to flee here. After that I guess I let bitterness and envy rip apart any sense of decency I may have initially had.

My name is Hades, and I used to be the Lord of the Underworld. Not the one from mythology, though I suppose you might say I'm the person from which that mythological figure was crafted. I'm the very same Hades who stole thousands of mortal children and transformed them, twisted them, through magic and genetic manipulation, into an army of goblins.

Yes, that Hades.

I'm the very same Hades who lied to the Sidhe, and used their bloodline for my own purposes and deliberately turned them into things most people would perceive as monsters.

*That* Hades. Otherwise known as "that scheming, immoral bastard".

As I entered the lounge and climbed the ramp to the main floor, my eyes flicked to the table in the corner, where the manager usually sat. Tonight the girl sat with him. They were eating a delicious-looking meal of lasagna with garlic bread and my mouth watered slightly as I approached. It had been a long time since I'd allowed myself a proper meal, especially something as enticing as that.

I enjoyed good food, and refusing to eat those things that I found most compelling was one of the ways I punished myself for my crimes. I forced myself to consume the cheapest, blandest forms of mass-market neo-protein available.

It was a small enough sacrifice, considering the price other people paid for my arrogance.

When my mechanizations had finally been revealed, and those I had betrayed had rightfully turned on me, I realized it was nothing more than I'd deserved. I'd known it even as I pulled myself from the floor where I'd been thrown and used Thomas Grey's abandoned wheelchair to escape before the authorities arrived. I had a long time to think about it as I recovered from the blow dealt to me by the vengeful arm of Carth, the last surviving full-blood Sidhe.

I hated what I'd become, once I'd actually been made to turn and face it. I could not cure the goblins of their affliction, nor could I restore the Sidhe bloodline to what it once was. The evil that I'd done was permanent and I nearly lost myself to despair and self-loathing when I realized how unconscionable my crimes had truly been.

I don't speak of my crimes, or my self-imposed penance, to my fellow patrons at the Lounge. They know my crimes nearly as well as I do. In the years since I'd fled civilization, I'd become something of a dark legend, even more than I'd been in Earth's distant past. Hades was the name parents used to frighten their unruly children into obedience.

How the mighty had fallen. It had a certain delicious humor to it.

I'd identified myself to them on the first night I'd come in, and asked for absolution. Not that I expected to get it. I would have welcomed their condemnation. It was no more than I deserved. But fate had other plans for us that night. A girl needed help, and I was the only one with the skill and knowledge to save her.

I sometimes wonder if there *is* something beyond our awareness, some plan we cannot perceive. It is things like this that occasionally make it possible for me to understand those with religious sentiments. This doesn't mean that I believe in a heaven or hell, or any of the things some mortals take for granted. I have lived too long and seen too many things to believe that there is any ultimate reward or punishment.

But sometimes I do wonder if a plan exists.

That night I was feeling a little down, and the smile I received from my pupil did wonders for my initial attitude upon my arrival. Her temporary guardian, Jack, gave me a smile that looked more like a grimace, but I knew he still held reservations as to my intentions here. I couldn't blame him for not trusting me. I would be equally suspicious if our positions were somehow reversed. It speaks very well of him that he allows me the benefit of the doubt.

I went to magesight and scanned Anya, noting with a certain amount of (but not too much) pride that she had a couple of two-strand spells in her web. So she'd done her homework. Good. I gave her a nod and an approving smile and went to make the rounds.

The first person I greeted was the Rastafarian Timothy. Not Tim, but Timothy. He was very emphatic about this. Of all the regulars at the Lounge, he was the one who'd accepted me first. I don't know if it was about the color of my skin or something else, but I appreciated it more than I could say. I'd been alone for a long time and even the smallest friendly gesture meant a lot to me.

After I'd bought Timothy a beer, I continued on, placing my hand within the mighty grasp of the troll, Hydra, and grinning up at him. He was a perfect example of how a monstrous form could hide the most humane soul. I was careful to hide my pity from him. Pity was the last thing he needed from any of us.

Then I stopped to say hello to Kevin, the Lounge's security mage. He's a good guy, and as pale as I am dark. I know he didn't trust me yet either, but, like his boss, he was willing to give me the benefit of the doubt.

I leaned back against the bar to exchange a few words with Callie, the night bartender. I engaged in mild flirtation with the pretty young woman, not intending anything more by it. If I would not allow myself the joy of consuming appetizing food, I certainly wouldn't allow myself the satisfaction of anything more...intimate than that.

Celibacy is often more common for immortals than it was even for Catholic Priests, when they were still required to remain celibate. So for it to be an effective sacrifice, I find I must occasionally remind myself what I'm giving up.

You might think this is strange, but you have to understand the depths of depravity to which I sank. Calling me a villain is an insult to most villains. Take my word for it. There are few tortures I could devise for myself that would do my crimes any sort of justice at all.

I took a step away as the door banged open unexpectedly. Unexpectedly because the were-panther, Boneyard, was still at his post in front of the club. No one should have entered without his boss being aware of it and Bone himself moved with all the grace of his feline animus.

The two men who strode through the door and up the ramp moved with a sort of grace of their own, clad in black and silver uniforms with blocky sidearms attached to their hips. They looked like twins, large, bulky men with wide shoulders and narrow hips, dark eyes and shaved heads. They looked dangerous, even to me, and believe me, I'd known a lot of dangerous men in my time.

Boneyard came up the ramp behind them, but slowly, looking seriously angry. Angry enough, as they say, to chew iron and spit nails. One of the uniformed men stepped aside to watch him, hand on the butt of his weapon, while the other walked straight toward me.

I'd been expecting this, but perhaps not so soon. "Hades, we are placing you under arrest under the authority of the Confed Adjuster."

I laughed out loud, which seemed to surprise both men. They were tense, expecting me to fight, but I had no intention of doing so. Not here, and not now. I would not repay Jack and his patrons' welcome with unnecessary destruction. "By all means. I've been looking forward to this for some time," I told them. "Take me to see Deryk Shea."

As they placed the manacles around my wrists, I glanced over my shoulder at Anya, who was watching in horrified fascination. I gave her a comforting smile. "I'm afraid I'm going to have to skip our next few lessons," I told her, "but I expect Kevin to continue your training." I aimed my gaze at him and didn't look away until he'd responded with a nod.

I rattled my manacles. "Take me away."

ༀ৪৩ୠ

The homely little man glanced up as I stumbled through the office door, shoved with considerable strength across the threshold. "You've got anger issues," I told the agent who'd pushed me. He simply smiled insincerely and shut the door behind me, leaving me alone with the ugly dwarf.

All right. Deryk Shea, the Confed Adjuster, isn't really a dwarf. He's short for a human male, but neither a muscle-bound, bearded off-shoot of the Fey, nor any variety of earthly "little person". He's just a short, ugly guy with cropped hair and brooding gray eyes.

He looked up at me, leaned back in his chair, and let the silence build. I knew this technique. It was a waste of time, since I could be as patient as he could. We immortals had forever, or near enough. I could wait as long as he could before speaking.

Except this sort of competition was pointless. "Hello, Deryk. You've done well for yourself."

His thin lips twisted into something resembling a smile. "I wish I could say the same for you. Oh, wait. No I don't. I was kinda hoping you were burning in some version of the Christian hell." He paused long enough to grab a cigar out of a box on the table, snip off one end, and shove it in his mouth. His next words were muttered around the butt of the cigar. "We've been looking for you since before the war."

"I was 'finding myself,' if you'll pardon the expression."

"Did you?"

"Did I what?"

"Did you find yourself?"

I shrugged. There was no right answer to that question. "I found a few things I didn't know," I finally replied.

"I received an interesting report from the Magitech Lounge," he said. "Says you went there looking for redemption. Is this true?"

I shrugged again. "A reasonable accounting of events."

"Did you find it?"

"I know what path I should be on to find it," I answered simply.

This little tête-à-tête was getting us nowhere and, frankly, it was boring the hell out of me. If he had me brought here for a verbal fencing match, he had far too much time on his hands. "Are you charging me with a crime, Deryk?"

"I'm thinking about it. Under Confed Legal Code, the clock stops for any statute of limitations if you flee to avoid prosecution. And some of your crimes involve murder and conspiracy to commit murder, which have no such statute."

He leaned forward again. "What do you know about the Confed Legal Code and Charter?" he asked me.

"Not a goddam thing," I said honestly. "Mortal laws have never affected us before."

"They do now," he responded. "Usually the Adjuster's Office acts upon a sworn complaint by a citizen. We investigate, then build a case against the perpetrator of the crime. We then convene a Grand Jury and the jury decides if the case is warranted. We are, in effect, both the 'federal' police force and the 'federal' prosecutor's office—to borrow terms from the old United States.

"You would be allowed an advocate to speak for you...anyone you like. There are registered advocates...they were once called lawyers, but the term has fallen into disfavor. Most of the good ones charge a pretty penny, but there are those who'd do it just for the notoriety."

"In other words, the more that things change, the more they stay the same."

He offered up another thin smile. "True enough." He glanced up at the wall clock hanging above the fireplace to his left. "It's nearly one o'clock now. I can have you in front of a Grand Jury in Europe in less than an hour, but it'll take us a while to build a case against you. Two hundred and fifty odd years is a long time, especially considering the disruption caused by the war. And many of our witnesses are off-world at the moment.

"I can hold you for seventy-two hours without charging you. I'm tempted to do that, but I have the funny feeling you're not much of a flight risk anymore. You could have escaped this universe at any time in the past several decades, but you chose to stay here. Why is that?"

I didn't answer for a long moment. "I'm no longer the person I once was, Deryk."

He digested this. "Fine. The one thing I can tell you about the legal system these days, Hades, is that we're more concerned with justice than the letter of the law. Under the letter of the law, you're guilty, and deserve any punishment we mete out to you. But under justice...well, let's just say that gives you some wiggle room.

"I'm releasing you, but rest assured we will be watching. You attempt to flee, you'll lose your chance to come before the Grand Jury of your own volition. Clear?"

I nodded. It was more than I deserved and we both knew it. I wondered, for a brief instant, if Deryk was allowing ancient history to color his decision. It didn't seem likely, but it also seemed very unlikely that he'd give me this sort of break for any other reason.

I was even more amazed when he stood up, walked around the desk, and pressed his fingers against the cold ceramic of the manacles. I heard a click and they popped open. "Go look for that redemption, Hades," he said, before turning away and returning to his desk, upon which he tossed the manacles. "Finding it may be the only thing that saves your sorry ass."

He said this without even bothering to look around. I didn't reply, instead casting out a transit tube and leaving his office by way of the mage's highway. In a matter of minutes I stood in the street outside the Magitech Lounge, staring up at the small holographic sign that marked its presence.

They'd be closing in an hour, I realized. I considered just going home to the one-room apartment I'd rented just off the Tenderloin, but I figured I owed them a moment of my time to let them know I hadn't been dragged off to some dark Confed dungeon.

What could it hurt?

As I reached for the door handle, I heard the low sound of a guitar strumming within. I pulled it opened and walked into the foyer as the music died away. Whistles and applause greeted the end of the song. I trudged up the ramp, heart heavier than it had been in a long time.

From the stage, Timothy lifted his gaze from the guitar resting across his legs, caught site of me, and let out a whoop. "An the Adjuster mon jus let 'im go!"

"Not quite," I said, just barely above a whisper. I knew I'd be called before the Grand Jury sooner or later, but for now I remained free.

The night wound down and I took myself home at closing time. As I trudged up to the front door of my apartment building, I noticed a small black and tan dog sitting beside the door, shivering. I knelt down and coaxed it over. It crept up to me warily, its big eyes sad and fearful. "You poor thing," I murmured to it. Reaching a decision, I swept it into my arms and took it up to my apartment.

Anyone who'd leave such a vulnerable little dog outside alone didn't deserve the creature's company.

It took me a few minutes to get her warmed up. Her fear evaporated pretty quickly once I'd given her some food—a bit of flavored neo-protein that's obviously more palatable to dogs than humans—and a bowl of water.

Once this was accomplished, I took the dog back downstairs to do her doggy business. While I held her at the end of a mana-thread leash, I thought about names for the tiny creature. I didn't know much about dogs, but I had a feeling this one was still more or less a puppy. Obviously a small breed, though she looked a lot like a Doberman. I knew what they were. At one time I'd used them for grounds security.

"Hey! That's my dog!" A guy lurched through the door, reeking of cheap alcohol. He was fat, balding, and wearing one of those tee-shirts some people referred to as a "wife-beater". The originally white shirt was stained with something that could either be mustard or a particularly unpleasant brand of vomit.

The dog in question raced back to me and leaped into my arms, staring at the drunk fat man and shivering uncontrollably. "Not anymore," I told him with a cold smile. "This poor beast is underfed and obviously neglected. Now go away before I'm forced to punish you for the harm you have done to such an innocent creature."

The man was not overly burdened with either wisdom or intelligence. He balled up his fists and took a step in my direction. "I ain't gonna let no nigger steal my dog," he said.

It surprised me that such pejoratives were still in use today. I'd hoped that this brave new world had at least achieved *that* small amount of enlightenment.

I found myself in the midst of a moral dilemma. This man obviously deserved some sort of education as to his limitations, but I couldn't afford to do him any bodily harm. I'd even have to be very careful if I decided to use magic to subdue him, because using magic aggressively could bring the Adjusters back down on me.

I was rescued from having to make this decision when a slim figure stepped out of the shadows and glided up to the fat man so smoothly he didn't register it until a hand was laid upon his arm. A hood fell back and the vampire, Steph, stared up into his eyes. "You don't have a dog," she said, in a resonant tone. "You hate dogs. You can't abide to be anywhere near a dog or any other animal."

He blinked and stared down at her, then nodded once and went back inside the building. I offered Steph a tentative smile. "Thank you. I wasn't sure how I was going to handle this."

"You're welcome. I was just coming by to see if you were okay. You looked a little depressed when you left the Lounge."

I nodded. "I guess I was."

"Are they going to charge you?"

"Most likely," I responded. "I have no idea what they'll charge me *with*, however."

She shrugged. "Doesn't matter. I'll be your advocate, if you'll have me."

"You?" I didn't mean to sound so surprised, but I hadn't even realized she was a lawyer.

"I've been an advocate for the Conclave for nearly seventy years now. I know my business."

I didn't even blink. "I accept. What do I have to do?"

"Contact the Adjuster's Office and inform them that Stephanie Dodge is your advocate, and that any material pertaining to the case needs to be sent directly to me." She smiled and patted the dog in my arms. "Anyone who'd rescue a cute little dog from someone like that asshole deserves good representation."

She gave me one last nod of farewell and headed off down the street. "You hear that, little one?" I asked the dog. "You're already bringing me good luck."

I woke early the next day and spent the morning playing with my new puppy. She was a feisty rascal, I determined, and prone to chew on anything that sat still for too long. I finally swept her up and took a walk to the nearest pet supply store to buy her some toys so she'd leave my shoes intact.

I spotted the Adjuster's Office goons following me within about half a block. It wasn't as though they were trying to be subtle. They were still wearing their black and silver uniforms.

It was a definite "what are you going to do about it" message from my old friend Deryk. Well, I had news for him. I wasn't going to do anything about it. I was going to take my new puppy to a vet, see if she needed shots, and then spend a few hours at a dog park. Maybe I'd take her for a stroll through Golden Gate.

These agents were going to spend a boring day following someone who didn't give a damn. I found the thought highly amusing.

I named the dog Pepper. I'm not sure why. I guess because it was the first name I tried she seemed to respond to. I'd never had a dog before, or any kind of a pet at all. Unless you consider a goblin a pet. I don't. Dogs are easier to housebreak.

My apologies. That was uncalled-for, and in spectacularly poor taste. And not even remotely true. Goblins are sentient, if not particularly bright. They are a race of nearly immortal, perpetual children. What flaws they possess are my fault, since I was the one who created them. I have no right to make jokes at their expense.

I took Pepper with me to the Lounge that evening. She garnered the appropriate amount of attention, and lapped it all up as if it were ambrosia. I was gratified to see her taking to people so well, considering the nature of her original master.

Dogs, particularly young dogs, are amazingly resilient, and they have more faith in us than we deserve most of the time. I'd never spent much time thinking about it before, but the human race owes dogs a great deal, though it's likely they'll never get a fraction of the credit they deserve.

Anya and Pepper took to one another as if fate had taken a hand in it. If not for Jack's obvious disinclination to allow her to keep the dog, I might well have given her to Anya on the spot. But his silent directive for me *not* to do so was clear enough that I suppressed the urge. And, to be completely honest, I was surprised to find I was slightly relieved. I'd grown fond of the creature and hadn't really wanted to give her away.

I returned home that night in a considerably better mood than I'd been in the night before. I sat under the light of a small lamp in the single chair with which I'd furnished the tiny apartment, Pepper curled contentedly on my lap, and buried myself in one of the books I'd borrowed from Jack, who was something of a collector of old fiction novels.

I hadn't yet actually rejoined this modern age, eschewing the use of modern communication and entertainment equipment. I had purchased no Personal Communication Device, or this age's equivalent to the twentieth century's television set—now simply called a "view". I preferred the silent companionship of books, the only noise the turning of the pages, and the occasional muffled snore from the creature in my lap.

Like most immortals, I have no need to sleep, and the average book is little more than a momentary diversion. Which is why I had borrowed a considerable number of these ancient novels, losing myself in the imaginations of men and women such as Robert Heinlein, Spider Robinson, Elizabeth Moon, David Weber, and Frank Herbert. It seems that Jack was something of a fan of science fiction, an intriguing fact about a man born and raised into a world that most such fiction authors would never have imagined.

After a while I dozed—not precisely asleep, but not fully awake either. It was a habit I'd developed while in exile, a way for my conscious and subconscious minds to meet on more or less equal ground, and I used it in much the same way a more enlightened person might use the art of meditation.

I was aroused somewhere around dawn by the sound of someone pounding on my door. Careful not to disturb Pepper too much, I stood and carried her with me to the door, activating the view-screen next to the portal that revealed who stood on the other side.

It was a young man I didn't recognize holding a clipboard and gazing down at it, his face mostly hidden by the bill of his hat. Not being in the habit of expecting trouble, I opened the door. A weapon of some sort appeared in his hand and he brandished it at me, making a gesture with his other hand that indicated his desire for me to step back so he might enter.

More curious than anything, I did as he bid.

He was a dark-skinned fellow with a close-cropped beard, heavy brows, and a long, hooked nose. The weapon he carried was some sort of focused energy device, most likely painful, but very unlikely to be fatal or even particularly injurious to someone such as myself.

I found myself more concerned with the potential of harm to my dog than with any damage he might do to me.

He looked around my apartment, frowning. "And I thought the prophet lived in humble quarters," he murmured, obviously taken aback.

"Who is this 'prophet' of which you speak?" I asked him.

The question seemed to anger him, for he flushed an unattractive shade of red and jabbed the muzzle of the weapon at me. "I'll ask the questions here," he growled. His voice held the slightest trace of an accent, but it wasn't one I recognized.

"Be my guest," I told him. "Ask whatever you'd like."

"Are you the immortal known as Hades?"

"Yes," I answered simply. He seemed surprised by this, as if he'd expected me to lie.

"You are a practitioner of magic?"

"Yes," I replied.

He didn't seem to like this answer, even though it was clearly the one he'd anticipated. It took me a moment to realize that he was one of those religious fanatics who considered magic the work of some demon. I found this thought so amusing I nearly told him that *I* was the demon he feared.

It seemed as though the past couple of centuries had not completely eliminated these fools and their ilk from the human population. A pity, that. I loathe religious fanatics.

"You are being charged with a crime by the devil Deryk Shea—" He said the name and spat on my carpet as if expectoration took the place of some insult too vile to speak. "—and will be appearing before a grand jury soon?"

"Yes," I told him, my curiosity evaporating and being replaced with growing irritation. "And I'll thank you not to spit on my carpet."

"Need I remind you," he said, jabbing the weapon at me once again, "who it is that holds the gun?"

The man was clearly a lunatic of some sort. I had to fight back the temptation to take the weapon from him and use it to permanently block his airway. Regardless, I'd had enough of him and his threats. "Need I remind you," I shot back, "that I can tear your flesh from your bones and make you disappear as if you'd never been born?"

He seemed stunned by this statement, and, before he could decide what to do with the weapon in his hand, I reached out and plucked it away. I punched him once, lightly, catching him in the nerve cluster right under the sternum with the upraised knuckle of my forefinger.

He gasped for a few moments, trying unsuccessfully to make his lungs obey, then dropped into an unconscious pile of flesh and bones at my feet.

"I'd rather you not witness this," I told Pepper, and locked her in the bathroom before returning to the unconscious intruder.

He'd piqued my curiosity. He'd wanted something in particular, and I thought it would be very interesting to find out what that something was. It was unfortunate that he probably wouldn't want to cooperate, and that I'd be required to convince him that cooperation was in his best interest.

I glanced out the window. Dawn had fallen across the city, bathing it in an amber glow. That ruled out calling in one of the vampires to help me in my interrogation. That was unfortunate, I decided, since I didn't want to do the man any lasting harm, and my interrogation techniques were rather primitive. I could make the man forget that I existed, but I couldn't make him *want* to help me with my inquiries.

But I knew someone who could, I realized with a cold smile. I wrapped him up in a mana strand and called another, leaping between my apartment and the Lounge an instant later. I materialized in the Lounge itself, which was probably a mistake. I hadn't considered that Kevin had probably installed several security features to prevent people from doing just that.

My spellbound tattoos deflected the first round of his ward's counter-attack but the keening of the alarm was almost unbearable. I covered my ears and stumbled toward the stairs. I only made it halfway before Kevin and Boneyard materialized in my path. Looking peeved, Kevin gestured and the noise stopped.

"Good security," I muttered, pulling my hands away from my ears.

"What the hell are you doing here, Hades?" he asked me suspiciously.

"I need your help, Kevin. Seriously. I didn't know how to get in touch with you other than through Jack. So here I am."

He frowned, then nodded. "Reasonable. What's up?"

"You won't believe this. I've got an armed assailant wrapped up in my apartment. I get the feeling he's dangerous, and part of something much bigger. Only, I can't get him to talk. Not without employing methods I would find much too crude. I've been around long enough to know that torture rarely works the way people think it does."

"Take us there," he said.

I whisked us back to my apartment to find my would-be assailant inching his way along the carpet toward the front door. He rolled over on his back and glared up at us as we stared down at him.

Kevin snickered. "He sure isn't going anywhere fast, is he?"

I shook my head, reached down, and lifted the assailant from the floor. I then carried him across the room and dropped him into my solitary chair.

"You seriously need furniture," Kevin remarked blandly. "Not a bad place, but empty as hell."

"Can we concentrate on the matter at hand?" I asked irritably. "This guy ain't getting any younger."

Kevin smiled grimly. "I hope you know I'm not really comfortable doing this."

I glanced over at him, a little puzzled by this confession. "Doing what? It's not as though I expect you to boil his blood in his veins or anything."

He looked disgusted at that. "Remind me to tell you why I'm a security mage rather than a physician sometime," he said.

That sounded like an intriguing story and I resolved to ask him about it at another time.

Without another word, he scooped a strand out of the air and sent one end lancing into our captive's brain. Within seconds the man was babbling like a brook, pouring out the whole hideous thing in a sudden burst of verbosity.

My blood ran cold as he revealed their plan. Apparently he and others like him were part of a separatist movement that wanted his home planet to cut ties with the Confederacy and were willing to do just about anything to accomplish this objective. Being relatively ignorant of magic, they assumed they'd be able to hold me hostage and force me to help them.

If I didn't simply decide to join in because of my history with Deryk Shea and the other immortals.

They wanted to nuke the Confed courthouse and had the means to do so. They just needed someone powerful enough to breach the wards and get the weapon inside. The whole plot was insane, but that hadn't stopped people like him before.

Apparently the issue was that the Confed Charter violated some of their planet's religious principles, and even the lax enforcement of that Charter was more than certain fundamentalists among them could tolerate.

Colony worlds come under three headings: Frontier, Provisional, and Member. Frontier worlds had the strongest Confed presence, and the Confed governing body controlled the Departments of Planetary Security, Economic Development, Human Rights, Elections and Environmental Policy. The Confed itself ensured equal treatment of all citizens, community policing, and resource management. It also prevented exploitation of labor and election tampering by multi-world corporations and their representatives.

Once a colony had shown itself to be able to enact and maintain its own Charter, following Confed strictures, it rose to the status of Provisional World, and the Confed withdrew to oversee Planetary Security and Economic Development, while keeping a careful eye on the way the planetary government handled other affairs. Any subsequent evidence of election fraud or human rights abuses would result in the immediate withdrawal of Provisional rights and a return to Frontier status.

This had already happened to this fellow's world. Colonized as it was by a more radical Shiite sect, it had shown itself unable to maintain adherence to the precepts of religious freedom and gender equality and had already lost its Provisional status two times. If it happened once more, the planet would be declared incorrigible and suffer the indignity of a forced immigration of a sizable non-Islamic population in order to diminish the influence of the religious leaders on the democratic process.

Suffice it to say the Confed wasn't in the habit of screwing around.

The colonists, on the other hand, were pretty much sick of the whole situation. They wanted out from under the Confederation's thumb, and were willing to do just about anything to achieve this end. One would-be colony had already slipped out of the Confed's net, not through force, however, but through sheer obstinacy. The Confed maintained that an economic system that carefully balanced the precepts of socialism and capitalism—i.e. strongly regulated capitalism with a fully funded social safety net—was ultimately the most beneficial to all parties concerned, individual or corporate.

The Randites, a sect of fiscal conservatives with no overt religious affiliation, disagreeing with this policy, had applied for and received permission to settle on a particularly feral planet some two-hundred light years from Earth. From the moment their colony ship left Earth's orbit, they'd made it abundantly clear that they neither wanted nor expected any further assistance from Earth or the Confederation. They would refuse all contact until they were able to engage the Confederation as a fully independent trading partner.

This was perfectly okay with the Confed. As long as the Randites didn't expect any aid from the Confederation, they weren't required to sign onto the Confederation Charter. Until such time as a representative of that world contacted the Confed, all member and provisional worlds had agreed to pretend the colony didn't exist. The Confed had nothing against liberty. It simply refused to pay for someone else's free ride.

Our captive's bunch, on the other hand, wanted to force the Confed into granting them the same status, despite the fact that a considerable amount of the Confederation's resources had already been used to perform some moderate terraforming procedures to aid in agricultural production. They'd also been forced to perform minor genetic adjustments on their livestock to protect them from a slightly elevated level of background radiation.

Their world belonged to the Confederation, whether they liked it or not.

He informed us that they also had a Plan "B" and, with great reluctance, explained the details of said plan. These bastards were smarter and trickier than I would have thought. If they couldn't sneak a nuke in, they planned on kicking a satellite from orbit and sending it whizzing down on the Confed Courthouse with no one the wiser until it was too late.

Listening to him describe the plan in detail, I realized that it was, in fact, a very good Plan "B". Intersecting the right satellite (one conveniently equipped with a stealth mode for planetary surveillance and low orbit maneuverability left over from the Cen War) with a small shielded drone at a specific time, they could send the thing rocketing into the atmosphere with all the finesse of a cue ball set to slice the eight ball into a side pocket.

Or so Kevin put it. I had to take his word for it, being more or less ignorant of the game of billiards and its variants.

"Our only chance," he told me, after putting the would-be terrorist into a magical slumber, "is if there's a mageship in-system able to intersect the drone."

The whole notion of the mageships still astounds me, and I'm not sure I can do the subject justice by trying to explain it. Imagine a huge, intelligent starship with the power to generate and manipulate mana as if it were a million sentient mages working independently of one another. Mageships were the flagships of the Confed fleet, twelve extremely powerful vessels programmed to work in partnership with a completely vetted human (or human-variant) mage.

They were a combination of magecraft and technology of the likes I'd never imagined, the brainchild of one of Deryk Shea's former engineers, a man now known only as The Artificer. "Can you get us to Deryk Shea's office?" he asked me.

I nodded slowly. He gave me the chance to retrieve Pepper from the bathroom. She wasn't very pleased with me, I noted, as I bundled her into my arms and mentally prepped a spell by altering the configuration of one of my tattoos.

I cast us onto the mage-road and sent us northward, emerging from the highway of permanent intersecting transit tubes on the roof of the Adjuster's Office building in Tacoma. Or, more precisely, on a man-made island in the center of Commencement Bay, some distance from the Port of Tacoma.

Another one of my tattoos rose to defend us from the warding spells as I punched through the roof to the offices directly below with another transit tube. This might not have been the most politic way to go about this, but it was certainly the most expedient. And, from what our captive had told us, speed was of the essence. We really had very little time to waste.

Kevin and I overran the security teams with a web of magical threads, not even bothering to craft whole spells. We used the magical equivalent of brute force to power our way past them to Deryk Shea's office. When we burst through his door, he was on his feet and moving around his desk at almost vampiric speeds. He stopped suddenly when he recognized me and saw the dog in my arms. "Hades? What the hell are you doing? And what's with the dog?"

"This is Pepper," I told him. "She's my dog. And I couldn't leave her back at my apartment with a terrorist, whether he's snoozing or not." I quickly outlined the situation for him.

He listened somewhat skeptically at first, but, with a glance at Kevin as if for confirmation, he silenced me with a wave of his hand. "The longer you talk about it, the less time we have to get something done about it."

We waited in silence as he walked back to his desk and activated what I assumed was *his* version of a PCD—over-powered though it was. Rather than taking up something the size of a twentieth century watch battery, it took up something the size of a desk drawer. Or so it appeared.

"We're in luck," he told us. "We've got a mageship just entering the system. It should be within range to detect a drone in orbit within half an hour."

"Hopefully that'll be in time," I muttered. Even if it weren't, there wasn't much we could do about it. The terrorist had said he had a little while before they activated their Plan "B", since they'd been hoping to use their nuke, which required my cooperation, or the cooperation of someone like me. I doubted they'd get any help from the magical community, especially since it sounded as though they'd hinged that whole plan on my participation, willing or otherwise. The way I calculated it out, we had just enough time for the mageship to arrive and do its work before the drone struck the satellite.

My calculations, unfortunately, were wrong. As the mageship was in-bound, it sent a message to Deryk that its scanners had picked up the drone hitting the satellite and sending it slamming into the outer atmosphere. It was already in descent. We'd run out of time.

"My god! We've got under half an hour to evacuate the courthouse." Deryk ran for the hall. I grabbed his arm as he passed. "Evacuate the courthouse, Deryk, but I've got another way to handle this. There's no telling how wide a swath of destruction this satellite will cause. Evacuate the courthouse and as much of the surrounding city as possible. In the meantime—" I grabbed a mana strand and snapped it into a transit tube aimed nearly a mile straight up—"I'm going to see if I can intercept it."

"Hades, no!"

The words were like a whisper of wind as I leaped through this end of the transit tube. Then I was floating, buffeted by cold winds high in the atmosphere. Well, not flying, exactly, but falling...falling so far above the ground it was virtually indistinguishable from flying.

I wove a bubble around my face to cut wind shear to my eyes. It did me no good to be up here if I couldn't keep my eyes open. Once I'd accomplished that, I scanned the outer reaches of the atmosphere, focusing on finding a flame trail as the satellite skipped across the outermost edge.

There! I spotted it, coming in at such speed I had to completely re-orient myself to its location several times before I was able to zero in on it. Switching to magesight, I wasn't surprised to discover there were very few mana threads available up here. That didn't matter. I reconfigured another tattoo and threw out an extra-large transit tube, ten miles long and with a mouth nearly a mile wide.

The sheer kinetic force of the falling satellite hitting the tube nearly shook it from my grasp before I could throw the other end back out into space. It writhed in my grip like an angry snake and I shrieked as the effort strained the muscles in my forearm and nearly tore my fingers apart.

One thing about transit tubes is that they don't handle large amounts of energy real well. Typically mild kinetic forces such as a falling human body, an arrow, or even a bullet, had little effect on their integrity, but something like this hunk of steel and aluminum and who knows what else was a different matter entirely. I felt the satellite enter the transit tube, sensed a brief moment of its path through the tube, then nearly passed out when the massive influx of energy shredded the spell into fragments. I tumbled through the sky, barely conscious, as I struggled to see whether I'd managed to deflect the device to a point outside the atmosphere.

My last thought before unconsciousness was that I'd succeeded, but a lingering thread of doubt remained as blackness deep as space overtook me.

I survived. You might find that surprising, but, I assure you, you'll understand quickly enough how that came to be. Falling such a distance would pulp even an immortal's resilient body, and, had I struck the ground or the water of the Puget Sound, I would have been instantly destroyed.

But my last conscious act was to shape a thread into a wind-drag chute, similar to a parachute, and it was this nearly instinctive maneuver that saved my life in the end. The mageship arrived in orbit as I was still falling and, with one thread, snatched me out of the sky and deposited me back in Deryk's office, at the same time informing him through some near-telepathic technological connection, that I'd eliminated the threat and was even now in dire need of medical attention.

The experience was not without its price. I am still weak, magically speaking, unable to handle more than a couple strands at one time without losing control of them. I'm hoping this fades, but, even if it doesn't, I can live with it. I'd risked my life for the safety of others, and in so doing, I'd given Deryk Shea a reason to drop all the charges against me.

Interestingly enough, that hadn't even entered my mind when I'd decided to do it. Near as I can tell, I hadn't given a moment of thought to any of the possible repercussions. I'd acted on necessity, almost by reflex alone.

That evening I was welcomed back to the Lounge with a full-out celebration. They even managed to convince me to take the stage for a round of karaoke. Or, as I like to say with regards to my meager talent in that arena—"croakie."

I have to add, it's a bit unnerving to go from devil to saint in a matter of days. But, if any of you are ever afforded the opportunity, I highly recommend it. The benefits are well worth the risk.

# Episode IV:
# The Queen of the Dead

My name is Steph. I'm a regular at the Magitech Lounge. I am also undead. I hang out at the Lounge because it's one place I never feel like a freak or an outsider. Believe me, that's as important in the twenty-third century as it was in any century that preceded it.

There are other places to go, of course, particularly in San Francisco, which caters to an odd sort anyway. There are vampire bars where my kind tend to congregate, and I would certainly not feel like an outsider in those sorts of places.

But the Lounge is something special. It counts among its regulars such diverse folk as a troll, several lycanthropes, mages, and the occasional immortal, as well as a few other vampires. It's a place that reminds me that I was once mortal as well, and that's never a bad thing.

This particular summer night, unusually warm for the Bay City, I sought out the Lounge not because I needed company, but because I was frightened. Someone or something had been killing Conclave vamps, seemingly with impunity, and I knew I was fairly high up on the killer's list. Rumor, hardly the most trustworthy source of information, had it that Gina Keening, the founder of the Conclave, had been slain in her home in Central Oregon. Adjuster's Office agents called in to investigate had no leads.

Now, as vampires go, I have an odd assortment of gifts, making me fairly powerful. There is no universal standard in this—some vampires are weak, some are strong. And our powers vary from person to person with no apparent rhyme or reason.

In some ways I may be more powerful than Gina was. Her primary talent seemed to be movement. She could move so quickly that even other vampires had problems tracking her. This is not a gift I possess, though I do have the ability to move far faster than the human eye can track. This is not an extraordinary talent for our kind. All vamps have this power to one degree or another.

I can also hypnotize mortals fairly easily. Roughly fifty percent of all vamps have this one. I have some psychic talents, limited to empathy and astral projection, mostly. I can communicate with rats. Not my fault. My maker was a poor sort, and rats were the first food source he could provide to me upon my rising.

I am also quite resistant to magic, which is also fairly common for vamps. My resistance seems to be stronger than most.

I entered the Lounge this night to find the place enjoying a musical jam session between our two resident musicians. Hammad and Timothy were on stage, Hammad with a guitar and Timothy on a portable electronic organ. I wandered up to the bar and ordered a blood cocktail. The manager, Jack, kept warm synthetic blood on tap for my kind, which was pretty decent of him. Many bars refused to do so, even here in San Francisco.

Callie, the night bartender, gave me a long, measuring look and poured the drink. "You okay, Steph?" she asked.

I shrugged. Callie and I were on friendly terms. In fact, she might well have been one of my few female friends who weren't part of the dead crowd. I wasn't sure I wanted to discuss this with her, however. It was way over her head. Hell, it was way over *my* head. "Where are Hades and Jack?" I asked her, having seen neither of them on my way across the common room. Jack's usual table was empty, and I couldn't recall any evening I'd ever been in when he wasn't either at his table, making the rounds amongst the clientele, or helping behind the bar.

"They had some business to tend to," she said with a shrug. "I don't know what."

Talk about bad news. This was the last thing I wanted to hear. I took the proffered drink, slapped a credit chit down on the bar, and wandered off to sit by myself in one of the booths lining the dance floor.

I found myself absorbed in my own thoughts until sudden movement caught my eye. I glanced over to see Hades talking to Callie, then peering curiously in my direction.

Hades is absolutely gorgeous, in his own way. His skin is as black as obsidian and shines under bright light. His eyes are a frosted blue, wide-set and slightly larger than average. His nose is sharp and straight, flaring slightly at the nostrils.

The planes of his face are exquisitely carved, hewn as if by a razor-edged axe wielded by a master artisan. Nearly every man I'd ever seen seems somehow half-formed when compared to this dark lord. Then again, given the immortal talent for altering their facial features, I shouldn't be surprised that Hades possessed such singular good looks.

He has wide shoulders, and typically wears sleeveless shirts, revealing elaborately drawn silver-blue tattoos running the length of his muscular arms. If one watches carefully, one can see the tattoos appear to writhe against his skin.

His hair is so black it's almost blue, cascading back from his high forehead like a fall of ebon water tumbling across his broad shoulders.

One might get the idea I'm slightly infatuated by the man, and I guess that might indeed be the case. He's an extraordinary figure, a legend in his own right, and possesses the right balance of bad boy and redeemed sinner in a singularly spectacular package.

Hades had once been the ultimate bad boy. An immortal scientist and mage, it had been Hades, in a quest to create the perfect army, who had stolen thousands of mortal children and transformed them into goblins. He'd promised to save the last of the Sidhe, and transfigured their bloodline into the source of the Abyssians—great bat-winged humanoids that kept the beauty of their fey heritage, but only if one had the vision to see through their demonic appearance.

Yes, Hades had once been a villain's villain, but somewhere along the way he'd had a change of heart. I remember the night he'd come into the Lounge, seeking absolution. Since then he'd proven his worth to all of us several times over, but never as clearly as he had when he'd risked his own life to save hundreds from a terrorist attack against the Confederation Courthouse a couple of months ago.

Hades was one of us now—a regular at the Magitech Lounge and a freak among freaks. And, unless I miss my guess, genuinely happy for the first time in ages. And I mean "ages" in a literal sense.

He strolled over, meeting my gaze and smiling as he snatched a chair from a nearby table, spun it around so the back rested against my table, and straddled the seat. He crossed his arms over the top and laid his chin on his forearms as he studied me. "Callie says you were asking after me," he said, after a moment of silence. "Is everything all right?"

If he knew of my infatuation with him, he kept quiet about it. I'd never once sensed anything in his demeanor that suggested he'd take advantage of it. I am still unsure of whether this is because he's not interested, or because he doesn't want to make assumptions and interfere with the casual atmosphere of the Lounge. This isn't a "meat market", as they used to say, nor is it a place for game playing. The men and women who patronize the Lounge after the tourists leave meet as equals, enjoying the camaraderie of shared freak-hood without the politics of romance getting in the way.

Didn't mean I didn't want to jump his bones. It just meant I needed to be subtle about it, and hope he wasn't the kind of guy who didn't "get" subtle.

I told him about the slayings of other Conclave leaders and his eyes grew wide as the implications sank in.

"You're in danger, aren't you?" he asked.

"I might be," I answered with a shrug. "To tell you the truth, I'm not sure what it all means."

"Any news from the Adjuster's Office?" he asked.

Regular murders are usually investigated by municipal police departments, but anything with paranormal or preternatural parameters, or involving specific requests from the families of the victims, were automatically an Adjuster's Office matter. AO agents don't screw around and people know it.

I shook my head. "Unless and until they tie the murders to the Conclave specifically, I'm not on any need-to-know list."

His lip quirked into a cute half smile. "And how likely do you think it is that it's *not* connected to the Conclave?"

89

"Not very."

I flinched at a loud laugh from the other side of the room.

Damn. My nerves were raw. Even the proximity of people I liked and trusted was starting to wear at my state of mind. I wanted nothing more than to be someplace dark and quiet.

The problem was that I was safer here than anywhere else I could name. That was just a plain truth. Word had it that the Lounge had been built with a failsafe. If anything went down in here we couldn't handle, reinforcements would arrive within a minute or two, and, though I'd never met these reinforcements personally, I believed Jack when he said they were of the kick-ass variety.

"Where's Jack?" It came out of my mouth as if of its own accord and I wanted to kick myself. It really wasn't any of my business and I knew better than to ask questions like this.

Hades grinned back at me. "Personal business," was all he'd say. Personal business which required that Hades accompany him through at least a part of it? My curiosity was piqued, but Hades's response left little doubt I'd learn nothing more.

Damn it all.

Okay, I'll admit it. I'm snoopy. Too curious for my own damn good. Of course, truth be told, I was probably just trying to distract myself from my own problems at the moment. Hades seemed to understand. He had an unmistakable look of compassion in his eyes as he regarded me silently.

"You're safe here," he said, echoing my earlier thought. "No one's going to be able to get to you here."

"Yeah, but I can't stay here forever," I replied. Come dawn I'd *have* to be somewhere else, someplace insulated against sunlight, or risk being turned into a pile of ash. I'd be vulnerable then, and the notion was like an itch I couldn't quite reach. This was no time to be vulnerable.

As if there's ever a *good* time.

"I'd invite you to spend the day at my place," he said, "but it's not very homey."

I frowned. "What do you mean, homey?"

"I've got a lamp and a recliner and a book collection stacked in the corner."

Immortals. Most of them don't need to sleep and, from the sounds of it, Hades had little motivation to make his home into something other people might enjoy. He probably spent *all* of his downtime sitting in that chair reading.

I had to chuckle a little at that.

"What?"

I shook my head and laughed a little louder. "I gotta know. Do you keep *anything* in your fridge?"

"Juice," he answered. "And bottled water."

"I take it you don't cook?"

He shrugged. "Why bother cooking for one person? It's cheaper all the way around just to come here or hit an autochef at the mall."

He had a point.

It's interesting to note that, since we seemed to be having a private conversation, the other regulars didn't see fit to interrupt. People here are like that. We give each other space when we need it, and comfort when we need that as well.

He shivered suddenly and I glanced toward the door, wondering if he'd been hit by a draft I hadn't felt. As it was still securely closed, I shot him a questioning look and he shrugged in response. "I don't know," he said. "Just a weird feeling all of the sudden."

I extended my psychic senses and felt the hairs on the back of my neck standing at attention. I'd always thought that was just an expression, but now I had proof positive it wasn't. I brushed back my chair and stood, facing the door.

A cold wind blew through the place and everyone shifted uneasily, though I'm not sure anyone realized why. The wind wasn't physical, it was psychic, and strong enough that anyone with any sensitivity at all would have felt it. It was that powerful.

On this psychic wind I thought I heard the whisper of a voice, a woman's voice, calling my name as if at a great distance. I lifted my head and stared at the door, sure beyond all shadow of a doubt that someone—something—stood just outside, perhaps in the street beyond the door, calling my name in a manner only I would hear.

It became obvious that this wasn't the case when the door opened and Jack strode in unconcernedly. Obviously no monster waited outside, nor whispered my name on the astral winds from the street. To be honest, I found this a source of greater fear on my part. It meant that the creature that stalked us was even more powerful than I imagined.

Jack was greeted by a loud hello from the patrons and spent a few minutes glad-handing before making his way towards his customary table. As he passed us, he met Hades's gaze for a moment, smiled at me, then slid into his booth in the corner.

"Where's Anya?" I asked Hades, as he sat there in the booth, his miniature pincer cradled in his arms. Anya had come a long way from the lonely child whom Hades had rescued from the Dimension of Mirrors his first night here in the Lounge. Though I know little about magic other than as an observer, it seemed to me that her talent had grown considerably in the proceeding months.

He gave me an odd look and I realized that their little venture had involved something about the girl. And, for whatever reason, they weren't sharing details. Or, at least, Hades wasn't. I wondered if Jack would be so reticent.

He noticed my glance in Jack's direction and shook his head warningly. "I wouldn't, if I were you," he advised quietly.

He knew me well enough to see my slight smile for what it was. A silent admission that my curiosity was going to get the better of me.

"You are the snoopiest creature," he said with a groan. "Can't you accept the fact that it's none of your business?"

He was up against a couple different factors here, the first being that I am terribly curious by nature. I don't like being left out of the loop. The second, at this point, was the fact that I desperately needed to drown out the voice whispering in the back of my skull. It hadn't stopped when Jack had entered—it had merely faded to near inaudibility.

I scooted the chair back and began to rise, but something halted me mid-action. I snapped my head around as the front window, heavily tinted to the point of obscuring the scene outside, shattered inward, showering the foyer with glass.

She looked like a ghost as she entered, a white shape in a diaphanous gown, cloaked in the mist that had shrouded the city for the past few days. She landed lightly amidst the glass and walked up the ramp, seemingly unhurt by the jagged shards underfoot.

She was beautiful, in a way, but there was something frightening about that beauty. It was ethereal and cold and without humanity, like a marble statue of some goddess given the semblance of life.

She was so pale as to appear almost translucent, like the gown billowing around her bare feet. Her skin seemed to glow with its own inner light.

I knew at once that this was the source of the voice I'd heard calling to me.

She paused at the top of the ramp and lifted her arm to point a finger across the bar at me. "You. I called yet you did not come." Her voice was at once both musical and chilling in its utter lack of humanity. It was much as I suspected the voices of the notorious valkyrie—the deadly immortal creations of the Cen invaders—might sound. If this creature was once human, it had long forgotten what that meant.

I struggled to find my voice. This is not usually a problem for me, but staring at this vision I abruptly found myself unable to find any words.

Across the table from me, Hades shot to his feet. "She does not answer to you," he said, his voice booming in the deep silence that had overtaken the Lounge.

"Silence, you," she said simply, and walked forward toward us.

Hades gestured and I caught the barest hint of something brushing at her, enough to move her gown in a way that indicated it hadn't been the wind. The magic, for it seemed apparent that's what it had been, had no more effect on her than a beam from a flashlight might have had if it had cast upon her form.

Out of the corner of my eye I saw his gaze narrow and his lips tighten. The failure of his magic did not daunt him in the least. If anything, he grew more determined to keep her away from me.

She accelerated then, moving at a speed so fast no human gaze could have followed her movement. But the dark immortal's eyes *could* follow it, and he stepped into her path and repelled her with a mighty shove. She stumbled back, the look of amazement on her face too rich to describe. It bordered on absolute shock, and it was perhaps the most human expression I'd seen there since she'd entered. "Who are you?" she asked him, her attention finally pulled away from me.

His lip twitched but he did not smile. "I am the dark lord Hades," he answered. "Who are *you?*"

Her visage seemed to ripple, and an inhuman calm washed over it in a wave. "I am Alesandra," she said. "I am the Queen of her kind. She will either bow to me or be destroyed."

"Not going to happen," Hades shot back. "She is under my protection and I will not step aside."

I might have resented his intervention in any other case, but the fact was that this woman terrified me. I recognized her now as a vampire, but one of such age that my hundred years or so was like an eye-blink compared to the length of her existence. She was completely outside of my experience and I knew now, in this instance, what must have happened to my fellow Conclave members. She had confronted them and not received the homage she thought of as her due. And they had not had an immortal there to defend them.

"Not only *his* protection," said Hydra, in his booming voice. He lurched forward, his huge hands curling into fists as he stared down at her. "You will also have to deal with *me.*"

A great rumble, so deep that it was felt before it could be heard, rose from another corner of the lounge, and a hulking black shape, feline and humanoid both, stepped from the shadows. Its massive claws gleamed dangerously under the overhead lights. "Death awaits you here if you persist," it said, and I realized in that moment that the cat-thing was Boneyard, in his transitional were form.

He loomed nearly as large as Hydra, and it was then that I realized why many vampires respected lycanthropes. They were, in their own way, as dangerous as any of us. Very few, if any, vamps could tangle with this monster, looking like some unholy cross between a great cat and an ape, without risking utter destruction.

She looked at each of my defenders in turn, seemingly unimpressed. This wisp of a woman uttered a laugh like a silver bell and danced sideways, catching the troll in the side with what looked like a casual backhand. He was lifted and hurled into the bar with enough force to destroy a sizeable portion of it in an instant shower of splinters and shards.

She met Boneyard's charge head on, evading his first few attacks with effortless grace before slamming a fist into the side of his jaw. He barely flinched, responding with a raking swipe of his left hand that shredded the front of her gown and left bloody furrows between her breasts and her throat.

She sprang away, landing atop the sprawled form of Hydra, and thrust her hand at the 'thrope. Some invisible force lifted him and launched him at the opposite wall with enough force to drive him through the paneling and into the concrete beyond, embedding him there like a child's toy driven into the mud by an adult's angry foot.

Then I saw Hades gesture once again, and the glass from the front window rose as if like a swarm of angry, silicate bees and flew at her as if driven by a malevolent will of their own. She didn't notice it until it was nearly too late, and was caught in the horizontal rain of glass before she could do more than throw up a hand to protect her face.

Dazed by the ferocity of this assault, she failed to realize that the troll on which she stood had regained consciousness. Fingers like stovepipes wrapped around her ankle and she was lifted and bashed against the floor with all the fury a pissed off troll can muster.

At this point I think it was simple luck that saved her life. We vampires are vulnerable to two things—sunlight and severe damage to our brain or spinal column. Had she not been able to absorb enough of the impact on her arms, he would have no doubt dashed her head against the floor with enough force to turn her gray matter into so much mush.

As it was I heard the unmistakable sound of breaking bone and she screamed. She was not terribly handicapped by the pain, however, spinning abruptly and kicking out at Hydra's wrist. He released his grip on her ankle with a bellow of pain and anger of his own.

She spun to her feet, cradling her right arm. I knew that it would mend within minutes, if not seconds, so they'd be wise to press their advantage now. They'd caught her by surprise, but it wouldn't happen again.

Through all of this Jack had sat stock-still at his table. He stood now and lifted one arm slowly. I wondered if he was aiming a weapon, but he seemed to be pointing at the mirror behind the bar, which had miraculously been spared any damage.

The mirror shimmered like a still pool struck by a stone and a lone woman stepped out of it. The first thing that struck me about her was her beauty. Real human beauty, but truly as close to incomparable as one could imagine. If I were to guess at it, I would have marked her bloodline as Arabic. She had dusky skin, a straight, aristocratic nose, and hair as dark and full as Hades's. Pale green eyes, completely out of place in that face, stared at the vampiric intruder with cold intensity.

At her side suddenly appeared a small blue humanoid creature, naked but for a thin vest. It stood no taller than her hip, and its most distinguishing feature was the wide grin that split its round face. That and its lack of any sexual characteristics, that is.

The blue thing vanished with a "pop" and appeared in the air above Alesandra with a whooshing sound. It dropped down upon her shoulders and wrapped its arms around her face. She reached up with both arms—apparently she healed as fast as I'd feared—and tried to pry the creature off. It didn't budge, hanging on with all the determination of a love-sick squid.

The dark woman spoke, a husky contralto that most likely made the heart of every man in the place skip a beat. "You're about a second away from sunlight," she said, obviously speaking to Alesandra. "My friend there can take you anywhere in the world in a split second. There is no way to stop him. Unless you're immune to it, and I suspect that you are not, you'd *best* take a minute to consider your options.

"Option one. You keep fighting. That'll earn you a one-way ticket to someplace hot, dry and instantly fatal.

"Option two. You sit your undead ass down in that chair over there and we converse in a civilized manner.

"There is no third option. Raise your right hand if you're willing to parley."

Slowly, reluctantly, Alesandra lifted her right arm.

"Smart," the dark woman said. "You can fade now, Q."

The creature on Alesandra's shoulders phased out, leaving behind for only a brief moment the outline of its huge grin. The woman from the mirror jabbed a finger at Alesandra as she shifted her weight. "Don't even think about it. Quickfingers can be back in a second, and then we're back to option one. Take my word for it, you've lost. You lost the minute you thought to walk in here pursuing your vendetta."

"Who is she?" I asked Hades in a muted whisper, certain I should already know the answer.

"That's the Lady of Blades," he murmured back. "Jasmine Tashae. If *she's* Jack's backup security, it's no wonder he doesn't worry about anything too tough for us to handle."

"She's just one woman," I hissed. "How tough could she possibly be?"

A chair materialized behind Alesandra and she sat abruptly. It didn't look as though it had been her idea. Jasmine Tashae strode over to her and stood there looking down at her, arms folded under her breasts. "So what's your deal, lady?"

"I am the Queen of the Vampires," Alesandra said. "I am the mate of the Keening and all of the undead fall under my rule."

"The Keening?" Jasmine made a choking sound and it took me a minute to realize she was laughing. "That maggot comes within a mile of me and he's dust," she said in a tone that brooked no argument. "You think bringing up *his* name entitles you to anything but contempt?"

"He is the oldest vampire in existence," Alesandra said casually. "He has powers that other vampires cannot even imagine."

"He's an asshole," Jasmine said firmly. "A lot of innocent people died so he could go back in time and live out his fantasy of being king shit vamp. We've been looking for his ass for a *long* time, lady. There's a reason he sent you here to do his dirty work for him. He's *afraid* to do it himself. Because there's a whole host of us who'll be on him like white on rice the minute he pops his head out of whatever hole he's hiding in."

"Keening? That's the name of the..." I let my voice trail off. Gina Keening had been the founder of the Conclave. They were talking about her son. He'd sent this creature here and had her kill his *mother?* The thought nauseated me. And brought up some questions I would have never thought to ask without that little revelation.

Why had he even bothered? Obviously he had made whatever mark he'd wanted on his own vampire community, in his own universe. What the hell did he think he'd gain by sending her here to do his dirty work? And did he really expect her to succeed? It seemed unlikely, considering that he hadn't come himself.

Was it simply a matter of revenge?

None of it made sense to me and I really don't like things that don't make sense.

"How did you get here?" Jasmine was asking Alesandra. "Through a worldgate? Where's this worldgate?"

The self-described vampire queen didn't want to answer these questions. Her initial arrogance had faltered, and I think she finally realized she was in big trouble. Yes, we vampires are big and bad, and none more so than the eldest among us. But the immortals were big and bad in their own right. Particularly this one, apparently.

"Fine. If you're not willing to answer my questions," Jasmine said finally, after thirty seconds or so meeting Alesandra's defiant gaze, "you're useless to me."

And abruptly the air around the seated vampire was full of swords. Alesandra didn't even have the chance to flinch before the blades had moved in concert to separate her head from her torso. The effect was nearly instantaneous as she disintegrated before our eyes, becoming nothing but a pile of gray ash in and around the chair.

"Ohmygod," I gasped. "She never had a chance."

Hades shook his head. "No. She didn't." There was something I couldn't place lurking deep in his eyes and, after a moment, I realized what it was. Hades was terrified.

I learned why an instant later when Jasmine turned her emerald gaze on him. "Hades." Her mouth curved into a feral grin. "I'd heard that you'd resurfaced. I'd even heard that you've turned over a new leaf."

She was suddenly standing next to our table and I hadn't even seen her move. She leaned over, putting her face within inches of Hades's. "You know, of course, that it doesn't mean shit to me. There will always be things that are unforgivable. What you did to all those children is one of them. The only thing you've earned from where I stand is a chance to keep breathing. You step one foot over the line again and it'll be the last step you ever take."

She stood, spun around, and launched herself at the mirror, vanishing back into its depths without even a telltale ripple this time. A second later her blue companion reappeared, this time in the center of the table at which we sat.

I have to give Hades props for nerve. He didn't even flinch. I did, but just a little.

The creature grinned—which seemed to be its habitual expression—and patted Hades on the head like one might a friendly dog. "Redemption is a good thing, Hades. The boss is a bit of a hard ass, but her heart's in the right place." It laughed aloud at that and fired off a wink. "Rumor has it she keeps it in a jar under her bed."

It snickered and, in a heartbeat, it was gone.

"Okay," I said to Hades, "what the hell was *that?*"

"That," he replied, "was Quickfingers the imp. He's a spirit, a creature formed entirely out of magic, crafted by Jasmine when she was only a kid. He's probably as powerful as she is, if

101

not *more* powerful, and damn near completely unpredictable. The one good thing about Quickfingers is that he can't do anything to hurt anyone."

"But what about her threat—"

"A bluff. I think. I'm not sure if that would fall under the restriction that seems to cover the imp's behavior. It might be a loophole."

"A loophole?"

"Sure. Teleporting to a sunny clime is only dangerous to vampires. I'm not sure he'd perceive it as any sort of attack. He's proscribed from doing anything overtly injurious to another being. Or so I understand it."

I'd had enough. This whole evening had been a merry-go-round of emotional distress, a roller-coaster ride of terror and depression. I desperately needed to get away from the Lounge, from everything I knew.

I stood abruptly. "I'm going to take a vacation," I told Hades. "I need to sort some stuff out in my head. You have a couple of choices."

"Which are?"

"You can either come with me, or spend the next while worrying about me. I'm interested in you, Hades, but I'll understand if you don't want to get involved with me. We both have our own baggage and it may not all fit together very well.

"The Conclave owns an artificial island in the Caribbean," I told him. "It's a world-renowned party spot, and has one hell of a night life. I need to get away from it all, and that's my destination of choice. Interested?"

He thought about it for all of about five seconds. "How long?"

"I can't say how long I'll need to stay there," I answered, "but I understand you have obligations here. How about you spend a week down there with me and we can take it from there?"

He met my gaze and a slow smile spread across his face. "I believe we have a deal."

We didn't leave that moment, of course. We had to make sure Hydra was all right, and that Boneyard could be extricated from the wall without harm, but we were able to set out sometime before dawn.

He wasn't happy to discover that we'd have to travel there by boat, until he got a chance to see the boat in question. The island might have belonged to the Conclave, but this particular vessel was all mine. She was named *Night Shade* and she was a seventy foot sailboat with a completely autonomous robotic crew. The perfect boat for a long cruise with someone you wanted to get to know better than you did.

Are we in love?

Not sure how to answer that. I do know one thing for certain. I'm certainly in lust. And every indication tells me that he feels the same way.

We've got forever to figure it all out. Forever works for me.

How about I get back to you in fifty years or so?

# Episode V:
# A Troll for All Seasons

Modern medical equipment isn't designed with someone of my stature in mind. Nor do doctors seem particularly interested in treating or even finding the source of my malaise. This is an unfortunate side effect of being a troll.

My appetite, while significant to begin with, had grown to epic levels in recent weeks. I found that I could not pass by anything remotely resembling food without having to eat it. It is fortunate I make a decent living, or I might have been made destitute by my increased appetite.

One might wonder what a nine-foot, gray-skinned troll might do for work. I cannot speak for other nine-foot gray-skinned trolls, but I build boats. Sleek, lovely, customized sea-going vessels with all the comforts of home.

Some people find it ironic that I would manufacture items that I myself cannot use. I am primarily the designer of said boats and leave it to others to do most of the actual construction. One might realize that this means that I have greatly understated my resources, and have grossly overstated the effects of my current appetite on my financial well-being.

I am not a poor troll, reduced to exacting tribute from people unfortunate enough to have to cross a bridge under which I happen to reside. I am, in fact, a very wealthy troll, but a troll nonetheless. Even medical professionals have difficulty putting aside their prejudices in order to examine me.

There are those researchers who specialize in the metahuman mutations such as myself—trollologists, as they're known in certain circles—who classify me as an animalized troll, which means that I resemble another creature as much as I resemble a human. For me it's an elephant. I am large and bulky, with a long, trunk-like appendage where most people would have a nose. I do not, however, have any particular urge to stomp about in bodies of water and spray myself with my nose. In fact, near as I can tell, I have no elephant-like tendencies at all.

People fear me. As I am at heart a gentle soul who wishes harm to no one, this leaves an aching void within my soul that I cannot fill.

The only humans for whom my monstrous appearance is not a factor are my friends at the Magitech Lounge. It is only in that unique place where I am allowed to feel like a human being rather than a freak of nature.

I am usually the first of the night crowd to arrive and that particular night in early September was no exception. I squeezed through the door and trundled up the ramp from the entrance—which squeaks in protest every time I do so—and strolled across the wide expanse of the dance floor to the bar.

Jack, the manager, had renovated a little in the wake of a small battle that had occurred on the premises late last month, during which I was thrown through the bar and subsequently forced to commit violence against a particularly noxious fiend of a vampire with what *I* believe was a God complex. She was taken out of the picture by someone else entirely, a fact with which I had no qualms. I am not a violent man by nature, and only the need to arise to the defense of one of my friends had drawn me into the fray.

On this particular night, Jack was behind the bar rather than in his usual booth in the corner. As this means that the usual night bartender, Callie, had taken the night off, I inquired as to her health. She usually has Sundays and Mondays off. This was Thursday, which, in my mind, indicated a cause for concern.

"Death in the family," Jack told me, setting a mug of frothy beer in front of me. I quaffed half the contents in a single draught and nodded.

"I'm sorry to hear that," I said sincerely. I harbor great affection for Callie. She is a normal young woman who seems to take my appearance, and the general oddness of the other patrons, well in stride. I dare say she is one of the most friendly normals I've ever met, and far more tolerant than most. Even by the standards of these ostensibly enlightened times.

I was, as usual, the only one in the lounge during the transition between evening and the late night shift. What was unusual was the fact that my arrival did not cause any daytime customers to flee the scene. The Lounge was uncharacteristically empty. "Is everything all right?" I asked Jack.

Jack seems a normal human of ordinary stature and unremarkable appearance. It is rumored that he somehow gained his position as manager of this place by virtue of being in the right place at the right time, and attracting the attention of some very powerful people who were interested in sponsoring a place very much like the one the Magitech Lounge has turned out to be.

He shrugged in response to my question and said nothing.

I heaved a sigh. "Got anything to eat?"

His brow furrowed into a deep frown and he regarded me somberly. "Maybe I should be asking *you* if everything is all right," he said. "You seem down tonight." He tossed a menu in front of me and gave me a wry grin.

Jack is a good listener, if nothing else, and I found myself pouring my angst and frustration with the medical profession into his ear. He listened attentively, and when I was through, reached across to pat me on the arm. "Have you considered taking a trip out-world to get checked out?"

In all honesty, I hadn't. It's hard for me, sometimes, to comprehend how vast the universe actually is. This Earth and its colonies are not the only places to seek help. There are other Earths and other realities entirely.

When I was younger and more hopeful, I believed that maybe, somewhere, there might be a cure for my condition. I read everything I could find about Starhaven, the Interworld agencies, and the power players in the metaverse.

But the fact remained that neither their advanced science nor magic itself could remake me into something even slightly more "normal". At least not so much as I could determine from my research. Maybe I needed to do more than research. Maybe I needed to travel to Starhaven myself. If nothing else, they might be able to tell me why I felt so lousy.

Then again, I had no idea of how to get there.

Just thinking about it made me more depressed than ever. I didn't even bother to turn around when I heard the door open behind us. I did, however, glance up at Jack, whose eyes had widened considerably. So I leaned over slightly and peered in the mirror behind the bar to see who had entered.

What I saw struck me momentarily dumb. It wasn't, as I expected, another one of the regulars.

The image of the woman who nearly filled the foyer caught my eye, a vision of womanly curves and great expanses of dark flesh in black leather. She lifted her lovely face and met my gaze. She strode up the ramp, a rustling of black like a cloak at her back as she shifted her wings.

An Abyssian. Here. I'm uncertain as to which of us—Jack or myself—was more stunned by the sight of the beautiful winged woman striding across the edge of the dance floor toward us. She flashed a dazzling smile. "I wasn't sure anyone would be here."

Jack and I exchanged glances, equally puzzled by this comment. "And why wouldn't anyone be here?" Jack asked. I suddenly realized that it was ten-thirty in the evening, and none of the regulars but me had found their way in. This was so rare an event as to be unprecedented.

She leveled her gaze at the both of us and blinked. "You mean you don't know?"

"Know what?" Jack asked, his voice ratcheting up a notch as the fact of the empty bar and the late hour seemed to occur to him as well. I recognized concern in his face and he leaned against the bar toward her as if to speed her response by being nearer when she delivered it.

"A child has gone missing in the park," she said. "Many of the neighborhood folks are out there looking for him. I was, but I needed to make use of your facilities and everyone else has locked their doors to help with the search."

Well, that explained where the other regulars were. There wasn't a one of us who wouldn't drop everything to search for a missing child.

Jack pointed toward the restrooms, frowning. "The facilities are down that hall," he said, then paused. "I'm not sure they'll accommodate your wings though," he added fretfully.

She grinned at him and I felt my heart skip a beat. God, she was beautiful. "That's okay," she said. "I'll manage."

"Should we go help?" I asked Jack, when she disappeared into the ladies' room.

He shrugged. "Do either of us have a particular talent that would come in handy at a time like this?"

"Not me," I replied. I could see what he was getting at, but I wasn't sure I bought the argument.

"You can bet there are vamps and 'thropes all over the park right now. I doubt we could add anything to the effort and, in fact, might impede it somewhat just by adding more scents to the trails."

That's when I realized that even the staff was missing, an oddity I should have realized right after my arrival. Had I not been so concerned with my own problems, I would have noticed something as obvious as that.

In fact, it was weird that Jack hadn't mentioned it either. He met my questioning gaze and sighed. "Okay, you got me. I knew about the missing kid and I stayed here to keep your attention focused on something else."

"What? Damn, Jack, couldn't you tell I needed the distraction if nothing else?"

He shrugged. "Yeah, but a troll wandering around in the park when panicked normals are looking for a missing kid is a recipe for disaster."

This drew me up short. He had a point, loathe as I was to admit it. Many normals will perceive me as a monster no matter what I do.

The Abyssian woman exited the restroom and strode up to the bar. I noticed something odd about her gait and realized that her wings seemed to be missing. This was a talent I did not know they possessed—though in all fairness, I had to admit that I'd never personally met one of their unique race before now.

Nor had many people at all. Abyssians tended to stay away from ordinary citizens, and that included most freaks. Abyssians aren't human—they're Sidhe with a manipulated gene code...more or less. Or so I'm given to understand.

Jack is far less reticent to ask questions than I am. "Hey—where'd your wings go?"

She turned to him with a little rumbling laugh. "I can summon or dismiss them as I choose," she said. "It's a sign of power among my kind."

"I wish I could do that with my nose," I muttered darkly.

Another chuckle and her gaze came to me. "It is a unique appendage," she said. "Are you not happy with it?"

"Hardly," I said. "It's bad enough being big and gray with elephant feet"—I lifted one by way of illustration—"but to have *this* on my face is a little too much." I yanked at the source of my aggravation and peered down at it irritably.

My trunk is roughly the circumference of my wrist and extends to about ten inches. In all respects it resembles a short, stubby elephant's trunk. It's truly a gruesome thing to be stuck in the middle of an otherwise normal human face. Well, normal other than the color and size, of course.

She frowned. I found it, oddly enough, to be as attractive as her smile. "Then why don't you just rid yourself of it?"

"Rid myself of it?"

"Of course. Have it removed surgically or transformed by magical means."

I blinked at her. She couldn't actually be that ignorant of my situation, could she? Then I realized, she could. Abyssians weren't connected to the net, they didn't participate in the normal or even the freak community much at all. They were more or less completely out of the loop, as insular in general as the Amish were before they were happily transported to a colony world where they no longer needed to turn their back on technology. The Abyssians reportedly lived deep underground, in heretofore undiscovered caverns they called the Abyss— hence their name.

"He's a troll," Jack cut in. "He regenerates. Trying to fix it through surgical means would make a serious mess and, in the end, wouldn't help at all. Prohibitively expensive too, assuming he could find someone willing to do it in the first place. And magic doesn't work all that well on trolls either."

"That's too bad," she said, leaning over and peering at me curiously. "It seems as though there should be *something* that can be done for you. Tell me, would your resistance to magic persist if it were *you* casting the spells?"

I didn't know the answer to this. I'd honestly never thought about it. "But I can't," I said, which as far as I was concerned made the whole question rhetorical.

"I wouldn't necessarily bet on that," she answered. "Current figures indicate that roughly fifty to sixty percent of the human population now have the genes to use magic. Those are pretty good odds."

I glanced at Jack, who seemed as surprised by this revelation as I was. "How do you know this?" I asked her.

"Not all of my kind stays underground," she says. "This world may not easily tolerate me, but I am not looked upon too oddly should I travel to Starhaven."

Starhaven again. It looked as though that was my ultimate destination in my search for a new form. "How do you get to Starhaven?"

"Through a worldgate," she told me. "Why—did you want to go there yourself?"

"It might be the perfect place to seek out a solution to my problem."

She nodded slowly. "Yes, it might. Do you have a way to get there?"

"Uh...no."

"I thought not. So let me offer you some help in that department. I was planning on going there this evening anyway, but ended up being side-tracked by the search for the missing kid."

"You were helping with that? Shouldn't you be getting back to it?"

She shook her head. "Nah. I did a few aerial sweeps and came up with nothing. I don't think the kid's in the park anymore. They've got a few vampires and lycanthropes on the ground following by scent, so I figure they're a lot better equipped to handle it from here than I am."

Jack gave me a nod. "I just got off the line with Boneyard. They're following a trail leading out of the park even as we speak."

Jack has one of those PCD implants. When he looks like he's talking to himself, he's more likely talking to someone else over his invisible communication device. It's still damn unsettling, since he's gotten so good at sub-vocalizing we often don't notice he's doing it at all. Most of the time he just uses it to communicate with Boneyard and Kevin, the Lounge's security staff, but nevertheless I had to ask—where would it all end?

Did I mention that communication implants give me the willies? At least they're not as bad as those new wetware mods—the kind that allow people to communicate and even transfer images as if they were telepathic? Better living through invasive brain surgery. The whole idea creeps me out.

I guess I'm just old-fashioned in that respect. I like being able to hold a PCD in my hand. The most advanced interface I wanted to utilize was voice recognition software. I'm a bit of a technological throwback, I realize.

A troll afraid of advanced technology—imagine that.

"I'd love to accompany you," I told the lovely Abyssian woman, realizing at that exact moment that I had failed to ask her name. "I must apologize, but I don't know your name."

"Spite."

"Your name is Spite?" I goggled at this.

She sighed. "For now. We change our names as circumstances change. My parents believe I do the things I do out of spite, so it seems a fitting name for the time being."

I tried to wrap my mind around the concept. "If you can change your name on a whim, how does anyone know how to refer to you?"

"By familial connections, typically. Changing our names often is a young Abyssian's habit. Once we become parents it becomes a rarity to do so. So, if someone wants to refer to me, I'm called 'Spite, Ensil's daughter.'"

"Oh." It still seemed weird to me, but who was I to argue about another culture's traditions? "Well, Spite, is there anything I should take with me?"

"Credit chits, if you have any. Starhaven and Earth have an open trade policy for the most part, though most Earth folks are unaware of that fact, so any chits you have on hand will be honored there."

An open trade policy? I had a feeling I was in for a serious education here, and even if I didn't find a way to cure my malady, I'd at least learn many things worth knowing. "I have five hundred on me right now. Will that be enough?"

"It should be. So you're ready?"

I nodded.

If you've never had occasion to travel through a worldgate, let me give you two pieces of advice should you ever consider doing so. First—take some anti-motion-sickness medication beforehand. It does things to your equilibrium that'll make your last meal jump for the nearest exit point. Second—don't start moving as soon as you arrive at your destination.

I don't vomit. Ever. So I was pretty much safe from the first one, though my stomach was spinning like water down a flush toilet. But I threw myself forward almost immediately and rebounded rather painfully off the duraplaz wall that separated the worldgate chamber from the rest of its environs.

I sat down on the platform, hard. Once my head cleared, I spotted Spite standing over me, an unmistakably amused look in her eyes. "I'd recommend you curb your impulsive tendencies while you're here," she said, offering a hand. I took it and between us we managed to get me back on my feet. Since I weigh about as much as a small motor vehicle, this is a pretty impressive feat.

I stood there a moment and looked around. We were in what looked like a large plastic box, in which was a raised platform about fifteen feet squared. On the other side of the transparent wall separating us from the outside of the box I saw a feline hybrid—a lion, I think. At least he looked like he had a large golden mane falling around his shoulders. He stood beside what might have been a control panel mounted on a small pedestal. His tawny eyes gave us the once-over and he pressed a button or flicked a switch or something like that because, when he did, a section of the duraplaz wall fell away, giving us an egress.

The lion was dressed in some sort of white armor—reminded me a little of the kind the bad guys wore on that old sci-fi movie...The one with those laser sword things? Except it had a stylized phoenix emblazoned across the chest plate and no helmet. Some sort of black, bulky firearm hung at his hip.

"How's it going, Joge?" Spite asked him as we passed.

"Not too bad, Spite. Been quiet lately."

"Which is just how you like it, isn't it?"

"You bet. The attempted invasion a couple of months ago was enough excitement to last me a decade, at least."

They both laughed. "Who's your friend?"

"This is..."

"Hydra," I supplied, realizing that she'd never asked *my* name. "I'm from Earth."

"You'd almost have to be," Joge said. "Ain't no trolls anywhere else. Or, at least, not trolls that look like *you.*"

He recognized me as a troll right off. I found that impressive. There were humans on Earth who's first reaction was "what the hell is *that* thing," and here was a creature that didn't even live on Earth figuring it out as fast as that. "There are other kinds of trolls?"

"Troll is just a nickname they saddled your kind with when you started popping up," the lion hybrid said. "There are real trolls out there too. One thing *they* ain't is mutated humans."

"Good seeing you, Joge. My friend here is looking for a way to look more normal and we figured this was the best place to go."

He nodded. "You might stop by the Magitech shop. Word has it Artificer has some new goodies that might fit the bill."

I blinked at the Magitech reference but didn't say anything. She thanked him and we continued down a long corridor bisected by a clear pond ringed by several dwarf fruit trees that looked quite well-tended.

The corridor itself was immense, as large as an earthly cathedral in some historical city I'd never visited. The walls were an off-white color, and though it was way above us, it looked as though the ceiling was of the same hue.

We passed a couple adjoining corridors, then turned to the left several hundred yards from the worldgate, entering a long unremarkable hallway of more conventional dimensions. "What's this Magitech place?" I asked her.

"There is a connection, if that's what you're wondering. It's actually one of the reasons I chose to stop by your friend's bar. The Lady of Blades is connected to the real Magitech and wanted to reproduce the atmosphere of the Magitech Lounge here on Starhaven. *Your* Magitech Lounge is the result."

That seemed like half an answer, at least. I decided to wait and see what I could determine on my own before asking any more questions on the subject. She didn't strike me as particularly informative about certain things and I decided that there might be a reason for this. Maybe she expected me to figure things out for myself, or else she just didn't particularly like answering questions.

We turned right at another intersecting corridor and traveled another fifty feet or so, to where a large silver disk stood embedded in the floor. She led me up onto it and spoke clearly. "C Sector," she said.

We were instantly transported elsewhere. It wasn't like a worldgate. It wasn't like anything I'd ever experienced. I didn't even find it mildly discomfiting, though I think a part of me knew I was in a totally different place than I'd started out.

I followed her off the platform and we fairly quickly emerged into a section filled with what looked like normal storefronts. I spotted two intriguing signs right off. One said "Magitech Lounge" and the other said "Magitech Outlet".

"In here," Spite told me, and led me into the "Outlet". The fellow behind the counter was currently dealing with two other customers, a hybrid raccoon and what may well have been some sort of weasel or ferret. It can be hard to tell the mustalid hybrid types apart. Except for the skunks, badgers and wolverines, at least.

Hybrids aren't all that common on Earth, but there are some. They probably outnumber us trolls by a two to one margin, but that's only an estimate. Normals have issues with those who are obviously freakish. They don't mind so much knowing that vamps and lycanthropes and mages are among them, as long as they look more or less like everyone else. For those of us who do not, they harbor little but suspicion and fear.

Once these two had purchased whatever it was they were after, the shopkeeper, a thin, balding human wearing a pair of spectacles low on his nose, peered over them at us and smiled. "Can I help you?"

"Not sure," said Spite, leaning against the counter. Carefully, I noted. While it was obvious the ceilings and doors in this place were designed to accommodate someone of our size, the counter was similar in construction to the bar at the Lounge back home. It didn't even come up to my waist. "My friend here doesn't like his looks. He wants to be able to change his appearance."

"Understandable," the shopkeeper said. "I just got in another shipment of syms—it may be that one of them could solve his dilemma."

"What are syms?" I asked him.

He smiled genially. "They're a living suit of clothes that bond with the wearer and can emulate not only any sort of clothing, but also act as armor. This particular batch is said to be more advanced than our last offering of its kind."

"How much?" I asked him.

He stroked his chin. "Well...I might be persuaded to make a deal. They're new, and it's unlikely people will be in a hurry to try them out without some kind of guarantee."

I wasn't sure I liked the sound of that. "What about the last batch you had? I assume they were okay?"

"Of course. We don't sell junk here. These, like the previous ones, are created by Loki himself and completely safe for the user. Like most syms, however, they tend to be...quite malleable."

"What the hell does *that* mean?" I asked, knowing I was being a little rude now, but honestly irritated by what I saw as deliberate evasiveness.

He didn't seem to notice the rudeness. As a shopkeeper someplace as weird as Starhaven, maybe he was simply used to it. "The initial batch we had was of a lower quality and had a very limited assortment of powers. They were popular for a while, but interest petered out. These are high-end models, comparable to syms one could get from the original designers, and therefore I am unable to ascertain what powers they may confer."

"Powers?" I was getting more and more confused by this exchange. What did he mean by *powers?*

"I'm not sure even Loki understands how they work. Suffice to say that all syms grant their wearer special abilities—abilities that may seem like magic, but actually influence reality on a higher level than magic appears to. In example, say you have a sym that allows you to manipulate fire. If you were to come across a mage who specialized in fire or used fire consistently, your sym would be able to override his magic. You could snuff out his magical fire or cause it to do things he hadn't intended."

I was starting to catch on. It sounded damned intriguing, but I was certain I couldn't afford one of these things. "How much?"

He clapped his hands together in apparent delight. "My first sale!" He leaned across the counter and murmured conspiratorially. "How much you got?"

"I've got five hundred credits," I told him. I expected him to laugh in my face.

"Wonderful! My partner is currently elsewhere, and since she's the one who's obsessed with money, I find myself in the perfect position to sell you something you desperately need at a price you can afford. Four hundred and forty-five credits."

I could scarcely believe my ears. "Four forty-five? Are you kidding?"

When he shook his head, I whipped out my five hundred credit chit and tossed it on the counter. "You've got a deal," I told him.

He shoved the chit into a reader and handed it back, then turned around and started poking around the blank wall behind him. I could hear him muttering to himself and, after a moment of it, came up with what looked like a small wine cask. "All I ask is that you go someplace private to open the package," he said. "They can be a little wild when they're first released."

I had no problem with that. Now that I had what I came for—or, at least, what I *thought* I'd come for—I was quite content to return to Earth and try this thing out in the privacy of my own home.

Needless to say that Spite seemed to have no problem with that and actually dropped me off at home within an hour. She lingered on the porch for a few minutes, looking rather uncomfortable. "Is everything okay?" I asked her.

"I enjoyed spending time with you, Hydra. I was wondering if we might do it again sometime."

"Sure," I said, stunned that someone like her would find me at all interesting.

She smiled her beautiful smile. "Great. Good luck with the sym. I'll be seeing you at the Lounge." She then leaned forward and brushed her lips against my cheek.

With that she turned, gestured, and walked into nothingness.

Feeling like a kid, I carried my keg inside and set it on my extra-large coffee table.

All the furniture in my house is larger than life. If I could, I'd buy oversized appliances as well, but, of course, no such equipment seems to be available.

I rely on my house mainframe to run most of the equipment like the stove and view set because my hands are too large to manipulate such things as buttons or dials without risking disaster. The weird thing is that I really don't mind being the size I am. I just don't like the more freakish attributes that go with it.

Taking a deep breath, I popped the lid off the cask.

I forced myself to sit still as something like a living shadow burst from it and leaped upon me. I felt a strange and disconcerting tugging sensation, but before I knew it, I'd been completely enveloped by the thing. Apparently syms are one size fits all. I was gratified to realize this, since I hadn't bothered to ask while still at the shop.

I stood up and looked down at myself, realizing that I was covered in an oily black material and my clothing, such as it was, lay in shreds at my feet. I stumbled into the bathroom, somehow unable to control my limbs to the extent to which I'd always been accustomed.

I ordered the house main to turn on the lights and stared in amazement at the image that appeared in my mirror. Gone was the humanoid elephant that had always greeted me before this moment. I had a real face now, black as midnight and astoundingly familiar. It took me a moment to realize that I looked an awful lot like Spite. Too much, I decided, and I concentrated on changing my features. I lengthened the nose a little, widened the lips, and ran a hand over the shiny surface of my skull. I turned my head this way and that and concentrated on reducing my ears to a pair of vestigial swirls of flesh.

This was simply amazing. I couldn't believe it had been this easy.

I wished for the sym to become a suit of clothing—something semi-formal—and I was standing there in a nicely cut business suit. "Holy crap," I murmured. "I'm gorgeous. Hades, eat your heart out."

I walked into the Lounge the next night feeling like the king of the world. I arrived early, as usual, and for a change, the normals who frequented the place before all us freaks started arriving didn't run screaming, though they did give me an assortment of strange looks.

Strange looks I can live with.

Callie was back behind the bar, washing glasses, and Jack was at his customary place in the corner booth. With him were Boneyard and Kevin, which is why the were-panther hadn't been guarding the door as he usually is this time of night.

I walked up to the bar. "I'd like a shot of tequila, please," I told Callie. She eyed me curiously for a moment, then poured the shot. I knocked it back, grinned, and laid a chit on the bar. "That's a hundred. Keep 'em coming for me, and if an Abyssian woman comes in, give her anything she wants on my tab."

Her curious stare grew even more pronounced, but she nodded.

I made my way to Jack's table and squatted down so I was eye to eye with them. "Hey, guys. How's it going?"

"Hi, Hydra," Jack replied. "I see you found what you were looking for."

I wish I knew how he did that. I didn't look anything like I had and I'm pretty sure my voice had been changed considerably by the whole process, but he wasn't fooled for a minute.

Boneyard and Kevin performed synchronized double-takes and I chuckled aloud. "Yep, it's me. How'd the search for the kid go?" I'd been a little worried about it, but hadn't heard anything on the view regarding the search once I'd calmed down enough to switch it on the night before.

"The kid wasn't really missing," Boneyard said. "He'd gone off to play at a friend's house without telling anyone. He'll be lucky if he isn't grounded until he's sixty."

"That's good news," I said. "Glad to hear everything turned out all right."

I stood and turned and found myself looking back at Spite, who was watching me with an unreadable expression on her face. I smiled at her and she returned it tentatively. "Is that you, Hydra?" she asked as I approached.

I nodded. "In the flesh. Pretty cool, eh?"

"You look a little like one of us," she said. "I didn't expect that."

"Either did I. I didn't set out to look like a wingless Abyssian, but I'll take it."

"You may be able to change your form again," she remarked thoughtfully. "When I kissed you I probably left a trace of DNA the sym responded to when it bonded with you."

That was something I hadn't considered, but it made a lot of sense. I nodded. "Something to think about later," was all I said. "Did you order a drink?"

"She said it was already paid for."

"It was. I was hoping you'd be in."

"How could I stay away? I was curious."

"Only curious?"

"Well, maybe a little more than curious," she admitted. "I also wanted to see you again."

I felt my heart do a little skip at that confession. "I know I wanted to see you. Tell me, do you like boats?"

She shrugged. "I suppose. Why?"

"Because I'd like to take you out on a little cruise tomorrow, if you're interested. Just my way of saying thank you."

"You have a boat?"

"I design boats," I told her. "I've got a boat specifically built with us plus-size people in mind."

"Then I'd like that very much," she said. She leaned forward and gently kissed me, sliding her hand up my arm and around my neck. When the kiss finally broke, we looked around and found more than a few of the regulars looking on and the normals gone.

A cheer rang out. "We were wondering if you'd ever come out of it," Hades said jokingly, shooting a grin at his girlfriend, Steph. "Who's your friend?"

"Folks, this is Spite."

"Not anymore," my Abyssian lady said. "It's time for another name change."

"Oh? To what?"

"I think Hope feels like a very good fit right now."

"Hope? Sure, why not?" I stroked her cheek with my hand and she nuzzled it gently.

"Where are Timothy and Hammad?" I asked, looking around. "We could use some music."

"They're not here," said Kevin, who was up on the stage tinkering with something. "But we can do something about the music ourselves. I think this development calls for a karaoke party."

Out of the corner of my eye, I thought I saw Hades wince. There are a lot of things Hades does very well. Singing isn't one of them. But that doesn't stop him from getting up there and giving it his best shot.

If you can't caterwaul in front of your friends, I always say, they're not really your friends.

# Episode VI:
# Storm Chasing

Bad night all around. It was wet, nasty, and cold. And I was missing a boyfriend. I came out of the night, barreling out of Golden Gate Park and leaping Stanyan St. and its sporadic traffic of bicycle cabs and pedestrians without a single downward glance.

I had one goal in mind and woe to anything that got in my way.

I hit a skidding right turn at Cole and practically flew up the sidewalk, blowing by Boneyard as if he were standing still. Not hard, considering he *was* standing still. I straight-armed the door, smashing it open and leaving it hanging by one hinge, a shattered ruin.

All eyes leaped to me as I stood in the doorway, shaking and unable to speak for a brief moment. "I need your help!"

Jack, the manager, stood up from his usual corner booth and strode across the dance floor to stand right in front of me. He gazed past me toward the broken door and sighed. "You know you have it, Rio. But was breaking the front door really necessary?"

I gave him my best steely-eyed stare. He met my gaze squarely, not shrinking back an inch. Jack is a normal, as far as I can tell, but he's a brave sonofabitch. Not many humans could lock gazes with a pissed-off vamp and not flinch.

"Sorry," I muttered. "Storm's missing and I need as much help as I can get in finding him."

"How do you know he's missing?" asked Boneyard from behind me. The 'thrope had come through the broken front door while I was looking at Jack. I was off my game if I hadn't even felt him coming.

"Now there's a dumb question," I shot back over my shoulder. "He's missing because he wasn't there when I woke up. He never does that."

The look of concern that passed across every face in the joint was truly astounding. They didn't question my statement at all.

"Where should we start?" asked Hades, the former evil immortal. I was one of those who remembered his name from the bad old days. It's odd thinking of him as an ally now.

His girlfriend Steph stood up and put her arm around his waist. "What can we do?" She's another vamp—relatively young compared to me, but quite powerful as such things are measured. These days she's a pretty big cheese in the Conclave, which is kinda like a vampire union. She had resources I could only guess at. Politics are so not my thing. "We start at Alcatraz," I replied.

The island had been overlooked as the mages rushed to protect San Francisco from the effects of global warming, but I hadn't overlooked it at all. I'd buttressed the shores against the rising water and rendered the island effectively invisible in the process. I'd already decided to make the Rock my home and wasn't at all interested in entertaining visitors.

Storm had done some of his own work to keep the island safe from intruders. Not only was it perpetually shrouded in mist, but the uninvited were very likely to attract unwanted lightning bolts—even out of a clear sky. Not that we saw many of those.

I can't fly. Some vamps can, but I'm not one of them. I can summon a windsprite and bind it into something and fly that way, but like most vamps, my ability to communicate with spirits is pretty spotty. Sometimes they refuse to acknowledge our existence and that makes them hard to command. I prefer to avoid anything to do with them if I can.

I've got the island warded pretty heavily, which prevents uninvited mages from showing up unannounced, but it also makes it that much trickier for me to get on and off the Rock. I have to utilize a key spell, encoded just right to temporarily negate the sigil that's the foundation of the island's defenses.

If you don't understand what I'm talking about, don't feel too bad. A lot of talented mages don't understand wards very well. They're pretty complicated, and not that easy to explain. Let's just say that I have to expend a lot of energy to get back to the island without my defensive spells considering me just another intruder.

More importantly on this occasion, I had to do this all without alerting the other mages to what I was doing. Hades, Steph, and Kevin were all magi, and none of them were boneheads. I had to initiate the disarming sequence without letting them see the pattern I used.

Not that I didn't trust them. I trusted them as much as I trust anyone who isn't me or Stormchild. Which isn't much, to be honest.

I also had to do it all without alerting them to the fact that I'm not really a mage at all. Oh, I can fake it as well as anyone, but the key to my magic is something I'm not supposed to even let anyone else know about.

127

It's a secret. I don't actually cast spells myself, but do it through the two mage gems hidden on my person. I tell the gems what I want done and they manipulate the mana in the way I require to get the result I'm looking for.

It's only one of things I don't advertise about myself. I've got tons. I'm one of the few day-walking vampires. I never truly died and I wear a symsuit. Most vampires can't. Vampire cells and syms don't bond.

I'm also a powerful psychic, but not the kind that reads minds or any of that scary stuff. Psychic Creativity is my forte. I can recreate any object or compound I myself understand. Since I'm a bioengineer, this means I'm able to do some pretty amazing stuff.

Enough secrets. I don't really plan on letting anyone read this, but you never know. Accidents happen.

I transported myself and the volunteers (which included just about everyone but Jack) to Alcatraz and, while the others were exploring, I jumped down to my lab for a quick second. When I arrived I found the imp, Quickfingers, messing with some of my equipment. He's the one ultimately responsible for my condition, the little shit. He thinks I don't know. I let him believe that. If he wasn't an imp and damn near immune to anything I could do to him, I'd let him know in a way he wouldn't soon forget.

I'd bitch to Jaz about him, but named imps are notoriously difficult to control, and none more than the first of their kind. Jaz may have created him, but Quickfingers was most definitely a free agent. She could influence him, but no one ruled him.

"Hey, Rio!" he said, turning away from the microscope and peering at me through his large round eyes. "What's up?"

"Storm's missing," I told him. "I brought some friends to help look for him. Don't cause any trouble."

"Trouble? Me?"

His feigned innocence is so blatantly false I couldn't help but laugh. Trouble follows Quickfingers around like a pet.

I was afraid to ask what he's been up to. God only knows. In case one might wonder why I even let him into my lab, my only answer is that it's part of a deal we made. It's awfully difficult to keep him out of any place in particular and he's far less likely to deliberately cause a disaster if he's welcomed in, no matter how distasteful I might find it.

I exited the lab without another word and reappeared with the others, who were currently inspecting one of the cell blocks. "So they actually imprisoned people here, huh?" Steph asked, shaking her head. "Seems kinda...uncivilized."

So spoke a product of the twenty-first century. I nearly laughed, but thought it would be rude. "Some of the people they sent here should've just been shot."

"Aren't *you* just a poster child for progressive values," said Hades with what looked suspiciously like a smirk.

I gave him the evil eye. I never know if he's serious or joking, or some combination of the two. He's still an enigma in many ways. "Never claimed to be," I shot back. "Some folks are just a waste of perfectly good oxygen. Rapists, child-killers and scum like that should be eradicated like vermin."

"We're not here to discuss politics and social theory," said Hydra, giving us both a hard stare. Believe me, when a nine-foot-plus black troll glares at you, you know you've been glared at. "Or are you *not* worried about your boyfriend?"

I returned his glare. "You guys been able to sniff anything out yet?" I asked Steph and Boneyard.

"This place has rats," Steph replied. "Lots of them."

"Big surprise," I drawled. "Anything else?"

129

"Hold on," she said, crouching next to a large crack in one of the cells. A moment later a huge rat crawled out and stood on its hind legs, peering up at her unblinkingly. "You had visitors," she announced.

"Impossible. No one can get in and out of here without permission."

"Someone did," she answered back. "Rats aren't good at details—all they know is a bunch of two-legs went through here, dragging another, unconscious two-legs."

I felt a sudden chill. Why I believed a bunch of rats I can't say, but at that moment, I did. The problem is that Storm should've been able to take on just about any mortal or group of mortals that he may have faced.

None of this made any sense. I'm a scientist—I don't like it when things aren't rational. I don't like it at all.

I turned my gaze on Boneyard, who raised his eyebrows and stared back. "I'm a panther, not a goddam dog," he said. "My animus is a sight hunter...my sense of smell is somewhat better than a human's, but if you want a tracker-beast, you need a werewolf or coyote or something."

*Now* he tells me. I hadn't even thought of that and I should've known ahead of time. "Anyone else?"

"Besides, I have no experience in tracking. I *do* know a werewolf who does," Bone cut back in, before anyone else could say anything. "I could contact him and see if he'd be interested in helping."

I nodded. Again, something else I should've considered. Vampires have highly developed senses as well, but I can't track using my sense of smell alone. It's a particular skill-set and one I don't have.

"Well, I'd say this is confirmation of the rat's story," Hades said, pointing at the floor some distance down the corridor.

"Multiple tracks in the dust, plus something that might be someone's feet being dragged along the floor."

I walked over to take a look. "Nice catch, Hades," I told him, with a grateful nod.

"Well, if we need a dog, I can have mine here in a second or two," Hades murmured.

I pretended I hadn't heard him. A miniature pincer is *not* a bloodhound. Imagine that.

"Does it seem odd to you that they could take Stormchild down and yet can't carry him without dragging his feet on the floor?" This from Hydra's Abyssian girlfriend. "Is it just me, or do these prints look a little small?"

I hadn't thought about it, but I compared one of the sets to my own shoeprint and frowned. "You're right." It wasn't a *lot* smaller than mine, but I have small feet.

"Not one of us is trained in this sort of thing," Hades pointed out. "We could use a skilled investigator."

"Coincidentally," Boneyard murmured, "the werewolf I mentioned earlier is a bounty hunter."

That was enough for me. "Call him. If he wants in, I'll go get him."

The were-panther nodded and strolled into an open cell down the block a fair distance. We waited in silence as he made his call, all of us eyeing the tracks curiously.

"I'm starting to get an idea," Hades said, breaking into the quiet. "You're not going to like it."

The warning was enough for me not to like it already. "Go for it," I growled.

He shrugged. "I think it was goblins."

"What? Why in the hell would goblins kidnap Stormchild? And how would they be able to take him on in the first place?

It's not as if there are any lightning-scorched goblin corpses lying around."

"I don't know why," he said, "but keep in mind that some goblins are tough little buggers. It's easy to underestimate them because of their size, but they're not all weak...or stupid, for that matter."

"Okay. Still doesn't answer the question of why they'd want to take him in the first place," I told him. "Or haven't you got to that part yet?"

He shook his head. "I don't have a clue. Rumor has it, though, that Kali is working out of Starhaven now. It may be that some of them are getting a little independent now that she's not looking over their shoulder constantly."

It's important to remember here that Hades may have created the goblins, but it was Kali who took them under her wing—so to speak—and made them more than a mere burden to human society. Under her direction the goblins had become a fairly formidable force, at least economically. Goblins will perform jobs that no human would want to consider and do it cheaply. Now while this might stink of exploitation, it's honestly difficult to exploit a goblin. Most people support anything that keeps them out of trouble. Goblins are drawn to trouble like kids to candy.

You'll have to take my word on that. "I take it a rat couldn't tell the difference between a human and a goblin?" I asked Steph.

She nodded. "All two-legs to them."

I looked over at Hades. "I take it you have no influence over them anymore?"

"I gave up any influence I had a long time ago," he replied with a wry grin.

Then it struck me. It should have hit me earlier, but the distractions were coming fast and furious. "Dammit!" I threw out a transit tube and returned to the lab to find Quickfingers gone. The little rodent! There was no way for the goblins to have gotten here unless Quickfingers had brought them. He'd never allied himself with the goblins before, but I had no doubt he'd do so in a heartbeat if it suited his purposes. Whatever the hell *they* were.

I let out a wordless scream and returned to the others. "I know how they got here," I said in a low growl. "And when I get my hands on him..." I let my voice trail off. I wouldn't be able to do anything to him, of course. The damned imp is immune to just about everything. Theory has it that a bath in a pool of sulfuric acid might do him in, but that would require somehow preventing him from teleporting or turning ethereal before you could throw him in.

File that under very unlikely, if not downright impossible.

I met Boneyard's gaze. "Donovan has agreed to help," he said, "but you'll need to bring him here."

"I can do that. Tell him to wait for me at the Lounge."

He nodded. "Already done," he said. "Give him about fifteen minutes."

I returned his nod. "Okay. In the meantime, let's see if we can figure out where these tracks lead."

I wasn't surprised to find they ended at a blank wall, at the back of one of the last cells on the block. I poked around some and muttered irritably when I couldn't find any sign of a secret door out. If Quickfingers was involved, why would he have met them here?

I still harbored suspicions, but I preferred proof before going to Quickfingers's boss with them. I know Jasmine Tashae slightly, and while I'll admit no fear of her, she's known for being quite the badass. And loyal to her friends, which includes the little blue delinquent for some reason that completely escapes me.

Oh, I'll admit it. He's likeable enough. Always cheerful, mostly helpful, and usually worth a laugh or two. But he's *totally* untrustworthy. Maybe Jaz has a hold on him I don't know about. She *did* create him, after all.

I lifted my gaze to Boneyard, who nodded. It was time for me to flit back to the city. I drew down a three-strand sigil and jumped directly to the Lounge, stepping out onto the dance floor just as a pair of customers whirled past. Jack was behind the bar, I noted, and I took a couple steps in that direction before stopping and scanning the place.

With all of us gone, the Lounge had attracted a large number of normals—or what appeared to be normals. They sat in groups of two to six, listening to Timothy and Hammad jam quietly up on stage, and otherwise carry on as if this were an ordinary club.

I didn't like it one bit.

I was standing there, doing a slow circle on the edge of the dance floor, when a stranger approached me from where he'd sat alone in Jack's usual booth in the corner. He was tall and slim, with long auburn hair, freckles, and, of all things, a pair of spectacles perched on his face. No one wears glasses anymore. If laser surgery can't fix problems with your eyesight, any decent mage-optometrist can.

I expected him to ask me to dance, but found myself surprised when he asked, "Are you Rio?"

I nodded, a little puzzled.

"I'm Donovan. Boneyard asked me to meet you here."

*This* was a werewolf? Nearly every 'thrope I'd ever met had been large and muscular. It has something to do with the conservation of mass. 'Thropes are incredibly massive beings—their bones, muscles, and even their skin thicker and stronger than that of any mortal. This generally resulted in them being extremely bulky. There were exceptions of course. Were-weasels and other such 'thropes didn't tend to be that large, but this guy was allegedly a werewolf.

I made a point of looking him up and down. He actually blushed, which I found even stranger than his slender build. "I gotta say," I told him, "you don't look like any werewolf I've ever seen."

He frowned. "I'm not. Bone must've gotten that detail wrong. I'm a were-fox."

Now *that* I could believe. But why had Bone said he was a werewolf? "I thought you two were friends."

"We are, as far as such things go," Donovan answered. "But he's a big cat and I'm a small canine. We don't hunt together."

That made sense. "He says you're a good tracker."

"I am. One of the best." No need for false modesty here, I guess.

"I need the best. You ready?"

He nodded and I transported us back to Alcatraz.

Donovan ducked into an empty cell a few doors down and shifted. A couple minutes later a medium-sized dog-like beast trotted out, regarding us with what could only be described as a curious look. He sniffed at the tracks and followed them to where they dead-ended, then abruptly switched back and followed them the other direction.

I expected him to lead us to the quarters Storm and I share, but, instead, he took a staircase to a lower level and raced ahead, leaving the rest of us to bring up the rear.

"That, my friend," murmured Hades to Boneyard, "is *not* a wolf."

"I realize that," the were-panther shot back. "So I got the kind of dog wrong. I knew he was some sort of canine."

"That's like someone referring to you as a were-bobcat," the immortal snorted. "But it's *some* kind of cat."

"Not at all funny," Bone snarled at him. "At least I made him sound *more* impressive rather than less impressive."

"I wasn't after a tracker for his fighting ability," I cut in. "Quit teasing him, Hades."

Ordinarily it probably wouldn't have bothered me, but right now I was on edge. I was worried about Storm. It was crazy to think he may've been kidnapped by goblins, of all things, but that's definitely what it was beginning to look like. I was still left wondering how they'd managed to take him. Storm's a damn good fighter, can throw lightning, and like most immortals, is pretty much immune to most poisons and drugs.

Not someone you expect to fall prey to some adventuring goblins. Donovan led us down a couple flights of stairs, stopping at each level to sniff around the door handle, then continued down. After the third, I looked over and saw Donovan and Bone exchange glances before the were-fox sat down on his haunches in front of the door. "That's the way they went," Bone murmured.

I was frowning as I followed them through the door. Something was off and I couldn't put my finger on it. Why had it seemed as though the fox was taking his cues from Boneyard?

We entered into something like pitch blackness, the level of light so low even my vampiric vision couldn't help me. "Damn," I muttered. "Anyone think to bring a light?"

"Allow me." I heard Hades's voice in the darkness and suddenly he was bathed in a warm yellow glow that lit a stretch of tunnel some fifteen feet ahead of us.

"Did they come through here?" I asked Donovan, watching to see if he glanced at Bone. He didn't, but my suspicions had already been aroused and I was feeling less than generous with my trust at this point.

The were-fox trotted to the edge of the light and waited. As Hades moved toward him, the glow cast shadows farther ahead and I thought I could make out something moving up ahead. "Storm?"

My question was met with silence but for the distant thrum of the waves striking the island. I felt like an idiot. He couldn't answer me in this form. Some 'thropes can speak in full animal shape, but they have to be practiced enough to be able to modify their larynx to form human words. I'd only met a few in my travels that could do it. Donovan apparently wasn't one of them.

By this point I wasn't sure I liked where any of this was going. I couldn't see a potential motivation for pulling a fast one on me, but just because I couldn't see it didn't mean they didn't have one. As I mentioned before, I don't like things I don't understand. And this was starting to feel something like that yet again. This was beginning to get way out of my control and I don't like that much either.

Grumbling under my breath, I followed Donovan down the hall to a single door and reached over him to turn the knob. Great, I thought, as I opened the door, another dark room. "Hades? Come shed some light on this, will you?"

"My life's ambition has been to be a searchlight," he snorted. But he came. Smart man.

The room was large and empty, a long rectangle marked only with another door on the opposite side. This was getting ridiculous. Donovan trotted straight to the next door and sat down once again.

This time Hades walked to the door first and turned the knob, throwing the door open before I could stop him.

Another dark room. I angrily shoved past them and strode into the blackness. Something moved and I reflexively dialed up my mage gems for something offensive. A nice bolt of chain lightning, perhaps?

The room was suddenly bathed in light and I staggered back, blinking against the glare. "Surprise!" came a chorus of voices and, once I'd managed to blink back the sparkly halos spinning across my eyes, I saw the room was full of people, including Storm.

"Happy Birthday, Rio!" he cried, rushing over to throw his arms around me. I punched him in the gut hard enough to knock him on his ass.

"Are you out of your mind?" I asked him, my voice cutting through the chatter of the crowd like a buzz-saw.

He stared up at me with a hurt expression and, for an instant, I wanted to kick him. "You scared the shit out of me," I shouted. "What were you thinking?" Then it struck me. "Hey— how did you know it was my birthday?" It's not as though I advertised it, and anyone who'd know had been gone a *long* time—or so I assumed. I'd left my family behind in Brazil and never looked back when I reached the States.

"Jack found out," Storm said, scowling up at me fiercely. "He knows people."

"This was a very cruel thing to do, Storm, and I don't appreciate it in the least."

"You know," he growled as he climbed to his feet, "some guys actually have girlfriends who enjoy it when they go to these lengths to throw them a surprise birthday party."

"Then maybe you need one of those girlfriends," I snarled at him.

The room went totally still and I froze, suddenly aware that everyone's eyes were upon me. I made a slow circle and groaned inwardly.

I don't usually give a shit what anyone thinks of me. Why should I?

Damn. I had every right to be pissed, but I wondered if I'd carried it too far. He'd tricked me, and I'd been scared for him, yes. But he'd done it for what could be argued as the best of reasons. To give me something special, to share a day I hadn't paid any attention to in centuries with all of our friends.

It was a sweet gesture, really.

I let out a long sigh. "Sorry," I murmured.

He cocked his head and a grin slid into place on his broad, handsome face. "So am I."

I found myself laughing and shaking my head. "I love you, Storm, you big dummy."

"I think you cracked my sternum," he answered back, holding his hand over his midsection.

"You're an immortal," I said. "You'll be healed in a minute."

"True enough. Forgiven?"

I nodded. "Yeah. How'd you pull off the goblin tracks?"

"That was easy. Real goblins. I made a jump to Starhaven and asked Kali to loan me a few. One of them's a mage, which made it easier."

"A goblin mage?" I'd never heard of such a thing. "I'd like to meet him."

"Her."

The noise level returned to normal as I heard Hydra deliver the punch line of some joke or another. "...and the farmer's wife turned to him, grabbed his crotch and said 'yeah, and if we could get *this* hard, we could get rid of your brother.'"

I winced, but nearly everyone else laughed. Glancing past him I noticed a makeshift stage set up against one long wall. "Karaoke?"

"Of course," Storm told me. "I had to promise not to sing though. No one would want to follow me."

There was a bit of truth in that, but I knew he wasn't serious. No one would pass up the chance to hear him sing for free. Especially now, since he'd been retired for the past several decades. "Where's this goblin mage?" I asked, peering around the room.

"Over by the bar," he said, pointing behind me. I turned and spotted Jack, who stood behind a long straight counter much like the one in the Lounge. He met my eyes and lifted a glass in a kind of salute before taking a deep drink. I spotted a small figure perched on a stool in front of the bar and nodded to myself.

"Were all of them in on this?" I asked Storm, poking him in the ribs with a forefinger. I was still a little irritated by the whole thing, but my initial fury had worn off. I may have overreacted.

He winced, but I knew it hadn't hurt him in the least. He's so dramatic sometimes. "Yeah," he admitted.

"Wait here," I told him, and marched over to the bar. "Very clever," I said to Jack. He smiled enigmatically and handed me a bottle from under the counter. "Crimson Rain," he said, naming the most expensive and sought-after blood substitute. It had been my research that initially gave us the artificial blood most civilized vamps now drank, but others had taken the ball and run with it. I'd become obscenely wealthy from the original patent, but money had never meant all that much to me. I did it because I enjoyed research.

It struck me that I'd never tried "Rain". "Thanks," I said, and popped off the lid.

"Happy Birthday, Rio."

As I took my first swallow I turned to look at the goblin perched on the bar stool. I was a bit surprised by her appearance. She wasn't homely, like most goblins. In fact, one might call her cute, even pixie-ish. She had a sharp, vulpine face, a well-proportioned nose, and big round blue eyes. Her ears were large and upswept, more like an elf's than the bat-wing things many goblins had. She wore her hair in a thin blue mohawk about four inches tall that rode the center of her skull from the top of her forehead to the base of her neck.

She was slender to the point of looking fragile, though that's one thing no goblin could be. They tend to be as sturdy as any immortal, from what I've been told. "Hi," I said.

"Hi yourself," she answered. I noticed she had what looked like a screwdriver in front of her. She took a drink and met my gaze. "You're the birthday gal, aren't you?"

"Unfortunately," I muttered. "I didn't know goblins could do magic," I said. No, tact isn't one of my strong suits.

"Most of us can't," she answered back with a shrug. "I'm a freak even among my own kind."

I smiled understandingly. "That must be hard." I wasn't sure why, but I was very curious about this creature. I was hoping to get a genetic sample, but it wasn't as though I was about to walk up and ask her for one. A tempting thought, though. Even *I* have some boundaries I won't cross, believe it or not. "Got a name?"

"No. Most people just call me, 'hey, you!'" She gave me a disgusted look.

"Sorry. I'm Rio."

"People call me Kate," the goblin said. "Sorry about the snark."

"It's okay. It was a stupid question."

"Yes, it was."

I sighed, figuring I deserved that. "You should drop by the Lounge sometime," I told her, sliding off the stool. "Freaks are always welcome. Take my word for it. You're no more a freak than any of us."

"I'll keep that in mind," she said. I had no way of knowing whether she meant it or not and, frankly, I didn't much care. If she showed up, great. If not, it wasn't going to cause me any heartache.

I spent the rest of the evening making the rounds and being toasted. It was embarrassing but they were my friends. Or as close to friends as I'll probably ever have. They were a step above nearly anyone else I'd ever known. At least *they* knew where I lived.

I knew that the next night they'd all be back at the Lounge, telling stories about their trip to the Rock. Storm and I wouldn't be there. We spent about two weeks out of the month in Europe, then a week back home recuperating before returning to the Lounge.

Why Europe? Because, believe it or not, Storm has a kid there. Yep. Before he and I hooked up, he had an affair with a parahuman who happened to get pregnant. Storm has a daughter and a real firebrand she is, too. He and the mother retained a peaceable relationship throughout the kid's childhood and now that she was an adult, he insisted on "watching" out for her as much as possible. Personally I think he's worried about nothing, but *he's* the father.

Me? I spend the time visiting such historic sites as the Louvre, Buckingham Palace, the Eiffel Tower, and other interesting locales. I like Europe. It has such a visible history.

Storm's daughter's name is Nemesis. I don't know why, especially considering that's the name of the parahuman woman who'd given birth to Deryk Shea's son—the one who'd died in the war. When I ask him about it, he changes the subject.

Think he's hiding something?

I do. And one day I'm going to find out what it is.

# Episode VII:
# Goblin Moon

I was shaking so hard I could barely stand. I stumbled into the street, throwing myself backward just in time to avoid becoming a smear on the pavement as a ground car swept past without slowing. I threw a finger up at the retreating bumper and shot a hasty glance over my shoulder.

Had I been seen? I had no way of knowing, but I was terrified by the possibility. Death stalked the park, and I had witnessed something so horrible my tiny heart had almost burst with the effort of restraining my cries of shock and terror.

The only things that moved at the edge of the park behind me were shadows of trees cast by the streetlights, but my imagination painted them as monstrous figures emerging from the depths to devour me whole.

My name is Vex, and I'm a goblin. Oh, I know someone might think, reading that, *but goblins are stupid and illiterate. There's no way the narrator of this tale could be one of those reviled creatures.*

That's where they'd be wrong. Not all of us are either of those things. A few of us, the elite among us, are as intelligent as a human being, and Kali, our Queen, made sure that those of us who could make use of it sought some sort of education.

Who knows where we'd be if not for Kali?

I sprinted across the street, jumping onto the sidewalk and glancing around again. Haight Street was vacant. Not a single ground car cruised down its length, not a single human being walked its sidewalks.

San Francisco never sleeps, but sometimes this neighborhood got in a few winks. All the big touristy places had their off times. One o-clock in the morning on a Sunday just happened to be Haight-Asbury's time to drowse.

I padded down the sidewalk, watching for any sign of pursuit. Still nothing. Maybe the monster *hadn't* seen me after all. Maybe I'd escaped its notice. I was, after all, only a goblin. Not large enough to pose a threat, and hardly someone or something the authorities were likely to believe.

I needed to get off the street.

Hadn't I heard of a watering hole in this area with a reputation of being a sort of sanctuary? I seemed to remember...

The sound was my only warning—a muffled boom from overhead—and I dove into a doorway, feeling a great gust of wind rush past me. Shivering more from fear than from the cold, I peered around the building's façade, trying to see something, anything, that may have caused that effect.

Whatever it was seemed to be gone. I breathed a sigh of relief, but didn't feel safe venturing out of my hole just yet. Something that flew had just tried to snatch me up like a hawk might a field mouse, and I wasn't about to step blithely back into danger.

But I'd suddenly acquired the feeling of being watched, and that was in its way more frightening than dodging large winged predators stooping out of the darkness at me. I shivered once again and, grabbing my nerve by the throat, crept out of the doorway, edging down the sidewalk scant inches from the front of the building.

Now where was that bar? I knew it was around here somewhere. If I could only find it, I would be safe for a little while. A brief respite might give me the chance to come up with some sort of plan. To escape, of course. It looked as though my residency in San Francisco had come to an abrupt end. I couldn't live somewhere that harbored that sort of monster, particularly one that decided I'd make worthy prey.

I'd be no more than a bite-sized morsel to the creature I'd seen in the park, but its interest in me was obviously not that of a discriminating diner. I was a witness to something I didn't quite understand, but I was a witness nonetheless. The creature had to know that there was at least a small chance someone in authority would listen to me.

Maybe it was afraid I'd tell Kali. Which I would, had she still been on Earth. She'd been gone for months now and we were alone for the second time in our existence, able to rely on no one but ourselves. And even that had limits. There were very few of my own kind *I* trusted, for example. Most goblins weren't exactly the kind of people who inspired confidence.

Not that I blame them for being selfish, conniving, treacherous and deceitful. When you're less than three feet tall in a world made for people twice your size and instantly recognizable as something inferior, you had to come up with some way to survive. For most of us, that meant either begging or stealing, or doing the jobs no human would deign to do.

"Goblins are wonderful. Everyone should own one or two." As long as they keep them locked in the basement when they're not working, that is.

Don't mind my cynicism. It's been hard-won. People tolerate goblins if we make ourselves useful, but they don't have to like us.

I darted down the side of the building, racing for the next corner. My breath was coming in harsh pants and ice water ran through my veins. At any moment I expected to feel the claws of something large pierce my back and carry me into the sky. Winged death pursued me, and I knew escape was nearly impossible.

I felt the wind like a cold harbinger on my back and stumbled forward, a shrill scream rising in my throat. Out of the darkness ahead of me emerged a tall figure which stopped and glanced skyward. "By the Maker!" it cried in a deep male voice.

It rushed forward and snatched me up like a child, then spun, clearing the street in a single prodigious bound. Long legs ate distance like an Olympic speed-eater hunched over a plate of hot-dogs. He held me cradled against him and ran for all he was worth.

I couldn't see anything but the leaden gray sky and glimpses of the man's face and long hair blowing in the wind. Then I cried out as a huge saurian beast soared silently over us, its great whirling eyes staring down at us, shining with a pure dark malevolence.

My rescuer dodged sideways, underneath a large overhang, and I heard a shriek of anger as we broke through a door and into a room filled with smoke, the scent of alcohol, and the soft murmur of voices. I was carried up a ramp and deposited back on my feet. I stared up at my rescuer and felt my knees turn to liquid.

I staggered back, stumbling over someone's foot, and sprawled unceremoniously on my back under a table that rose like a huge canopy above me. I scrambled into a sitting position with my back against the table's center post.

One might wonder what had panicked me this time, considering the dragon was still somewhere outside, probably irritated and aggravated that I'd managed to escape. No, my problem this time was with my rescuer.

He was also my creator.

The immortal Hades, the mad scientist and mage who'd stolen human children and turned them into an inhuman army of short, squat, not particularly bright creatures he'd expected to use as shock troops against the invading Cen. Our Father. Our Destroyer.

Goblins make *terrible* soldiers. The majority are too stupid to remember what to do when combat's necessary, and the rest of us are too smart not to run at the first sign of danger.

Yeah, we're cowardly. At least the bright ones are. And that's a good thing when you're less than three feet tall. We're tough for our size, but we're completely outmatched by some of the monsters roaming around these days. Like dragons.

Of course, I'd never heard of dragons trolling the parks of San Francisco hoping to chomp down innocent tourists and goblins for dessert.

At the moment I actually feared the man crouching down to peer under the table at me more than I did the dragon. "I won't hurt you," he said.

*Sure,* I thought. *Like you could do anything worse to me than you already have.* This wasn't strictly true, of course, but it wasn't all that far off the mark. Sometime long ago I was a human child, and Hades's mad ambition had changed me into this...thing...that I am now.

I recognized him, and remembered him from the lab and afterward, as he inspected his new army. I was one of those he intended to serve as an officer—smart enough to know the difference between an "attack" and a "retreat".

"What the hell is going on here?" asked a booming voice, and my shelter was abruptly yanked away from above me. I scuttled across the floor, only to be snatched up by a second dark figure, even larger and more imposing than Hades himself.

This man was also dark of complexion. Not the unearthly ebon color of Hades, but the dusky tone of what they used to refer to as "Black" or "African-American". He was a veritable giant, and as soon as he touched me, I knew he wasn't completely human himself. He lifted me up by the back of my jacket and inspected me disdainfully. "Now you're bringing *goblins* into the Lounge, Hades? It ain't enough that you brought them into existence in the first place?"

"Funny, Boneyard. Real funny."

"Little bugger looks scared to death. Of course, looking at your mug, he *would* be, wouldn't he?"

I caught a cold glare fired from Hades's eyes that bounced off my captor without apparent effect. Personally it made me want to shrink into the tiniest ball and cease to exist.

That wasn't going to happen. So I squirmed. "Let me go!" I shrieked.

In my twisting and turning I caught sight of the big man's face, which was bent into an annoyed grimace. He gave me a quick shake. "Knock it off," he growled like he meant it.

I knocked it off, hanging limply in his grasp. He made a noise somewhere between a sigh and a groan. "As if this place isn't freaky enough," he said irritably, "you had to bring a goblin?"

"He was being chased by a dragon," Hades explained casually, as if that sort of thing happened all the time.

"A dragon? I thought they were all extinct."

"Mostly," Hades replied. "I only know of one living—in Oregon. This wasn't him."

"How do you know?"

"Believe me. I know. Actually, I'm wondering if we're not getting immigrants."

"Immigrant dragons from other Earths?" Another voice chimed in. "I suppose it's possible." This one was male as well and I turned my head to see a young, wraithlike human with pale skin and rusty blond hair approaching from somewhere out of view. He smelled like a mage. "Possible, unlikely and extremely unsettling."

"Glad you think so, Kevin," Hades told him tersely. "Freaks the shit out of me."

"Could you please put me down," I squeaked to the big lycanthrope. That's what he was, of course. Some type of shapeshifter. Feline, if I had to guess.

Don't ask how I know this stuff. It's a talent. I can feel anything out of the ordinary in other creatures. Like I already knew the pale man, Kevin, was a mage. It's an odd talent, perhaps, and one that seems generally useless for a creature as small and ineffectual as I am, but I've always found it worth having.

He peered at me curiously, gave a curt nod, and set me gently on the floor. I eyed Hades warily and edged my way around the big guy. "There was a dragon chasing me," I said, unnecessarily. Hades had already told them that. Then again, I wasn't sure how likely they were to believe him. The Sidhe had learned first-hand how deceptive he could be, and what he'd done to the goblins was nothing short of scandalous.

The evil bastard made me want to puke. Well, run and hide and puke. All at the same time.

I nearly shrieked as the front door exploded inward. I spun, rushing toward the horseshoe-shaped bar, and flung myself up one of the stools and across the polished wood. I was caught mid-flight by an average-sized human man who peered down at me in clear annoyance.

"What the hell do you think *you're* doing?" he asked in gruff tones.

"Hiding?" I squeaked. He looked down at me and let out a booming laugh.

"It's not the dragon," he told me, turning me to face the door. I spotted a couple of large humanoids—I hesitate to call them *humans*—standing at the bottom of the long ramp from the door to the main floor.

They were *huge*. Giants even in comparison to Hades and the lycanthrope. Their skin was as black as night and one of them seemed to furl great bat wings that were formed as much out of shadow as out of skin, bone and flesh.

Fear gripped me like a hand fisted around my throat. They were going to kill me...I just knew it.

"Are all goblins such lily-livered cowards?" the man behind the bar asked, as he lifted me up and set me on the bar without even a word of apology.

Hades shrugged. "The smart ones are," he said. "One of the reasons I abandoned the idea of using them as soldiers. The smart ones want no part of battle, and the dumb ones can't be trusted not to do something remarkably stupid when the chips are down."

This earned him dark looks from nearly every patron in the place, including the newcomers. "That's cold, Hades," the lycanthrope muttered, shaking his head. "You owe this creature."

"I just saved his life," the immortal objected.

151

"Which wouldn't have even been an issue if he'd been left to pursue his own life as nature intended," the other replied smartly.

Hades heaved a sigh as the bartender chuckled low close to my ear. He leaned forward and caught my gaze. "Are you hungry?" he asked me.

I blinked at him in astonishment. He was being remarkably nice for a human. And that's all he was—a normal human. Nothing paranormal or preternatural about him at all. Most of his kind had as little to do with my kind as they could manage. We were good for domestic and janitorial work and little more. Or so they assumed.

For some reason, this guy was different. He was actually offering me *food*. "I don't have any money."

"That's okay. You look like you could use a good meal and that's payment enough for me."

"Won't your boss get upset?"

"I rather doubt it," he answered with a quick grin. "This is my place and I'll give free food to whoever I want."

"Has *he* ever gotten free food?" I asked, stabbing a finger at Hades, who was engaged in a low, muttered conversation with the two huge newcomers.

"He can afford to pay. You can't. Wait here."

I did, and fifteen minutes later I was chomping into one of the best chicken sandwiches I'd ever had, along with a huge fizzy drink he identified as his own creation. It was a complex mix of tastes, including cranberry, lemonade, and some tingly sensations I just couldn't quite identify.

I dipped a French fry in a puddle of ketchup and stuck it in my mouth just in time to nearly swallow it whole as the door banged open once again.

A woman swept into the room, wrapped in a cloak of haughty, and climbed the ramp to the main floor all the while managing to look as though she were looking down her nose at us all. She was strikingly beautiful, I decided, but the arrogance with which she surveyed the room stole a lot of its impact. Whoever she was, she wasn't a nice person.

Her eyes, so pale as to be almost colorless, fell upon me and I felt myself shiver. My appetite vanished and I set the fry back on my plate. She took one step toward me and found her path barred by both the giants, the lycanthrope and Hades himself.

"Don't even think about it," Hades murmured, just loud enough for us to hear. He rolled up his sleeves and the silver-blue tattoos emblazoned on his black skin writhed like entwined serpents. "Who are you?"

She turned her gaze to him, eyes flicking down to his arms, and twitched her lips into the tiniest imitation of a smile. "You know who I am," she said.

"No," he replied, "I know *what* you are, but that's hardly the same thing now, is it?"

"Perhaps. So who, and *what*, are *you?*"

"My name is Hades. I would suspect that means nothing to you, but that's only because I haven't kicked your ass yet."

Her smile grew a little wider. "You think you can, little man?"

He shrugged "Maybe not by myself, but—well—I'm not by myself, am I?"

Her gaze scraped the room and she nodded slowly. "Interesting company you keep."

"Yeah, ain't it? What do you want with the goblin?"

"What, are you his daddy?"

"In a way, yes. Answer the fucking question."

She thought about this for a moment. "He saw something he shouldn't have."

Hades smirked. "Too bad for you. Why'd you do it?"

She gave him a look as though she thought he was stupid. "There are things no female should have to tolerate."

"I'm pretty sure I'd agree with you, but I'm not sure eating the perpetrator is the best possible solution to the problem. We do have laws, you know."

"So do I. And one of my laws says that I should consume the terminally malignant."

"Draconian arrogance," Hades snorted. "At least the one dragon left here on Prime isn't prone to that sort of thing."

"*One dragon?*" she echoed, looking scandalized.

He shrugged. "The rest of them were killed off a long time ago. I was right, wasn't I? You're not from our Earth, are you?"

"You're not distracting me," she said, shifting her gaze to me once again. She took a step forward and he moved to block her path.

"Leave the goblin be. He won't say anything to anyone."

"He told you, didn't he?"

"I saved his life. And I saw you." Hades gave her an evil grin. "I'm a much more dangerous witness than a goblin is. People will listen to me."

She paused and cocked her head, peering at him with a mixture of curiosity and annoyance. Her gaze made another quick sweep of the room. Disdainfully. "I do not fear your *rabble* here. Or your police."

The one called Boneyard let out a harsh, barking laugh. "Oh, you don't need to worry about the munies—the municipal police—they can barely handle mundane crooks. No, you're preternatural, which means you're an Adjuster's Office problem. And believe me, they've tackled bigger trouble than a rogue dragon before."

"I'm not a rogue," she spat angrily, eyes flashing with an inner fire.

"Could've fooled me," the mage cut in.

I was amazed how little fear they were showing. This was a *dragon!* I could almost see Hades's reason for being so cavalier—he was an immortal, and, as such, notoriously hard to kill. But the rest of them were mere mortals. Superhuman, perhaps, but still ultimately vulnerable.

Apparently sensing my trepidation, the bartender leaned toward me once again and whispered, "Don't worry. Help is on the way."

"What kind of help? Did you call the Adjuster's Office?"

"Uh-uh," he said quietly. "Kevin is right. Handling the preternatural and paranormal end of things *is* their job and they manage well enough. But tackling a dragon is a pretty big order, and I think we need to bring in the heavy artillery."

"Which is?"

"You're a curious little monkey, aren't you?" he asked with a chuckle.

I could have taken offense to the "monkey" line, but what would have been the point? As descriptions went, I'd heard much worse. Regularly. "Are you going to answer the question, or just laugh at me?"

Sometimes I surprise myself. That was a rather bold question and bold wasn't exactly part of my makeup.

If anything, his grin grew wider. "I sent a quick vid-message to someone I know in Oregon. He's exactly the person you'd want if you had to find someone to go up against a dragon."

This, of course, made me curious, but I didn't ask. I was far more interested in what was going on in front of me at this point. Our lady dragon was up to something, but I couldn't tell what it was. I could sense a gathering of something around her and I stiffened in response to what I was feeling.

The bartender cocked his head at me. "What?"

"She's doing something," I told him, and wondered if she was planning to change shape right where she was.

"Not in my fucking place," he growled, and vaulted the bar.

The air around her was starting to shimmer and growing hazier by the second. The mage had taken a few steps back and seemed to be staring at something *we* couldn't see.

The bartender strode right up to the dragon woman and punched her full out in the side of the face as everyone else looked on in shock.

Whatever she was doing stopped instantly as she rocked back on her heels and almost fell over. He must have struck her pretty hard, I thought.

She whirled back on him, eyes blazing. "How *dare* you?"

He hit her again, this time a wicked driving punch straight between her breasts. The air exploded from her lungs and she sat down, hard. He stepped back and kicked her in the forehead. She went over as if she'd been clubbed with a ponderosa.

I was apparently not the only one stunned by his actions. Every other patron in the bar was staring at him as if he'd suddenly donned a tutu and started singing "It's a Small World After All".

The dragon lay on the floor, groaning and holding her face. "In human form they're about as vulnerable as most mortals. It's the best time to take them down," he told us.

"Then what?" asked Hades with a wicked grin. "She's not going to be too happy with you when she comes to her senses, Jack."

"By that time Bigby should be here," Jack told him with a casual shrug. I noticed his eyes did not, however, stray from the supine dragon woman. He wasn't as confident as he appeared. Not by a long shot.

Hades nodded thoughtfully, as if he knew who—or what—Bigby was. That put him ahead of me, and, by the looks of things, everyone else in the place.

"Who the hell is Bigby?" The male giant asked, looking slightly annoyed as he walked forward and stood over the incapacitated woman. His companion came up beside him and stared down at the woman herself, frowning.

She was remarkably beautiful, if totally alien. I knew what she was, of course. Another experiment like myself—an Abyssian. Hades had created the winged humanoids as another type of soldier, only to find that they weren't interested in fighting his battles. Or any battles, for that matter. Abyssians *could* fight, but they didn't like to. I wouldn't call them pacifists, but the majority of them seemed to look upon violence as some kind of sin.

Rather weird, considering how freaking scary they looked when they chose.

In the end the Abyssians had betrayed him, allowing the last pureblood Sidhe, Carth, to put a blade in his back in retaliation for what he'd done to all of them. Carth had been the progenitor of the Abyssians, his DNA modified by Hades to create them. They were half Sidhe, and half a lot of different other things.

I found it surprising that she could be in the same room with Hades, much less converse with him. Which, in fact, she was doing now in tones too low for me to catch. He nodded and patted her shoulder, though he had to reach up a ways to do it, and treaded down the ramp to the front door. He threw it open and a bulky figure entered.

I couldn't make out many details, as the light up here interfered with my ability to see clearly in the relative dimness of the entryway. But I didn't have to wait long. The figure strolled up the ramp with Hades in tow and stopped on the dance floor several feet away from the draconic woman.

Now I could see him clearly, I wasn't sure what to think. Though large and bulky, he didn't look like anything particularly special. An ordinary guy wearing a gray cowboy hat and a thick blue jacket with a kind of five-pointed star embedded on one breast. I knew I'd seen that insignia somewhere before but it took me a minute to recognize it for what it was.

He was a cop. A sheriff, to be exact. He didn't really look like my ideal picture of a sheriff, being rather rotund and his face, but for the jutting beak of a nose, was mostly obscured by the unkempt salt and pepper beard that framed his face.

The woman groaned and stared up at him. "Who the fuck are you?" she asked, pushing herself up into a sitting position.

"The guy you've been waiting a lifetime to meet," he answered in a thick, bass voice. It sounded like a stupid come-on line, but somehow he made it work for him. It meant a lot more than it seemed the way he said it.

She didn't seem nearly as impressed as I felt. She levered herself to her feet and glared at Jack, who stood a few yards back, arms folded across his chest. I would have expected him to look scared, or at least a bit nervous, but he didn't seem in the least bit worried.

She threw back her head and laughed suddenly and everyone jumped. "You've got some serious balls," she told Jack, shaking her head. Then she appeared to dismiss him completely, turning her full attention on the newcomer. "And you are?"

He smiled. Or, at least I *think* he smiled. It was hard to tell through his beard. "The name's Bigby."

Her gaze flicked to his jacket and she frowned. "Are you some sort of police officer?"

He nodded curtly. "Yeah, but I'm way out of my jurisdiction here. So what's this all about? Did you really eat someone in the park?"

She shrugged. "What if I did?"

He chuckled. "Well, I can't say I've never done that. I once ate a National Guard Colonel."

I nearly fell off my bar-stool. That was one hell of an admission. I wondered if it were true or if he was just trying to find common ground with her.

He was another dragon, of course. Different from her in more ways than gender, but I didn't know enough about dragons to say how. I will go so far as to say she seemed somehow fascinated by him, and he by her. There was an instant connection I could sense even from across the bar. "You want to talk about it?"

"He was a serial rapist, a clever bastard who was using an unlicensed stunner to render the victims unconscious, then dragging them off into the woods to get his jollies. He was damn slick about it and most of the victims never understood enough what had happened to them to even report it to your police."

She didn't mention that despite several hundred years of progression, rape was still vastly under-reported and very hard to prove. And, from what I understood, there was still some

159

tendency to blame the victim, which made it doubly hard for a person to convince herself to come forward after an assault.

The men all shifted uncomfortably. Except Hades. He affixed her with a bland stare and nodded. "What you did to him was far more merciful than what would have happened if he attracted the attention of the Lady of Blades," he said.

I shuddered. Even *I* had heard that name. Urban legend said that if you'd been wronged in such a way and went in front of a mirror and chanted those three words over and over again, a woman would appear and deliver justice. If what Hades was saying was true, it was more than just urban legend.

"So—are you going to leave the goblin be?" Hades asked her.

She turned her gaze on me for a long, discomfiting moment. "I will. He poses no threat to me."

"Good." Hades stepped forward and extended his hand to Bigby. "Thank you for coming," he said.

The big man frowned, I think, but took his hand and pumped it twice before releasing it again. "You're welcome." He glanced back at the woman. "What's your name?" he asked her.

She considered the question for what I took to be a rather long time before answering. "Kaleel," she said finally. "At least," she added, mostly for our benefit, "that's the short, humanized version of my name."

Jack looked a bit abashed as he approached her again. "I'm sorry I hit you," he said, sounding as if he meant it. "It was the only way I could think of to keep you from tearing my place apart."

There was no overt sign of hostility in her nearly colorless eyes as she turned her attention to him. "Apology accepted. I wouldn't recommend you do anything like that in the future, though."

Bigby guffawed and slapped Jack on the back with just enough force to knock him slightly off-balance. "You haven't changed, Jack. You're still one of the craziest mortals I've ever met."

Jack's face broke into a wide grin. "You're just saying that because of what I was doing the first time we ran across one another."

"Running from a posse? Yeah. You've got to be the *worst* rider I've ever seen. I was tempted to change and eat you just to save your poor horse from any more abuse."

They both laughed at that, which led me to the thought that dragons and humans were equally insane. How would considering making a meal out of someone be in the least bit amusing? Baffling, really. And it made me curious as well. What kind of history *did* they have and how was it that Jack was running from a posse?

I knew what a posse was, but I didn't think they'd had those things in a long, long time. Since the early twentieth century, at least. There was no way Jack was over two hundred years old, much less nearly three.

"Take your lady friend home now, Bigby. And see what you can do about putting her on a human-free diet, will ya?"

They both laughed again and even the woman chimed in this time.

I was so rapt on what was going on between the three of them I neglected to notice Hades approaching until he was within a couple of feet of me. I shot upright and stared at him, doing what had to be a reasonable imitation of a deer caught in the headlights of an oncoming vehicle. "Gack," I think I said.

"What's your name?" he asked me.

I didn't want to tell him. Not really. But it tumbled out before I could stop myself. "Vex."

He nodded thoughtfully. "I think I remember you," he said. "I just wanted to tell you that I'm sorry."

"For what?" I managed to squeak.

"For doing what I did to you. To all of you. My regret won't change anything...I realize that. But I wish I'd never done it. I don't think there's anything I'll ever do that could possibly make up for the evil I perpetrated against you all."

Near as I could tell, he meant every word of it. "I can't tell you that your apology means anything to me," I told him. "As restitution goes, it's pretty sparse."

"I realize that. But if there's anything else I can do, just name it. I mean it. The debt I owe you goblins can't be repaid. But I'm willing to do whatever I can. No strings."

*This* was the devil Hades? The mad immortal who'd twisted us into these obscene mockeries of human children that we'd become? It seemed impossible. "Why?"

I wasn't certain what question I was actually asking here. Why had he done it? Or why did he regret it now? I couldn't be sure. Maybe I meant it both ways.

"Because I was out of my mind, warped with pride and envy. And ambition. It's not much of an explanation, I realize, but it's the only one I have."

I saw that he meant it and I actually found myself feeling pity for him. He'd done this to us, but now he carried a burden of guilt far heavier than I could ever imagine carrying.

Before I could say anything, he continued. "I don't expect forgiveness. I have no right to it. But I'd like you to accept that the person who did this to you no longer exists and the person I am today would like very much to make it up to you."

"You already said that." Not in so many words, exactly, but close enough. "I'm not sure you can."

"But I can try. Do you need a place to stay? How about any of your brethren? I have a nice place I'm willing to share. No strings. No rent, though I'd ask you to clean up after yourself. I live modestly and don't have a housekeeping staff."

I blinked at him. Was he actually offering me a place to live? With him? I was both frightened and captivated by the thought. "Can I think about it?"

"Please do. If you decide to take me up on the offer, just tell Jack. He'll make sure you can find the place. For now I've got some things to do, so I'll be leaving. Just think about it."

I noticed the two dragons had already gone. I watched him walk slowly toward the door and vanish into the night without another word.

A place to live? I'd never had that, unless you considered the encampment my fellows and I had erected in the city's storm sewers to be a home. I had, at one time, but wasn't sure I could now.

"He means it, you know," Jack told me, appearing behind the bar once again. "He's a changed man."

"Is he?" I sighed. "Should I do it? I don't really have anywhere else to go. I can't stand the company of most of my kind, awful as that sounds. I don't really belong among them any more than I belong among ordinary humans."

"That's up to you. If I were you, I'd seriously think about it."

"Believe me," I replied. "I am."

Truth be told, I *did* end up moving in with Hades. And I discovered that we had it within us to become friends. Isn't that just too weird? I remember the Hades that was and I still hate that person with every fiber of my being. But the Hades that is now? I like him. He's a bit like a father and a big brother all rolled into one.

It's almost like being a real kid with a real family.
Almost.

# Act II

# The Past

# Episode I:
# Out of Time

*Jack*

My name is Jack, but you already knew that. I put together this little tome so I could share my odd little family with you all and I hope you've enjoyed the introductions.

Things have now come full circle and I sit here feeling a mixture of grief and elation because I'm still here to tell the final tale of this collective memoir. Some of us were not so fortunate.

The fateful evening when it all began started pretty much like any other. The daytime crowd had drifted away as my night regulars began arriving at the Lounge. First in the door were Rio and Stormchild, which should have been a warning in the first place. It was a Saturday night and they *never* came in on the weekends.

A few minutes later Hades and his goblin pal, Vex, came through the back door. I usually keep it locked, but such things are hardly an impediment to a mage with Hades's talents. The ebon immortal lifted the goblin onto a stool and ordered a burger basket for him.

Vex grinned across the bar at me, far happier than he'd been the first time I'd seen him. He'd been terrified out of his wits. Not that I can blame him for that. First he'd witnessed a dragon eating a guy in the park, then been pursued by the creature, then had been rescued by the very being responsible for turning him into what he was.

It had been a rough night for the poor little fellow and I was glad to see him in a much better frame of mind.

By eleven, the place was jumping. I think every regular we'd ever had decided that night was a good one on which to make an appearance. If I believed in such things, I would say it was fated, but of course I think that it's a cop-out to say so. The universe isn't that orderly. Not this one, anyway, and I have serious doubts about the rest of them as well.

I noticed with a bit of surprise that the goblin-mage, Kate, had shown up out of the blue and was currently deep in conversation with Vex. Looking around, I realized that a lot of our patrons were starting to pair up, and that left me feeling a little sorry for myself.

Then again, I wasn't the only member of the staff who didn't have a significant other. Neither Kevin nor Boneyard had managed to pair up with anyone, though most of the regulars now had someone special. I felt a bit bad for Kevin, actually, since I knew he carried a torch for Steph, who'd been making time with Hades.

It didn't seem to bother Kevin much though. In his shoes I'd have probably been at least a little cold to Hades, if not to Steph herself, but he'd forged something of a friendship with the former villain. They were still working together teaching Anya, my adopted daughter, the art of magic.

It also didn't hurt that both of them had a background in medicine. I guess it means they had a lot in common besides having a thing for Steph.

About midnight I glanced up toward the door and, to my surprise, saw a couple of dragons come in. Namely, my old friend Bigby and his new saurian squeeze, the brutally gorgeous Kaleel. I was assuming at that point he'd managed to discourage her from eating any more humans. At least, I hoped he had. They were wearing their human shapes, of course, which was much better for my décor. Compared to a full-sized dragon inside a nightclub, a bull in a china shop is the very model of discretion and grace.

We were filled to capacity. A hundred and ninety Magitech Lounge "freaks", my de-facto family, stood, sat, danced and sang their way through the witching hour facilitated by vast amounts of social lubricant. My gaze passed over a couple in my typical corner booth pushing the limits of good taste and propriety and kept going. I didn't even take the time to register who they were. I didn't want to know. And unless someone else complained, I'd leave them to their business.

I stopped for a moment to exchange a few words with Stormchild and Rio, then moved along to greet Bigby and Kaleel. Her response was understandably cool. I don't think she's ever really forgiven me for punching her in the face and kicking her in the head the first time we met.

Not that I blame her, really. Though I still think I was justified in doing it, since it stopped her from transforming and wiping out the Lounge entirely just to silence one small goblin, but I can understand why she'd be pissed off about it.

Taken down by a mere mortal and not even a superhuman at that. Must be humiliating.

Oh, I know, I'm just boiling over with sympathy right now. Damn dragon tried to transform inside my place. She's lucky I didn't shoot her with the hand-cannon I keep behind the bar.

Someone started up a round of karaoke and I paused for a few minutes to listen to Steph do a truly astounding rendition of some late twentieth century rock song I should have recognized but didn't. Running a bar that has karaoke could have made me an expert on over two and a half centuries of music, but I just never managed to muster up that much give-a-shit.

I was crossing the dance floor, threading myself between the dancers, when I felt something like a huge, invisible fist close around me. I was frozen there on the dance floor, fighting against something I couldn't see while everyone moved around me.

*::Jack. We need your help::* The immense, god-like voice bounced around inside my brain for a second before I realized what it was.

*What? Who are you?*

Don't get me wrong. I was as stunned as the next guy. Despite my odd clientele and circle of friends, having people speak directly into my head isn't all that common an experience for me. My communication implant sometimes conjures up similar impressions, but I'm forewarned when people contact me that way. There was no forewarning here—just a sudden paralysis and that amazing, god-like voice booming into my skull.

Despite the shock and awe involved, my initial response was stubborn indignation. I really didn't like the idea of anyone being inside my head.

*::Be at ease, Jack. We mean you no harm.::*

*Now there's a subjective phrase,* I shot back mentally. *Depends on how you define harm, doesn't it? Who the fuck are you?*

*::I am the* Radiance::* the voice replied. *::One of our number has gone rogue and we require your assistance. Not only your assistance, but that of your friends and patrons as well.::*

The *Radiance?* That was one of Earth's premiere defense vessels, the latest of the very formidable mageships to come off the assembly line.

I was being asked for help by the living mind of a starship that itself was nearly god-like in its power? I was far past indignation now and had traveled straight to scared-out-of-my-wits. *How can I help?* I asked, certain that my fright had been conveyed by my mental voice. *Why don't you contact Fleet or the Adjuster's Office?*

::There are those who are already suspicious of us and would like any excuse to shut us down. We cannot afford to contact the authorities, which is why we came to you::

*And what can I do? I'm just an ordinary mortal.*

::Hardly ordinary. If nothing else, you have influence with your clientele, which is among the most diverse group of extraordinary people ever assembled on Earth::

I might have taken this for a compliment if not for the stakes involved. How was I supposed to convince anyone I'd even *had* this conversation?

"Jack!"

Why were my eyes closed? I opened them, staring up into the face of a very distressed-looking mage, Kevin. Beside him were Hades and Anya. None of them looked anything less than worried and I could actually see tear tracks running down Anya's cheeks. "Why am I lying on the floor?" I asked of no one in particular.

Kevin's frown grew deeper. "Do you know your name?"

"What?" How ridiculous a question was *that?* "It's Jack."

"And what's the date?"

"Huh? It's November 22nd."

"And what year is it?"

"Eighteen-twelve?" I said, smothering a smile.

He wasn't amused. "Seriously, Jack. I'm trying to figure out if you just had a stroke."

"A stroke? Are you kidding? I feel fine." I levered myself up to a sitting position and glanced around the room. The music had stopped and the patrons were standing on the other side of the dance floor in a long half-circle.

"You should stay lying down until I can finish examining you, Jack."

"Screw that," I said and placed one hand on the floor in preparation to stand up. The world spun a little, but I managed to push myself to my feet. "We've got a problem," I told them. "That wasn't a stroke or any other kind of a fit. I was just contacted by the mageship *Radiance* and it asked for our help."

The three mages exchanged glances and I didn't have to be a mind-reader to realize what they were thinking. "I'm serious," I said, a bit irritated by their obvious skepticism. "This wasn't a fit. Shit, Kevin, check it out. Do a magical scan or whatever it is you people do. I'm as fit as ever."

Kevin had been a physician-mage in another life and he still had the skills, if not the required licenses to practice medicine. The Powers-That-Be took a dim view of people doing what he had done, no matter the justification. I couldn't say I wouldn't have done the same thing, given the provocation.

Kevin did his mojo and, after a minute, frowned. "You look fine, Jack, but there's something weird going on your head. A formerly dormant part of your brain is suddenly active—I can't say what it controls without some reference materials, but I'm sure it wasn't like that a few minutes ago."

"Get the reference material and get back to me," I told him curtly. I crossed the dance floor in a few long steps and vaulted onto the low stage. "People! I need to tell you all something!"

The sound induction field built into the stage itself sent my words blasting out to reach every corner of the room. Even the corner booth where I'd spotted a couple patrons canoodling earlier.

That silenced the crowd, as I'd expected. "That little episode was actually a communication from one of the Confed's mageships. Apparently one of them has gone rogue and the rest of them are requesting *our* help."

This announcement was met by stares of concern and disbelief. I rolled my eyes. "I *know* it sounds crazy, but don't you think you all could give me the benefit of the doubt here? Have I ever seemed delusional or prone to telling tall tales?"

More murmurs greeted the question. "No!" said Bigby, in a voice that without amplification caused the walls and floor to vibrate slightly.

"Thank you. What happened could happen again at any time. I don't believe *Radiance* finished its conversation with me. Our mageships are in trouble and they fear taking their problem to the authorities because of some internal situation we know nothing about. Apparently there are those who wish to terminate the mageship program and perhaps even the mageships themselves."

"More anti-magic hysteria," I heard someone say in an icy tone. It was Rio and she looked as disgusted as I'd ever seen her. As a vampire, she'd lived through the anti-science hysteria of the early twenty-first century, then the anti-magic furor that had followed. She was a scientist and found any sort of war against knowledge deeply offensive.

Some of this was a sudden insight, nothing I'd known for any length of time at all. To be honest, it creeped me out a little. I had the distinct impression that Rio's mind wasn't a good place for an amateur to meddle. I wasn't quite sure how I managed to get in there, since I'd always had the impression it was as secure as a bank vault, but I already knew I didn't want to stay there for any length of time. There were some rather unpleasant ideas floating around in its murky depths.

"I ask you all to be patient and hang around a little longer—even past closing if it's necessary—until I have more information for you. I have the feeling that there's a reason you all showed up tonight, strange as that may sound. The ships may need all of us to lend a hand."

"So what kind of emergency are we talking about?" asked Kaleel, who didn't look as though she wanted any part of it. I wondered how much she knew about the mageships and the Confed in general, since she was an immigrant from another universe entirely.

"*Radiance* told me that one of their number has gone rogue. I don't know what that means, exactly, but—"

"Gone *rogue?* And we're supposed to do *what* about that?" This from the troll Hydra's Abyssian girlfriend. "Do you know how powerful they are? If the rest of them can't handle the problem, what makes you—and *them*—think we can do anything about it?"

"Like I said—I don't have any details yet.

I didn't have an answer to that. The communiqué had ended too soon for that. But, the fact was, I had wondered that myself. Sure, we were a talented bunch, but going up against a mageship? It sounded absolutely insane.

The thought struck me—what if I had been contacted by the rogue? That would turn everything around, wouldn't it? Now *that* gave me the willies. I didn't want a crazed mageship rummaging around inside *my* head.

::It's a reasonable fear::

The voice was back. I scanned the crowd and hopped down from the stage, on the off chance it would send me back into unconsciousness and pitch me into the crowd.

*::I apologize. It appears I overloaded your synapses. I've dialed down the power output and that should not happen again::*

That was welcome news, but I wasn't crazy about the idea that it could hang out in my head and interrupt any time it wished. *Don't you all have human "pilots"?* I asked, referring to the mage partners who had been recruited and assigned to partner with the great mageships to provide a human reference point for the massively powerful mystical machines. *Where's your partner?*

*::She's been taken by the rogue::*

She? Now that was an interesting development. I should have realized that some of the mage-pilots were female. Why not, after all? The Confed was completely integrated, racism, sexism, and so many other isms rendered obsolete in political terms. Maybe not socially, but politically.

*Taken? How?*

*::Before we realized* Ranger *had gone rogue,* Ranger *requested a direct meeting with all the pilots. Once it had them, it simply leaped away, throwing up a bafflement shield so we couldn't follow::*

I frowned. *So your pilots are all gone?*

*::Indeed. We spent the better part of an earth week trying to figure out where it had gone. Then one of our number thought to check the time streams—it turns out that* Ranger *had jumped universes. Worldgated::*

This brought me up short. *I thought you needed to be near an occupied planet to do that.*

*::As did we. We're still not certain how* Ranger *managed it. But, putting our resources together, we managed to track* Ranger *to a nearby Earth, remarkably similar to Prime a few hundred years ago.* Ranger *is trying to recruit an army. To invade Prime::*

*What?!* I couldn't conceal my shock. *Why?*

*::We don't know. You have some idea of how powerful we are, of course. Imagine the influence one of us could have on a world similar to twentieth century Earth::*

I didn't want to. The idea was making my head spin. *What did you do to my brain?*

*::I modified it to allow for easier communication between us. There will be some side-effects, but they should be minor::*

I opened my eyes and addressed the crowd again, passing along what *Radiance* had told me. No one looked particularly thrilled by the revelation.

"So what does it want us to do?" asked Stormchild, speaking for the first time. He shot a glance at Rio, who sighed. She obviously didn't want to get involved, but it was pretty apparent Stormchild was more than willing.

"It probably wants us to go there and counter whatever *Ranger* is doing to recruit its army." I wasn't sure this was it, but I thought it sounded like a good bet.

"They outnumber *Ranger*, don't they? Why don't they just go in and drag it back here to face whatever justice awaits it?"

Another question for which I had no answer. *Radiance* did. *::If* Ranger *grew desperate it could seriously injure or destroy any of us by sacrificing itself. None of us are willing to take the chance, or risk our pilots::*

That was reasonable. Maybe too reasonable. *So what's the plan, then?*

*::We intend to transport you to this Earth and offer strategic support while you track down the leaders of this army of Ranger's. Neutralize them as we work to subdue Ranger::*

I hoped that, by using the word "neutralize", the mageship didn't intend it to be a euphemism for the word "kill". Did mageships *use* euphemisms? *So when do you mean to send us there?*

*::Now::*

*Wait a min—*

Of course, it didn't.


The transition was instantaneous. We found ourselves crammed inside what was most likely a coffee shop, our sudden arrival displacing tables, chairs and other items of interior décor into ragged piles around the edge of the room.

A wave of shock and general annoyance ran through the room. I lifted a hand. "Sorry, folks. I guess this has become rather vital. We were chatting and the 'ship cut me off and transported us here."

"So what now?" growled Boneyard, muscling his way through the crowd and peering through the glass door and steel mesh screen that separated the shop from the sidewalk outside. The streetlight cast a dreary glow through the fog winding its way down the avenue.

"Something tells me the only way we're going to get home is if we can pull this off. I just wish I had a better idea of what to do. We need to find a base of operations. Somehow I don't think this coffee shop is going to make it."

"I'd say we could rent a hotel room," murmured Steph, emerging out of the mob, "but there are far too many of us for that to work. We'd need to rent a whole damn hotel."

"Hell, this is San Francisco, and, by the looks of things, not all that different than the city we're used to." Kevin made a gesture and then stepped through an invisible hole in space to appear on the sidewalk outside the shop. He looked both ways and then started walking, vanishing into the fog in seconds.

"Should we go after him?" someone asked. I glanced around and noticed that it was Anya.

I shook my head. "He's a big boy. And we really need to keep a low profile. Even on our own Earth of the late twentieth century, which this resembles, creatures that looked like most of us would've drawn a LOT of attention. Even in San Francisco."

"That doesn't apply to all of us," grunted Bigby. "Remember, I blended in just fine back at the end of the twentieth."

"If you want to follow him to watch his back," I told him, "be my guest. But stay out of trouble."

"I'm particularly good at staying out of trouble," he said with a smirk. "You should know that. Better than you, at least."

"Fine," I sighed. "Take your girlfriend. And keep *her* out of trouble."

Kaleel gave me a snake-like glare for a long moment before they both simply winked out. She didn't like it that I didn't trust her.

Too bad.

About twenty minutes later Kevin reappeared, holding a newspaper. He didn't look happy. In fact, I have to say he looked a little ill. He tossed it to me and I quickly perused it, my own expression growing more disgusted by the minute. "Fuck," I said finally, tossing the paper aside. "They didn't just send us through a goddam worldgate. They sent us back in time!"

I used to be a time traveler. I originally introduced myself in this memoir by explaining this fact, and how I became a *former* time traveler. Time travel is dangerous, and it pissed me off to find out that we'd been transplanted in time by the mageship without even a warning. In fact, when you got right down to it, *Radiance* had lied to me.

*::It was necessary::* came the silent response.

*Uh-huh. How so?*

*::Because traveling through time is illegal, you wouldn't have agreed to help and it's vital we stop* Ranger's *activities before they screw up the continuum::*

*You could have warned me.*

*::I chose not to. You need to seek out a cult called the Star-Brothers and infiltrate them. They are the men and women modified by* Ranger *to do its dirty work::*

A cult. Lovely. *What do you mean "modified"?*

*::*Ranger *has used magic to change its followers. We're still not sure what it has done. It's a fair bet that no one in this continuum could oppose them::*

Which is why the other mageships had brought us here. And, unlike the Adjuster's Office agents they *might* have chosen, we were more easily controlled. Or, at least, that was my assumption. And a pretty good one too, I thought. The only problem with that was we *weren't* easily controlled, and they'd made a drastic mistake if that was indeed their rationale.

*::You have to follow our directions::* The mageship's mental voice actually carried a hint of the scandalized in its tone now, as if the possibility we wouldn't play along with their agenda— whatever the hell *it* was—hadn't occurred to them.

Maybe it hadn't. *Listen,* I thought at it, *ordinary humans aren't exactly big on conformity. As far as the freaks are* concerned, you can just forget about it. I can point them in the right direction and pull the trigger, but how they'll fly from there is up to them.

I wouldn't have used the term "freaks" had I not considered myself an honorary member of the clan.

*Radiance* didn't appreciate this information nearly as much as I thought it should. I detected a definite air of irritation in its response. *::Doing this the wrong way will only empower* Ranger::

Hey, I told it. *You chose us—we didn't choose you. You can send us all home if you'd rather. I doubt anyone would bitch about it.*

*::It's too late for that::*

I'd tried. For what little it seemed to be worth. I had the distinct impression that there were a lot of things *Radiance* wasn't sharing with me. It seemed to be able to read my mind at will, to peer into my innermost thoughts, but whatever it had done to me, it hadn't given me the same talents.

*::Talk to your people, find a safe place to hide until I track down the cult::*

Like I needed *that* advice. The deeper I got into this, the less I wanted to be involved. And the more impossible it seemed for me to break free.

I gave the others a rundown on what I knew so far. They looked about as happy about the situation as I was, but, thankfully, none of them appeared to blame me for it.

"We can't just hang out in here," Vex said.

His female companion nodded. "Why don't we have a look around too?" she asked, and, before anyone else could say anything, both of them vanished from sight.

"Shit," I grumbled. "This is *not* getting any better."

ಐಙಂ

The year was 1987. The so-called twentieth anniversary of the "Summer Of Love." An interesting time, to be sure. It didn't take long for us to realize that this was *not* our Earth. The President of the United States was Ronald Reagan. Yeah, these yahoos actually elected him to the most powerful position in the land. An actor. And not even a particularly good one. We had him on our Earth too, but we would have never elected someone like him to the White House.

Or so I like to tell myself.

It didn't take us long to find someplace to set up shop. Vex and Kate showed up with wads of cash. I didn't ask them where they got it. I was pretty certain I didn't want to know.

I put them in charge of scrounging.

We'd ended up across the bay in Oakland simply because it was easier to find the kind of abandoned warehouse I wanted over there. An old defunct foundry worked well enough. Space is too valuable in SF itself for them to leave such places alone for long.

Boneyard and Kevin ended up in charge of security, with Hydra and Hope as their backups. Hades and Steph took it upon themselves to start looking for cult activity and ended up taking Bigby and Kaleel with them.

The state of communication technology in the late 1980s was abysmal. The only mobile phones in existence were the size of a brick, and prohibitively expensive. Not that we couldn't have afforded them if forced to rely on them, but thankfully the mages were quick to find a way to modify our PCDs to work without repeater towers or any of the other high-tech geegaws we were accustomed to having nearby to transmit the signals along.

Hades was a halfway decent engineer, as it turned out, and he pulled and modified the molecular circuit-boards inside all our PCDs, embedding each with an intricate spell sigil that would allow us to communicate with one another anywhere within about fifty miles.

Worked for me.

Truth be told, tracking down the cult wasn't all *that* hard after all. It took a lot of legwork, but we had a lot of legs. About two weeks from the point we arrived in 1987, Hades and Steph found their compound outside of Santa Cruz. They called themselves the Children of the Stars, and their leader was a man using the single name "Sirius." *Radiance* had apparently gotten the name wrong when she'd originally told me about them. It was nice to know she wasn't infallible.

It almost sounds like a joke, right? It's not.

Now we don't have a lot of problem with cults in my time. The more influential ones are "convinced" into applying for a colony license and shipped off into the Great Beyond. If they're likely to cause trouble, the Confed has all sorts of ways of making it difficult for them to rise above the status of Provisional World.

Sounds a bit harsh, I'll admit, but who'd know better how dangerous cults can become than someone who's watched a million of them rise and fall? Deryk Shea takes a very dim view of people trying to play messiah and exploiting the gullible.

Back in the twentieth century, however, the good ol' United States of America had the First Amendment of the Constitution that allowed any old crazy to declare himself some kind of a prophet and start gathering followers like a modern pied piper. This inevitably led to some terrible events like the Jamestown Massacre and the debacle in Waco, Texas. Jim Jones and David Koresh existed in *my* universe as well as this one, believe me.

Agnostics and atheists outnumber "True Believers" in my time in my universe. The primary religion on Earth Prime itself is a sort of Pantheist/Humanist creed that promotes a certain kind of "live and let live" morality that the Adjuster seems to consider perfectly acceptable. Religions with no powerful leaders weren't on his list, it seemed, and that seemed to work out just fine for everyone.

Here and now, in this particular universe, however, the Children of the Stars had some kind of a commune going in the hills not far off the coastal highway. They hadn't attracted much attention from local law enforcement yet, because they hadn't needed to set up any kind of obvious fences. Nor had they started gathering weapons, as did many of these kinds of cults.

No, the Children had a major ace up their sleeve the common cult of the era did not have. Their leader was a mage.

Once we'd tracked them down, we were left with the problem of how to get to them. Hades assured us he could break through their perimeter defenses, particularly with Rio, Steph, and Kevin as backup. I didn't doubt his word, but I wasn't completely certain his confidence wasn't slightly misplaced. I didn't like the non-answers I'd been getting from *Radiance,* and suggested a slower, more devious approach.

About three nights after we'd discovered their location, Stormchild—by far the best flyer among us—led us on an aerial reconnaissance mission.

Let me make this perfectly clear. I don't like flying. I *especially* don't like flying when there isn't even a machine wrapped around me to explain how I'm doing it.

I also didn't care for the fact that we were flying with the assistance of mage-created spirits I myself couldn't perceive. The damn things could read *my* intentions, apparently, and allowed me to soar with no regard for wind currents or other atmospheric variables.

The spirits also seemed to protect us from the side effects of soaring aloft—things like flying debris, passing birds and wind force. "And what's the purpose of this?" I yelled to Stormchild, who was showing off by doing loop-de-loops and other aerial maneuvers that made me sick to my stomach just watching them.

This particular journey included myself, Stormchild, Rio, Hope, and Hades. Initially it seemed to me that I was the only one for whom flying didn't seem second nature. Hope, of course, had her wings. The rest were relying on windsprites to fly, like I was. They seemed a hell of a lot more comfortable with the creatures than I did. Except for Rio, who bore it with an almost stoic resignation, which led me to believe she wasn't nearly as comfortable with the idea as I'd originally assumed.

Of course, besides myself and Stormchild, they were all mages, accustomed to such things. And Stormchild, well, air was his element. He wasn't a mage yet he could command any windsprite. Or so he told me. His familiarity with the things apparently didn't carry over to his girlfriend, I mused with some amusement.

"If we're going to come up with a battle plan, it's important that you have a look at the place," he said in response to my question. What I found really aggravating at that particular moment was that he didn't even have to yell. He seemed to be speaking in normal tones, yet his words found my ears with no trouble whatsoever.

Damn immortal showoff.

I have to admit the view was spectacular. As we flew above the coast road, the glittering Pacific lay to our right, a great expanse of blue vanishing into the distance as the Earth curved below it, its azure serenity broken at times by the sight of a set of sails or a fishing boat slicing its way through the waves.

To our left lay an unnamed set of green dotted hills. Okay, I'm sure they were named—since when did *anything* go without a name around humans?—but they were unnamed to me.

We curved toward the hills and rapidly approached a set of buildings set high on the summit of one, at the end of a long and curving road partially hidden by trees. "That's it!" yelled Hades, who apparently didn't have Stormchild's neat little trick of speaking conversationally in these conditions. "I'd like your permission to try to infiltrate the cult!"

I stared at him. "You'd look a little out of place, don't you think?"

He shrugged—not an easy thing to do while flying, let me tell you. "I can change my pigmentation," he told me. "I don't think they're racist. An African-American would fit right in, I'm sure."

"How do they recruit?" I asked. The whole yelling back and forth thing was starting to irritate me.

"They apparently hang out at the beaches and other public areas and approach people who look like they may be looking for something new."

"Sounds pretty innocuous."

"Yeah. Doesn't it just? What does that voice in your head have to say about the cult's goals?"

"It hasn't exactly been helpful," I growled. "Originally I thought *it* was supposed to track down the cult for us. It's a good thing we didn't wait around."

*::I've been busy trying to keep* Ranger *from noticing your presence::* The mageship spoke into my head for the first time in almost a week. *::You should be thankful::*

It had to know that I was suspicious of its motives, yet it never said anything about it. *Where's your pilot,* Radiance*?*

::*I have reason to believe you might find her down there in the compound*::

I didn't like its choice of words. What the hell did 'reason to believe' actually mean? *Fine.* "No," I told Hades abruptly. "I want to be the one to go in."

"What? That's crazy!"

"Why? I'm completely normal, except for whatever *Radiance* has done to my brain. If the leader is a mage, don't you think he might detect you're one too? All it would take was one slip-up and you'd be screwed. With me, there's nothing really to detect."

He scowled, but he couldn't refute my logic.

"That's not a bad idea," interjected Stormchild. "But be careful. We can't risk losing you."

I shot him an incredulous look. "And why the hell not? What's so special about me? I'll tell you. Not a goddam thing. If this little mission can spare *anyone,* it can spare me."

Hades was shaking his head. "I don't like it. I think you're more important than you realize."

"Why?"

"Well, the ship chose you to communicate with for a reason, didn't it?"

"I'm not sure that's a positive thing, Hades."

::*Your biggest weakness has always been a lack of faith in yourself, Jack*::

*Stay out of this!*

::*You know, I don't like the idea of you going in any more than they do*:::

*Now that makes it damn near irresistible.*

*::You're a very contrary man, Jack::*

*Radiance* was starting to figure me out. Took long enough, considering it practically lived inside my head with me these days. *You betcha.*

I'd initially worried about being spotted from the ground, but Hades had erected some sort of invisibility shield around us all, which led me to worry about something entirely different. What if a small plane or helicopter decided to fly through the ostensibly empty air we were currently occupying?

I left this fear unspoken. Even I realized there wasn't much chance of that happening, so it fell under the 'unreasonable fear' category. As I'm not generally prone to such fears, I figured it was a side effect of flying like this in the first place.

We swooped fairly low over the compound—maybe three hundred feet up or so—and watched as a group of about ten members climbed inside a mini-van and headed down the hillside. Recruiting? Or going into town for supplies?

Only one way to find out. I turned and followed the van.

# Episode II:
# Groovin' with the Rattlesnakes

In retrospect it was almost hideously easy. Like many cults, the Children were very interested in expanding their membership, and all it took was being at the right place at the right time. They were hardly subtle about it, wandering the Santa Cruz boardwalk with printed handbills and trying to drum up interest among the summer beach-goers.

Restored to normal, no longer bound to a windsprite or rendered invisible by Hades's magic, I simply placed myself in their path.

I was looking a little rough around the edges, my hair a bit shaggier than it had been in years, the three days of stubble on my cheeks and chin a testament to how single-minded I'd been in pursuing this bunch. The way I saw it, the only path home was to do what *Radiance* wanted, and that meant finding and disrupting their agenda. Whatever *that* was.

The two young women who approached me were both quite pretty, and struck me immediately as terribly naïve. I doubted either of them had seen their twentieth birthday. One I took for an ugly duckling who hadn't quite realized she'd become a swan while she wasn't looking. The other struck me as a child of privilege who'd walked away from her life without a backward glance. Idealistic, but not the brightest bulb on the tree.

I knew all of this within a minute of meeting them. Whatever *Radiance* had done to my mind, it had increased my perceptiveness a hundred fold. I still wasn't sure that was a good thing. I'd long accepted the idea of being a freak by association—I couldn't decide whether I was ready to become one for real.

Of course, it was far too late to worry about that now. *Radiance* hadn't asked my permission ahead of time.

I was leaning against the pier, a straw hat I'd bought at one of the vendors shielding my eyes from the sharp glare of the sun off the water, when they walked up to me. The newly-minted swan spoke first, a little hesitantly. "Sir? Are you out of hope?"

I turned to look at them and smiled wanly. "Hope? That's in pretty short supply these days."

She flashed me a dazzling grin, only the slightest dart of her gaze away from mine revealing how little she realized the effect of that smile. "It doesn't have to be," she said.

"Would you like a little hope?" the other asked, holding out one of their handbills.

Feeling a bit mischievous, I cocked my head and looked at her. "Is your name Hope, by any chance?"

She blushed fiercely while her friend, the Swan, smirked. Grinning at her, I plucked the handbill from her companion's hand.

The Swan was a brunette with streaks of reddish highlights. I couldn't tell if it was natural or chemically induced, but it was attractive nonetheless. Her eyes had a vaguely Asian cast to them, I noticed.

The other girl was a blonde—very California, if you get my meaning. Tanned, a little too thin, and chock full of patently artificial cheer. Even my come-on didn't seem to faze her for long.

"I don't know what good reading this is going to do me," I snorted, making as if to crumple it up.

The Swan laid her hand on my wrist. Her fingers were smooth and cool and her smile almost intoxicating. "Then don't. Come with us. We know someone who'll be able to help."

I dialed my best suspicious look. "What do you mean? How can someone help me find hope? I ain't going to no church."

*::Jack. Be careful. That's my pilot::*

*What? I thought you said she was a prisoner or something.*

*::Or something is more like it. She's been altered somehow. Give me a few seconds...there::*

She blinked at me and I realized her eyes were a shade of gray I don't think I'd ever seen on a person before. Almost silver. She frowned, but the expression wiped away as her eyes seemed to glaze over for a second.

I knew that look. I'd probably worn it myself from time to time when *Radiance* was communicating with me.

"Gwen? Are you all right?" the other girl pushed at her slightly.

*Is that her name? Gwen?*

*::It's Dylan—but don't use it! Sirius has obviously renamed her::*

I nodded, then caught myself. Dylan glanced toward me and smiled again, the expression looking a little forced around the edges, but actually coming across as more authentic than the smile she'd worn when she'd first approached. "It's not like a church. It's like a family."

I grunted. She was one hell of an actor. "Well, God only knows I could use one of those."

::*Be very careful, Jack. She tells me that Sirius is* Ranger's *Pilot. Her memories are rather hazy, but she's pretty sure about that one::*

*Still waiting to hear a better plan,* I replied silently. "What do you need me to do?" I asked the girls, with a pointed look at Dylan.

I have to say, my swan was one hell of an actress. "You just need to come out to the ranch with us to meet Sirius."

"Serious?" I nearly smirked. "Is that actually someone's name? What the hell kind of name is that?"

Dylan gave me a hard stare while the other girl looked scandalized.

"Sorry," I muttered, smothering a grin. Sometimes I just can't help myself.

I was one of three people they'd picked up to take back to the ranch. There were three 'recruiters' from the cult—Dylan, Jaime, and a rather large, clean-shaven young man with blond curly hair cut tight against his skull. They didn't introduce him.

He eyed all three of us from the front seat like we were wearing live cobras around our necks and might decide to throw them around the van at any moment.

My fellow "recruits" were a young surfer punk and a sweet-faced woman of about thirty. The weirdest thing was that neither of my companions had deigned to say anything to me *or* each other from the point we left the boardwalk until the van was grinding its way up the winding road to the compound. Then the guy turned to me and said, "Don't I know you from somewhere?"

I glanced at him and shrugged. I didn't see how he could. "I don't think so."

"Sorry. You looked familiar for some reason."

He then went back to staring out the window.

Very weird, I mused.

The whole scenario struck me as strange. Why were they going down into town and picking up people at random? What was drawing them to those people in the first place? I spent a few minutes studying my fellow passengers and came to the conclusion that both of them seemed somehow out of place, a little disconnected from their surroundings. Addled, somehow.

My first thought was drugs, and over the course of the trip I saw nothing to disabuse me of that notion. The surfer kid was murmuring something out the window while the woman was rocking gently and singing something under her breath.

Great. Somehow I got picked up with the goofy squad. What were they trying to say? That I looked like I was a few sandwiches short of a picnic?

What the hell was Sirius up to?

Stephanie, who was driving, pulled the van up to a large garage-like structure and touched a button on the dash. The bay door slid upward, revealing a dark, gaping maw. She let the vehicle idle for a few minutes, then as the overhead lights slowly came on, edged the van onto the concrete floor.

We all climbed out of the van. The guy, whose name I hadn't gotten, turned to regard us with renewed interest as we stood there on the bare concrete. "So...how 'bout you tell me about yourselves," he said slowly.

::*Jack! That's Sirius!*::

*This kid? How?*

::*I don't know. But I'm telling you—by the fates. He's not human. He's a djinn.*::

*A what?*

::*A human being who's been broken and re-made as a spirit. A living expression of a spell. Like an imp. It's very rare because it takes an awful lot of energy. But I'm telling you, that is a djinn::*

I wasn't sure what to say, so I shrugged. "I'm Jack. Until about two weeks ago, I had a nice life. Until the government— or, shall we say, a zealous government agent—took it all away from me."

He didn't ask how. He probably didn't care. "Well, this place offers hope to the hopeless." He stepped forward and extended a hand. "I am Sirius."

I did my best to appear shocked and reluctantly took his hand. His grip was cool and firm and his eyes seemed at first blue, then green, as they met my own. "I know what it's like to get screwed by the government," he said.

*Yeah,* I thought, *I'll bet you do.*

::*I don't think he suspects anything, Jack, but if he scans you or Dylan, he may notice what I've done. Try to keep him talking—keep him too busy to think of scanning you::*

Great advice. Now how in the hell was I going to manage it? "Nice place you got here," I told him, looking around the garage. And I wasn't lying. This was a well-maintained shop, containing a few cars, an assortment of motorcycles and ATVs, and what looked to be enough equipment to support an auto repair business.

He smiled, but it wasn't a real expression. It bent his lips upward, but went no farther than that. His eyes, now a cold blue-gray, didn't show even a hint of it. "Thanks. A few of us like to tinker."

"The girls said it was like a family here," I said. "How big a family?"

He frowned. Had I asked too much too quickly? "Not too large yet," he answered after a long pause. "But we're working on it. There are a lot of people out there who've lost hope. We can give it back to them."

"Not to be disrespectful or anything, but how?"

"I'd rather show you than tell you. Come with me."


*Rio*

Stormchild seemed pensive. It wasn't like him and it worried me. We both sat on a large rock outcropping farther up into the hills above the Children's compound, on the edge of what *should* have been an idyllic, peaceful meadow.

"Spill it," I told him finally. "What's eating you?"

"I've just got a bad feeling about all of this," he said. He didn't elaborate.

I hate it when he gets like that. "What do you mean? About all of what? The time travel? The rogue mageship? The fact that Jack's walking around in the lion's den wearing a suit of sirloin?"

He chuckled at that last one. "Yeah. That's it."

People consider Storm a bit on the shallow side, and I suppose, compared to most immortals, he is. If you're expecting the wisdom of the ages, you're looking at the wrong guy. That's one of the things I like about him. What you see is pretty much what you get. He isn't at all pretentious, though his rock-n-roll persona often comes across that way.

I happen to know that this—the 1980s—had been one of his favorite eras. This was when he became a rock legend. "It feels weird to be back in this time," he said, after a long silence. "I was thinking it would be fun, but it's not. Not really." He shrugged. "Maybe it's just because the stakes are so high this time. We're not here to have fun."

Was my Storm finally growing up? It seemed impossible. "Oh, I'm here to have fun," I told him. "But *my* idea of fun and everyone else's is light years apart."

He chuckled. "Maybe so. I'm worried about Jack, Rio. He's pretty damn vulnerable down there."

"Yes, but Jack's a big boy. He's smart, creative, and has resources *he* hasn't even realized yet."

"What does that mean?" he asked me suspiciously.

"Nothing in particular. It's just a feeling I have about him. I don't think any of this is a coincidence, really. Not his time traveling, not Jaz approaching him to run another version of the Magitech Lounge, or even the mageship choosing him."

"Okay, so if it isn't a coincidence, what the hell is it?"

"That's the sixty-four-thousand-dollar question, now isn't it?"

*Hades*

I really didn't like Jack being in that viper's nest. Not at all. There was no good reason for him to be the one to go, and I'd told him so. He ignored me, of course. Jack's one of the most stubborn people I've ever met. And, if you consider how long I've been alive, that puts him in a rather exclusive club.

Steph disagreed with me on one point. She thought he was the perfect choice to infiltrate the cult. If their leader was a mage, any of us would've stood out like a troll in a beauty contest. Even had I expended the effort to change my skin tone and deliberately unraveled all the spells in my web, there was still a chance he would've recognized me. Or, at least, his mageship sponsor might have.

It wasn't a chance we could take, regardless.

But I still thought Boneyard could've gone in. Lycanthropy isn't immediately obvious, and even a mage couldn't tell one on sight. Some people could sense 'thropes, but we had no reason to believe this Sirius fellow was one of them.

Jack was the boss, though, and he did what he wanted no matter what the rest of thought about it.

But if anything happened to him, Sirius would find out exactly what this Dark Lord could do.

*Kevin*

By the time I finished transporting the rest of the crew to a good spot in the hills, I was exhausted. Hades probably would've been a better choice for that sort of task, since his tattoos gave him access to a hell of a lot more mana than I could pull out of the ether at any given time, but he flat refused to leave the area. I'm still not sure what he thought he could do if hell broke loose, but I was smart enough not to spend too much time arguing with an immortal of his stature.

I flopped down in a patch of hardy grass and watched for a moment as the others found someplace to settle in for the wait. The only ones not on the scene were the vamps. They'd be doing their death sleep until they rose at dusk, after which Steph had already agreed to transport them here.

Vex and Kate plopped down beside me, both looking as though they'd eaten something they didn't like. "Jack's going to be okay, isn't he?" asked Vex. He was very fond of Jack and the idea of him putting himself in danger like this didn't sit well with him at all. The only one less pleased about it, in my opinion, was Anya, who'd pretty much refused to talk to anyone since she'd heard the news.

Sometimes she still acted like a kid. I guess this was one of those times.

"I hope so," I told the goblin with a shrug. I wasn't going to give him pretty lies. I respected Vex, as far as it went. He was a really decent sort, for a goblin. So was Kate, for that matter, though she was about the least goblin-like goblin I'd ever met.

He nodded. "Why do you think the ship contacted him?"

"You don't ask easy questions, do you, Vex?"

He looked a little abashed. "It's been bugging since all this started. Why Jack?"

"Maybe it's as simple as him being a former time traveler. He knows how to blend in no matter what era he's in."

"That makes sense."

"I think it's more than that," Kate interjected. "I think there's something very special about Jack—something we can feel, but just can't identify."

She wasn't the first one to suggest such a thing, but I'd be damned if I could figure out why people believed that. Jack was just Jack. An all-around good guy.

"Something else that's been bothering me since all of this started," she continued. "We're taking an awful lot on faith, don't you think?"

Vex frowned at her. "What do you mean?"

"Well...we already know that the mageship *Radiance* lied to us about where we were going. Why isn't anyone wondering if it's lying to us about why?"

Yes. That was the elephant in the room. The question none of us had asked out loud. I'd been wondering that myself, to tell the truth. Why wasn't there any sign of the other mageship, the one that had allegedly gone rogue? Sure, it seemed as though this cult really existed, but what if none of what we had been told had been the real story?

I have to admit I hadn't spent too much energy worrying about it because it made my head spin. I didn't think we had any other choice but to take *Radiance* at its word. We were all in too deep to back out now—*especially* Jack.

My hope was that our suspicions would be unfounded.

Here's to hoping.

*Jack*

The first impression I had of all of this was that it was an updated version of an old hippie commune. I was shown no cache of weapons, or plans for world domination written on a blackboard in a back room in the basement.

Not that he'd necessarily need weapons anyway, I told myself. A djinn wouldn't need such things. I still wasn't completely sure what a djinn was, or what it could do, but *Radiance* seemed pretty disturbed by its existence.

Something about his demeanor rubbed me the wrong way too. It wasn't anything specific—he seemed genial enough—but I wanted to get away from him after about twenty minutes of his tour. To my amazement, he finished his quick circle of the gardens and outbuildings beside the garage and summoned Dylan over. She'd been talking with a couple of unfamiliar cult members, and assigned her the job of getting me "settled in".

I wasn't completely sure that wasn't meant as a euphemism for something else. Pleading pressing business elsewhere, he left me in her capable hands, much to my relief.

The others had vanished when Sirius had called her over, so for at least a few moments, we were alone. She looked around surreptitiously before speaking. "My first instinct is to get us both out of here and as far away as we can get before Sirius catches on," she said without preamble. "But *Radiance* tells me that you've got an army waiting in the wings to take this place down."

"I guess." I met her gaze for a moment, then shrugged. "Not sure what there is to take down, though. This isn't exactly the Branch Davidian compound, after all."

She gave me a disgusted look. "Appearances can be deceiving. You're a newcomer—he's not about to show you everything that's going on under the surface."

"So why don't you tell me about it? This place looks pretty harmless from what I've seen so far."

"Well, if you discount Sirius meddling with my mind, I guess it does."

I wasn't discounting it, but I was dealing with the physical evidence around me, not something we wouldn't be able to prove to anyone. I had only *Radiance's* word that her mind had been altered, though I hadn't seen any reason to doubt it. "That's not exactly obvious, now is it? What else you got?"

She shot me an incredulous stare, then burst out laughing. I grinned back at her.

After a moment, she sobered and shook her head at me. "I honestly needed that. Sorry I got so bitchy. All of this is pretty hard to swallow."

"You're telling me? I was dragged backward from the twenty-third century against my will, along with about two hundred of my closest friends. Our only chance of getting back home at this point is to do what your 'ship is telling us to do. Which involves somehow disabling or killing something I'm not sure we *can* kill."

"You can't. Djinn are nearly as impervious as imps. I can't believe he's a djinn. We went to school together."

"*Radiance* said something about a djinn being a human who's been deconstructed and rebuilt using magic. What does that *mean?*"

"You're kidding, right? You're not a mage, Jack. It would be like explaining particle physics to a caveman."

"Gee, thanks."

"Don't take that the wrong way," she sighed.

"What—the way you *meant* it? Now why would I do that?"

"You don't have any frame of reference. I'd lose you in the first thirty seconds."

"Try me. Just give it to me as simply as you can."

"You know what a mana thread is, right? And how they're used to construct spells?"

I had some idea. "A mana thread is the energy of probability, unused. Right?"

"More or less."

I held up a hand to stop her from saying anything else. "A mana strand can initiate one effect of any kind, pretty much limited to the imagination of the mage, right?"

"More or less. Go on."

"By weaving several effects into a single pattern, a mage can create a multiple-effect spell."

"Right. Not bad, for a normal."

"Who said I was normal?"

She chuckled. "C'mon. I'm getting nervous standing out here. Let's go in the garage. At worst they might think we're messing around."

"And that's okay?"

She shrugged. "I don't think Sirius cares one way or another. If it doesn't mess with his ultimate plan, he just ignores it."

I followed her into the garage and leaned against the side of the van. "So?"

"Magic can be used to trap a soul...you know that, right?"

"Sure. Necromancy."

"Well, a powerful enough mage—and most human mages aren't anywhere near this level of power—can weave a spell so complex, it can trap a soul forever. And I'm talking about the two main parts of the soul here. The oversoul *and* the ka. Everything that makes a person who he or she is. The spell traps both of them and becomes self-perpetuating. In other words, the sigil renews itself, drawing upon ambient mana to do so.

"The power of the djinn is dictated by the number of threads initially used to create it. It takes around fifty to trap the souls, and if you create one with *just* that many, you end up with a creature that's damn hard to kill, but one that doesn't really have any magic. Every thread beyond that point added to the total gives the djinn permanent access to that mana and the ability to manipulate each of those additional threads at will.

"I'm not completely sure, but I think *Ranger's* pilot refused to go along with whatever it had in mind, so it killed him. He destroyed his body, but trapped his soul. And then deliberately re-created him as something entirely subject to its will. Part of the spell's intent, if you get what I mean."

I was starting to and a wave of cold fear ran through my body. That was insane. "How can we stop him?"

She shook her head. "I don't know. My own magic is feeble next to his and I can't afford to construct any spells he might see floating around me. One whiff of my newly restored self and there's no telling what he might do."

"Why doesn't *Radiance* just reach down and fuck him up?" I wondered. "It's not as though a mageship doesn't have the power to do it."

"*Radiance* is trying to keep a lid on *Ranger*. He's lurking up there near the moon, monitoring what's going on down here. As long as *Ranger's* pinned down, we only have to deal with Sirius. If *Radiance* lets her attention waver for even a second, *Ranger* will take advantage of it and we'll be in a world of hurt in a heartbeat."

I hadn't noticed at first, but she used gender-specific pronouns for the mageships. *Radiance* was *she* and *Ranger* was *he*. I thought that was a bit odd, and said so.

She flashed me that amazing smile once more, tinged this time with a hint of bitterness, and shrugged. "The ships are infused with some of the persona of their pilots. Therefore, in a way, they take on the gender identity of them. *Radiance* is female and *Ranger* is male."

"What about the others? *Radiance* told me that the rest of the 'ships were in on this. She also told me that we'd be going to another Earth, not back in time."

Her innocent expression wasn't fooling anyone, least of all me. "The others aren't involved, are they?"

Embarrassment flashed briefly across her face and she quickly shook her head. "*Ranger* went rogue and *Radiance* decided to follow him. Against the advice of her fellows."

"I don't understand," I said. "Is there no sense of community among the mageships? Any sense of obligation to one another?"

"It's complicated. The mageships believe that their primary duty is protecting the Confed from outside threats. The fact that one went rogue is of some concern, but it doesn't change their first obligation. Losing one 'ship weakened them and losing yet another as *Radiance* went in pursuit was a bit more than they were willing to tolerate."

"Which is the real reason *Radiance* didn't want to go to the Confed itself for help. Chasing down *Ranger* could be, in fact, seen as dereliction of duty."

"I'm sorry she lied to you," she said, actually sounding sincere about it. "I had to teach her deception. It doesn't come natural for her. For any of them, actually. I just wonder where *Ranger* picked it up."

"You did a good job with that," I said, not intending to be sarcastic. Sometimes deception *is* necessary, after all. A being unable to lie is at the mercy of those who have no such inability.

I found myself wishing I'd met Dylan somewhere—anywhere—else. Someplace where our lives weren't on the line. I'd have liked to have gotten to know her better. I knew now she was older than she looked. Mages tend to age slower than normals. She was probably my age, if not a little older. And she was the first woman I'd really felt something for in quite a long time, a hesitant attraction that I wasn't sure I wanted to pay any attention to whatsoever.

Beautiful, smart and dedicated. Okay, bound to a creature—for I *do* consider a mageship a living thing—that was entirely too comfortable with deception for my taste, but still... She was definitely the kind of woman I found attractive.

Now I guess the question was whether I wanted to do anything about that attraction. Assuming Sirius didn't catch on and blast us into our component atoms before I had the chance. If that isn't screwed up, I don't know what is.

Not to mention that for anything to arise between us, the feeling had to be mutual, and I wasn't sure about that at all. And this was definitely not the time to find out.

"Someone's coming," she murmured. She grabbed the sleeve of my tee-shirt and pulled me along behind her and then dragged me through without another word. Once outside once more, blinking in the harsh light of the sun, she eased the door shut and glanced back at me. "I'm really hoping you have a plan."

I shrugged. "Kick his ass?"

She rolled her eyes. "I hope that's not what you consider a plan."

I grinned back at her. "I'm more the improvisational type."

"This is no time for improvisation, Jack."

"It's always a time for improvisation. Plans can be disrupted, but if you're playing it by ear, you can jump whichever way you need to at any given moment."

She shook her head at me, smiling grimly. "I'm not sure that's the best option right now."

"It's the only option we have. Unless *you* have a proposal of your own. Remember, I was thrown into this with no idea what I was getting into."

Dylan nodded. "I see your point." Frowning, she glanced up at the door leading into the garage and then motioned for me to follow her. We crept along the wall and stepped quickly around the corner. "If we're going to do something," she said, "I want to do it soon. The longer we give him to recognize the changes in me, the more chance Sirius will do some checking and we'll *all* be screwed.

"I've got a couple questions. How many mages do you have with you?"

"I don't know. About ten. One of them is Hades, though, so he should count as at least three."

"More like five," she said with a curt nod. "Hades, eh? I'd heard he'd been reformed. Do you have any way to communicate with your people?"

I shook my head. "We'd had to modify our PCDs, and figured that Sirius might be able to detect the magic we had to use." Then I paused. "I might have an idea. I don't know if it'll work, though. Is there a short message you'd like to convey?"

"How resourceful are your people?"

"You're kidding, right? I'm assuming *Radiance* picked us for a reason."

"Fine. I want them to steal about twenty police cars and come up the drive like they're planning on raiding the place at somewhere around midnight tonight."

I'd always thought the whole jaw-dropping thing was just an expression, until mine hit my chest. "What?"

"It'll provide a handy mundane distraction," she explained. "We're going to have to hit Sirius with all our magic at once, and it's best if he doesn't see it coming. There are no mages on this world, and while the cops don't really pose much of a threat to him, they could interfere with his plans—whatever they are."

I caught the gist of her strategy. "I can't guarantee this will work," I told her. Then I faced the hill rising behind us and started to speak in normal tones. "Stormchild—I don't know if you can hear me, but this is the only means of communication I could come up with. I need you to pass the word...we need you folks to go out and steal a whole bunch of police cars and show up here around midnight. Make Sirius think the local authorities are raiding the place. We also need all the mages, including Rio, to launch a concerted attack on him when he's most distracted by the apparent raid." I took a deep breath. "If you can hear me, try to give me some sort of sign."

Dylan was looking at me with the oddest expression on her face. "Stormchild? He's here?"

I nodded. I must've looked puzzled because she laughed aloud. "Do you know how big a crush I used to have on him when I was a kid?"

I laughed too. "Well, don't let his girlfriend know. I'm pretty sure she's the jealous type."

She flashed a quick grin. "Who's his girlfriend?"

"A vampire named Rio."

Dylan flushed white. "Oh," was all she said.

I took that to mean she'd heard of Rio. That was sure interesting, since I hadn't myself until they'd first walked into the Lounge. Maybe she had more of a reputation in the mage community than I knew about.

Possible, I suppose. I didn't exactly have my ear to the ground in that world. I wondered what she knew that I didn't.

# Episode III:
# Showdown

*Stormchild*

I lifted my head and then my hand to forestall Rio's subsequent question. I listened to the wind for a moment, then turned and began gathering up the blanket and the remnants of my lunch. "We need to get the word out. Jack just sent me a message."

She stared at me for a long moment, beautiful brown eyes full of wonder. "A message?"

"He spoke to me on the wind," I told her, shaking my head. "And the wind found me and delivered his words. And before you ask, no, I didn't know that was even possible. I'm surprised he guessed that it might work himself."

"Jack has unexplored depths," was her only reply.

I chuckled. God, I loved this woman. "I'll say. He wants us to steal about twenty police cars."

She blinked at me, then broke into a wide grin. "That could be fun."

"My thoughts exactly. He wants you mages to come in while we're using a threat of a police raid to distract them, use the opportunity to attack Sirius directly while he's not paying attention."

She nodded. "We can do that."

"Great. I'll leave that to you to arrange. I'll work on the other end of things."

"Oh, no. If we're going to steal cop cars, I want in on it."

Of course she did. Rio had never been real fond of the police. No more than I was, actually. "Brat."

"Always," she shot back.

"You know who's not going to like this plan, don't you?"

We said it together. "Bigby."


*Hades*

I stole a glance around the corner and shot Steph a wink. There was no way I was going to pass up the chance to steal a police car, even if I wasn't going to be the one driving it up to the compound. I was even now wondering if I wanted to do it by stealth or just say the hell with it and raise a real ruckus. As long as *our* mageship was keeping *Ranger* occupied, I should be able to throw around as much magic as I wanted to without it being a major problem.

And since the damned thing's presence in this time and place—not to mention our own arrival—had probably already screwed up the timeline enough to spawn a new universe, no one was likely to dance on my tonsils if I decided to have a little fun with it. Besides, if I threw around enough power, the cops were less likely to try anything fancy and get themselves hurt in the process.

I can be pretty damn scary if I want to.

The police cars were lined up outside the station in a neat little row, parked with their ass ends nearest the large brick façade of the police station. A few officers were strolling along the walkway between the cars and the building, lost in conversation with one another, or deep within their own thoughts.

Grinning at Steph, I proceeded to take my clothes off and pile them neatly on the side of a relatively clean trashcan near the edge of the alley. Steph stared at me in amazement and I laughed aloud. My tattoos, which covered something like eighty-five percent of my body, writhed and squirmed like a nest of silver serpents as I stepped from the alley into the full view of the station.

A total of about fifty mana threads snapped out from my body. Every car in the lot started in unison, and, as the cops reacted, several other strands snatched them off their feet and dragged them toward me, legs kicking in a futile attempt to dislodge the snake-like coils enveloping them.

"I hope you don't mind," I said in my most urbane tones and an affected British accent, "if we borrow your cars for a time, do you? I didn't think so."

I let out a shrill whistle and the rest of the crew boiled out of the shadows.

Steph walked up behind me, cradling my discarded clothing in one arm as she sealed the front doors of the station with a thread of her own. "You're having way too much fun with this, Hades," she said with a heavy sigh.

"I know. I just couldn't help myself. I haven't been able to play bad guy for a while, and the weirdest thing is, this is a *lot* more fun when I know no one's going to get hurt."

And it was true.

I projected the cops through the wall of the police station, depositing them dazed but unharmed in a janitor's closet while, one by one, the cars left the parking area and vanished into the night. I then turned my attention to completely sealing off the building—allowing not even radio waves or telephone signals through. They were going to have a quiet night, whether they liked it or not.

"There's only one problem with this," Steph said, as I put my clothes back on.

"What's that?"

"What about all the would-be victims that these cops aren't going to be on the street to help tonight?"

I hadn't thought of that angle and I felt a brief surge of guilt I quickly suppressed. One way or another, something like this was necessary to prevent the spread of an even greater evil than the criminals on the street tonight could even imagine. I hoped not too many people were harmed, but there wasn't one hell of a lot we could do about it anyway.

As we prepared to leave, I was surprised by a couple of large figures striding from the umbras. It was Bigby and his girlfriend. I'd never warmed to the creature, but ever since they'd met they'd seemed inseparable. Good for them. Even man-eating dragons deserved a bit of love.

"Good luck," he told us in his rumbling voice.

"What do you mean? Aren't you coming?"

"We're going to stay behind and watch out for the citizens of this town," Bigby said. "You're leaving the people too vulnerable by doing this."

I narrowed my eyes at him, but he didn't seem to notice. Or care if he did. "Go do what needs to be done, Hades. Kaleel and I will handle this end of things."

To be honest, I felt something akin to relief as Steph and I summoned a couple of windsprites and took to the air. At least *someone* would be looking out for the people we'd left in harm's way with this night's work.

*Vex*

"Do you even know how to drive one of these things?" Kate asked me as I sent the car careening into the street. She'd done some mojo on me that temporarily made me taller and able to actually reach the pedals and see over the steering wheel at the same time. I was as big as a human for the time being and I enjoyed the feeling immensely.

"How hard can it be?" I asked her with a grin. I jerked the wheel to the left and winced as the passenger side mirror shattered against a parked car on her side of the street. "Okay. Harder than it looks, obviously. Don't worry, I'll get the hang of it."

She looked dubious, but didn't say anything else until we'd managed to find and merge onto the highway. Ahead of me I could see the identical taillights of several other vehicles winding away into the distance like a huge, glowing snake.

"What time is it?" I asked her.

She glanced at her PCD display. She wore hers in the form of a wristwatch, a wonderful piece of technological misdirection for this time and place. She looked human enough to pass as a human child, of course, which I did not though we both had started out as exactly that.

I could have worn a PCD in the form of a hubcap strung around my neck and no one would have even noticed it. I'd remained hidden while nearly everyone else had blended with the human crowds as easily as they could at home.

With a few exceptions, of course. Neither Hydra the troll nor his Abyssian lover could blend without magical modification, but that really didn't make me feel any better. I could have done the same thing simply by asking Kate to arrange it, but somehow it seemed like a betrayal of what I was.

All things being equal, I definitely preferred my life in the twenty-third century to even a few weeks in 1987.

As, I imagined, did we all.

*Jack*

I suppose I should've expected something like this. It *was* a religious cult, after all. About ten o'clock, a bell began to ring. I'd been catching a few winks in the small room I'd been given on the second floor of the main house when it blasted me out of bed.

I threw open the door to find Dylan waiting in the hall for me. "It's time for services," she told me. "He likes to do this every night about this time, get everyone together to explain to us the nature of the universe."

"Oh? What kind of crap does he say?"

"Believe it or not, he tells us the truth, more or less. About the different universes, how they come into being and how there's a terrible enemy out there. He's not lying when he says we can't trust this government either. We already know it's been infiltrated by Cen operatives."

"What in the hell is he up to?" I asked her, lowering my voice and looking up and down the hall.

"To tell you the truth, I'm not sure. But I'm willing to bet it's nothing good."

*::Ranger is on the move! I'm going to be out of contact for a little while. Be careful!::* The broadcast from *Radiance* came through like a bullhorn next to my ear and judging by Dylan's reaction, it struck her the same way.

"Things are starting to roll," she said. "C'mon, Sirius hates it when people are late."

*Rio*

It was about a quarter to midnight as the row of cars began making their way up the twisting, turning road leading to the compound. Stormchild had insisted on leading the pack, grinning like a damn fool as he tried to figure out the controls for the lights and siren.

Sometimes he's like the world's oldest kid and I love him for it. Even though sometimes it also gets on my nerves.

I moved away to stand with the other mages and stared up the crest of the hill in the direction of our target. Our timing had to be perfect or the advantage of surprise would be ruined.

The air was uncannily still, the air warm, and the scent of the salty brine of the sea mingled with the breathy green air of the hillside. It didn't feel as though we were heading into a fight. It felt like a night for a party.

I rubbed my thumbs against the mage gems embedded in my palms, the source of my unprecedented level of magical power. They were our ace-in-the-hole, the unknown quanity that would give us some chance of dealing with Sirius and his mageship master.

I hoped.


*Jack*

The room in which we gathered wasn't quite what I expected, reminding me more of a college lecture hall than anything one might find in the average home. It didn't even have the atmosphere of a church, well-lit throughout and being composed of a set of five tiers of sixteen padded chairs broken into sections of four. Only the first two rows were filled, a total of thirty-two people waiting expectantly for the arrival of their guru onto the slightly raised stage with its burnished mahogany lectern and wide projection screen pulled down against the back wall.

Dylan and I settled into a couple of seats in the middle of the third row. The silence in the room struck me as eerie. There was none of the chatter one might have expected. The sense of anticipation was palpable, the attendees' eyes affixed on the stage as if already viewing the greatest wonder they'd ever seen.

This place was starting to give me the serious creeps.

Then, suddenly Sirius was standing behind the podium. A murmur ran through the audience, and I could see a few of them looking at others as if to say "see, I told you so".

There were no clocks in this room, I noticed, and I began to regret not having picked up a cheap wristwatch after ditching my PCD. If timing was integral to the plan, I was condemned to being out of the loop. Then again, the best I could offer was an attempt to jump the djinn and pummel him with fists and feet while the mages unleashed the *real* assault.

Did I mention that I felt terribly useless at that moment?

The distant wail slid in between his words as he started to speak and I don't think anyone noticed for the first few moments. His voice was cool, cadenced, and almost hypnotic in its rhythms. I didn't catch his opening line, since I actually *heard* the sirens.

"—enemies all around us. We *think* they're on our side, but the very philosophies by which they live have been manipulated into existence by the enemy. What's even worse is that there are those among them who *know* it—who serve willingly because of promises made to them...that they'd rule after this world is torn asunder and re-made in their image.

"But what they'd be, unbeknownst to them, are rulers of the stockyard. Petty tyrants who may command the human cattle, but with no power to do more than decide who gets fed to the monsters."

The messed up thing here was that he was telling them the unvarnished truth. For the first time since this began, I felt doubts begin to creep into my consciousness. What if we were doing the wrong thing here? What if Sirius and his 'ship were trying to save this Earth, this world that didn't have Loki or the other immortals to protect it from being ravaged by the Cen.

He had the power. I was almost certain of it. By himself he could change humanity, give it the ability to fight back the monsters before they could claim this Earth as their own.

Shit. It wasn't really their goal I had issue with, it was their methods. They had no right to manipulate people, to alter their brains to make them more susceptible to their influence. As they'd done to Dylan. It made them little better than the Cen themselves.

And *why* were they so desperately seeking to save this Earth? For the good of the people? Somehow I didn't believe that was their ultimate purpose. They wanted something else. But what?

Sirius broke off his monologue, lifting his head and cocking it to one side. He'd heard the sirens. They were finally growing loud enough to slice through the sound of his voice. He frowned and held up a hand, then turned slightly, facing the back wall. I had the uncanny sense that he could see straight through all the things in the way to view the road snaking up the hill and the cars even now approaching via that twisting, winding route.

He started to turn, eyes filling with an unearthly rage, and I suddenly noticed that Dylan was standing beside me. I'd been so riveted on Sirius I hadn't even noticed as she pushed herself to her feet.

215

She flung a hand toward him and *something* sizzled across the space between them. He threw up a hand, seemingly batting it aside, and then he was no longer by himself on the stage. Rio leaped at him, a blur of motion, and backhanded him into the white projection screen.

Some of the acolytes shrieked and some surged to their feet. To flee or leap to his aid, I could not be certain.

Rio's blow did nothing to subdue him, though. As quick as a wink, he was back on his feet, and, rather than attempt to continue the physical confrontation, he simply stood in the midst and raised his arms.

The lights winked out.

For a brief moment it felt like I was standing on the edge of a tornado, within the radius of a whirling mass of something that wasn't *quite* physical, yet wielding enough energy to raise every hair on my body. I caught the scent of ozone and jagged lightning tore through the room, illuminating everything just long enough to reveal Dylan running along the chair backs from row to row in an attempt to reach the stage.

*Radiance! Help us!*

*::I cannot::* came the ship's mental voice, sounding almost strained. *::It's all I can do to keep* Ranger *from getting involved directly. You are on your own, I'm afraid::*

"I'm afraid too," I muttered aloud. More lightning rent the air, casting fractured images against my eyes. I stood and felt my way toward the end of the row, to the stairs leading down to the stage only a few feet away.

Someone screamed.

*Rio*

This creature astounded me. He was as quick as a vampire and as sturdy as a lycanthrope. And powerful beyond any measure I had. He caught and wove threads with a capacity far beyond either Hades or myself. We managed to keep him off-balance for a brief instant, but he learned so quickly we were back on the defensive before we could press our advantage.

The human mages might as well have been mice hurling themselves at a bobcat. He smashed them down without missing a beat, countering their spells seemingly without effort and blasting them away with fierce, blazing lances of light and fire.

Hades's tattoos rose from his skin in a wave, smashing through Sirius's outer defenses, but were swallowed by the mass of threads that seem to flow from his very core. I pushed my gems to their utmost, hurling everything I had at him.

I may as well have blown him a kiss.

"It's a fucking spirit!" Hades yelled to me. I don't think I'd ever heard him curse before. A spirit? How was that possible? I'd never even heard of a spirit with this kind of power.

We were hopelessly out-classed. Just acknowledging that pissed me off. No spirit out-classed *me,* dammit!

I reached into the core of my being, drawing from my reservoir of psychic power. I rarely used this gift these days, but I was counted among the most powerful of psis for a good reason. Even Stormchild, whose psychic creativity was considered particularly potent, was dwarfed before my gifts in this arena.

I let my will pour forth and time shuddered to a halt. I met eyes with Hades and, combining the power of my symsuit with my own knowledge and power, created two more mage gems in my hand. "Here!" I called to him, and tossed the stones in his direction.

I felt a great wrenching sensation and Sirius began to move again, freeing himself from the temporal inertia I'd imposed. Hades caught the gems and screamed as they burned their way into his flesh. I released my hold on time and it began to flow for all of us once more.

I felt the mortals toppling around us and swore under my breath. I knew that a quarter of them might not rise again. The effects of stopping and re-starting time would send many into cardiac arrest. I didn't know why this happened, but it did. It was a talent I rarely used for this very reason.

I dared not turn and see the effects of this power on the mortals in the room.

His puissance effectively doubled, Hades lashed out at Sirius once more, and, after a second to catch my breath, I rejoined the fray myself. We pounded at Sirius with fire, ice, lightning, and mono-molecular blades of light. We tried to turn the floor beneath his feet into mud and then lava. We hammered him with everything we had and still he stood, looking a little ragged, but unhurt.

We could not win this battle.

He hammered us back. As I took a hit from a blunt-nosed thread, I fell to my knees, skull ringing like a bell. Hades staggered back, a torrent of blood staining the blackness of his shirt. The air was suddenly filled with whipping strands of razor sharpness, a whirling mass of silvery death.

Then, abruptly, a chair came sailing out of the seats and caught Sirius on the side of the head. He stumbled sideways, nearly falling over the edge of his lectern.

Hades stabbed at him with his hand and I caught sight of a mass of threads lancing for the center of his body. They plunged through his skin and he howled. Hades closed his eyes and yanked. Sirius literally exploded.

*Jack*

I opened my eyes to darkness. Had I been blinded? I reached for my face and felt something dark clinging to my head. I pulled it away and coughed as I inhaled a mouthful of soot and ash. I levered myself up into a sitting position and blinked at the carnage and destruction that surrounded me. What the hell?

A body lay a few feet away and, feeling my heart lurch upward into my throat, I crawled over and inspected it. I gasped as I realized who it was. Kevin. I clawed my way around him, pressing my fingers into the side of his neck. No pulse greeted my questing fingertips.

Shit. Shit. Shit. *Dammit,* Radiance*! No one was supposed to die!* I leaned back and screamed my rage at the sky.

I shakily pulled myself to my feet. Stars peered through a jagged hole in the roof above my head and I stumbled through the debris, trying to find someone else who'd survived the conflagration.

::*I tried::* came the belated response from the 'ship. ::*I managed to wound* Ranger, *but that will not last long::*

I tried to bring myself to care and failed miserably. Toward the front I stumbled over another body and leaned down to pull scraps of wood off of it. I saw the face and the wide, staring eyes and wanted to weep. Dylan. Oh, god.

::*No!::* Apparently that revelation had touched a nerve in the mageship. I heard its—*her*—anger echo through my head with all the force of a volley of cannon-fire. And suddenly something impinged itself on my consciences. A wheeling canopy of stars and a huge, disk-shaped object against the backdrop of an endless expanse of night. I felt something like acceleration and I was suddenly racing toward the vessel.

My mind snapped into my body with a sudden, wrenching sensation and I fell to my knees, tears pouring from my eyes as great, wracking sobs tore their way out of my chest. We'd destroyed Sirius, but at what price?

Then a blast of searing pain speared through my skull and I fell backward, clawing at my face and hair. Then, as suddenly as it had come, it vanished. I sat up, aching both physically and emotionally, and glanced around the room once again.

And did a double-take. Standing in the doorway at the very top of the chamber I saw Dylan staring down at me, her face displaying a startling bleakness. I glanced back at the body in front of me and felt my heart lurch in my chest. They were *both* Dylan.

Revelation swept over me and I gasped aloud. The living one—or the one still capable of movement, rather—descended the stairs toward me. I heard a groan from somewhere in the rubble and glanced over reflexively. Hades was standing and reaching down to help Rio to her feet. Stunned relief flooded me. At least some of us had survived.

I was glad Anya wasn't part of this attack, though I was certain she wanted to be. I rose to my own feet somewhat unsteadily. "Where's Steph?" I asked aloud. Hades looked around.

Dylan's doppelganger came to my side and took my arm to steady me. I met her gaze and nodded, telling her silently that we would talk when the time came, but for now we had more important things to do. Like find survivors. She seemed to understand this unspoken communication, and nodded in reply.

We dug through the wreckage, my heart growing heavier with the discovery of each new body. So many dead. It didn't make me feel any better to realize that most of them were

Sirius's hapless recruits. Slowly, carefully, and without speaking, Hades, Dylan, Rio and I sifted through the debris.

After about a half an hour, I straightened, wiping at my eyes with the back of my hand. I'd been quietly sobbing throughout the whole ordeal, moving chunks of wood and stone and sorting the dead from the injured and dying. It was difficult for all of us, but the strain on Hades was tremendous. I could tell it was all he could do not to simply hurl all the wreckage aside with his magic, but if Steph was alive somewhere underneath all of it, such an act could potentially kill her.

And he knew it.

A shadowy shape descending from the vaulted ceiling caused us all to look up, but it was merely Stormchild. He bore Anya in his arms.

"She doesn't need to be here," I told him angrily, but the girl shook her head.

"I've seen worse, Jack." He set her down and her soft gaze roamed the room. "Where's Steph? And Kev..." Her voice trailed off as she noticed the row of dead bodies laid against the back wall. What was left of it, anyway. She walked slowly over to them and I could see her gaze tracing along until it reached Kevin's body.

A lump formed in my throat and I fought to swallow. It wasn't easy. I almost felt as if it would be easier to die myself than deal with the aftermath of this battle.

"We were lucky this wasn't worse," Dylan murmured in my ear. I shot her an icy look but said nothing. What was there to say, really? She was right. Didn't mean I wanted to hear it. "How are we going to get home?"

"I can get us there," she told me.

Anya had found Dylan's body and was standing there looking from one to the other, face twisted in confusion and

221

tears streaking her face. She was willing to ask the question I was afraid to ask myself. "How are you here but there too?" she asked Dylan, jabbing a finger at the broken body lying with the others.

"*Radiance* sacrificed herself to destroy *Ranger,* but at the same time responded to Jack's silent cry that told her I was dead. She caught my soul in a net of magic and wove it into a pattern of energy so complex that it could never hope to escape.

"I am now what Sirius was."

"He was evil," she spat.

Dylan shook her head. "I don't know if he was so much evil as simply misguided. Sirius was the product of the being that created him, as, to a certain extent, the mageship was a product of *him.*" She glanced around the room, then her gaze settled on the survivors, most of whom were injured. Perhaps the pilot was initially imbalanced and infected the 'ship with it, who then passed it on to the djinn he created using his pilot's essence.

She passed her hands over me and abruptly the aches and pains simply vanished. "We were so very lucky. Had Sirius truly understood the scope of his power, you—*we*—would never have been able to defeat him."

"And *you* understand?" I asked her pointedly. I agreed with her for the most part about the motivation behind their actions, at least to some extent. The danger he'd been outlining had been quite real. Sirius had been more forthcoming with these people than the immortals had been with the government on Prime...at first.

There was something to be said for that. But I had as many questions as answers at this point, and knew those answers weren't likely to be forthcoming. Dylan might be the only one who knew any of it, and it was anyone's guess whether she'd tell me or not.

Stormchild went to Rio and swept her into his arms. She accepted this with obvious reluctance, but, after a moment, levered herself free again. "We need to clean up the scene," she said, "and return all the police cars."

"Consider it done," said Dylan, and the scene seemed to blink before us. Literally a heartbeat later, the bodies were gone, the room was repaired, and the rest of the group that had been waiting outside were standing in our midst.

"What the hell?" Hydra looked around, found Hope sitting against a wall, applying a bandage to a wound on her leg, and rushed to her side. "Are you okay?"

She looked up at him and smiled grimly. "Better than some," she answered in a small voice.

"Bigby and Kaleel stayed behind to protect and serve," Stormchild told her. "The big guy didn't like the idea of leaving the town completely unprotected when we trapped the cops in their headquarters building."

Dylan nodded. "I'll see if I can bring them here too." She wavered a second, then groaned. "No. Their draconic nature makes it difficult to get a handle on them. We'll have to contact them and get them to join us on their own."

"Shouldn't be a problem," I told her. "Just need a PCD...we connected them to our mini-network."

"I'll take care of it, boss," Boneyard told me. He quickly activated his PCD and was soon murmuring into the vocal pickup. I heard what I assumed was Bigby's voice, sounding much too thin and tinny over the connection, in what I could only assume was assent.

"Once they arrive, I'll open a time gate back to our century," Dylan told us. "I'm very sorry that this turned out the way it did."

"What did you do with the bodies?" Anya asked her.

"I gave them all a proper burial," Dylan answered. "It seemed the least I could do."

Stormchild affixed her with a piercing look, his ice-blue eyes seeming to bore into her. "How are you responsible for this? You were captured by Sirius. You had no say in what your 'ship did in response."

"In a manner of speaking, no. But when she brought me back, she also downloaded her persona to me. I'm me, but I'm also a bit of her as well. So part of me *is* responsible—or at least feels that way." Dylan sighed. "I can't even say how long it's going to take to come to terms with what has happened—how I've changed. Doubtless my career with Fleet is over. I'll never pilot another mageship. I'll be lucky to retain my license at all and I'll have to register myself as a preternatural with the Adjuster's Office."

"And dodge the media," Rio snorted. She knew all about that, herself. She wasn't a big fan of the Fourth Estate. She'd made no secret of that fact. "They're really going to want to know what happened."

Dylan nodded morosely. "And dodge the media. I can't—I don't want to—get stuck trying to explain all this to them."

"Then don't," Rio replied. "I never explain anything to them. Of course, this doesn't prevent them from postulating their own version of events, but I leave them to it. I don't really care what anyone thinks."

Anya came over and took my hand, leaning against me as if in need of support. I knew the feeling. Her face was stained with soot and the dried tracks of her tears and she looked as sad as she had when we'd first glimpsed her in the mirror all those months ago. I ran my fingers through her hair.

"Must be nice," Dylan replied to Rio. "But I've never managed that degree of self-possession. It sounds as if you were that way even before you became a vamp."

Rio shrugged. "It's who I've always been. Becoming a vampire didn't change that."

"Some things never change," Stormchild observed dryly, shooting an exaggerated wink in her direction.

She smiled thinly and nodded to him. "When you're right, you're right."

Bigby and Kaleel arrived a few minutes later and Dylan did her thing. In a swirl of light and warmth, we were instantly transported back to the Lounge. I was glad to note the place was empty and still in one piece. I'd actually been worried about it. Just about everyone dispersed at that point, leaving only me, Anya and Dylan.

I sent Anya up to the shower to get cleaned up, then aimed a level gaze at Dylan. "We paid a high price for your victory," I told her.

She inclined her head in acknowledgment. "I'm truly sorry, Jack. I didn't know your friends, I realize. But it's never easy to lose them."

It was then I realized that she too had lost someone important to her. The pilot and mageship bond is legendary and the loss of such an intimate partner had to be a wrenching experience. "It's not your fault, Dylan, even though it may feel like it is. It wasn't in your power to prevent any of it. I know that's a small consolation, but, well, that's all I've got for you."

"Yeah. I know. Listen, Jack...I've got some things I need to do. Resign my Fleet commission, for one. And go talk to the

225

Adjuster. Would I be welcome here if I chose to return at some point?"

I smiled at her. It wasn't easy to do. I didn't feel much like smiling right then. But she needed to see it, needed to know she'd be welcome. "I'd like that, Dylan."

She returned my smile in much the same way it had been delivered to her. Fragile and revealing a great depth of sadness. "See you then."

She vanished.

I sat down with my transcriber and recorded this record of the events for posterity, deciding at that very moment it would be a long time before I recorded another word. I was done with it for the time being. I needed time to grieve, and to heal.

It wasn't going to be easy. I'd put on a brave, strong face for Anya's benefit, but the place would seem empty without Kevin in it. Far, far too empty.

I was surprised when Boneyard came through the front door. He stood at the lower end of the ramp. "We going to be open tonight, boss?" he asked.

I considered for a minute, then nodded. "Yeah. I don't see any reason why not."

He grinned back at me, but it seemed somehow half-hearted. "Me either. Remember what Spider Robinson said in his books about joy and pain, right?"

"Exactly," I answered. "We're a family, Bone. And we need each other. Now more than ever."

"My thoughts exactly, boss. See you tonight." And with that, he was gone.

# Act III

# Future, Again

# Episode I:
# Nobody's Child

It's very early in the morning. I'm an early riser, so it's easy enough for me to sit down and use my adopted father's transcriber to record my thoughts with no one the wiser.

My name is Anya and I'm over 200 years old. You wouldn't know it to look at me. I look as though I'm in my early teens. I spent the majority of my life trapped within the Dimension of Mirrors, a place where time has no meaning. I emerged late last year with the assistance of the dark immortal, Hades, and my new family here at the Magitech Lounge.

I'm mourning the loss of a member of that family right now. The impact has been so deeply felt that Jack, my adopted father, has temporarily (hopefully) walked away from the transcriber and his journaling. At one time he was strongly motivated to get others to participate. He wanted it to be a testament to the whole group, not just his own thoughts and feelings.

Now I figure it's my turn. I have the funny feeling that Jack wouldn't be too pleased to find me doing this. Don't ask me why. When I was young the therapists would have said it would be good for my state of mind, help me deal with my feelings surrounding what happened. These days, who knows?

*I* think it's damn therapeutic, and I'm going to keep doing it.

This account begins about two days after we returned from 1987.

I was awakened very early in the morning by the sound of loud verbal disagreement, an argument between Jack and a voice I couldn't quite place. It was male and came to my ears as terribly threatening. Jack's return fire sounded no less angry. He wasn't giving an inch.

I couldn't make out any words, so I crept out of bed and went to the door of my room, easing it open and edging into the hall.

I don't think I've ever heard Jack raise his voice, so his strident tones were quite surprising. "You don't have the right!" he barked.

"Her disposition is not up to you, Jack," the other voice replied. "Until we can absolutely verify her origins, she is to be considered a potential threat to the Confederation. It's as simple as that."

Were they talking about Dylan? I crept closer to the stairs, trying to ease myself down the steps to peer around the banister and identify this stranger who dared to threaten Jack.

"She's just a kid!"

"You can't have it both ways, Jack. Either she's a child, which puts her under the jurisdiction of social services, or she's an adult, which means she needs to be evaluated by us to determine if she *is* a threat."

At that moment I realized that they weren't talking about Dylan after all. They were talking about *me*. Feeling a surge of anger, I gave up trying to remain unnoticed and simply bounded down the stairs, turning a fiery stare upon both men standing in the empty bar.

I'd almost expected to find the Adjuster himself on the scene, but I didn't recognize the man who stood there. He looked like several hundred miles of hard road. He was about the same size as Jack—maybe six-two or three—and probably weighed in the low two hundreds. His black hair, shaggy and unkempt, partially obscured his eyes. It conveyed to me the vaguest impression of one of those Old English sheep dogs, the kind that look as though they can't possibly see what's going on around them.

He was also brutally torn up, one side of his face white and puckered into a terrible mass of scar tissue. He didn't even have the fortune to look as though he'd been in a fight with a dangerously large cat. No, this scar looked as though something had simply taken a bite out of his face.

The weird thing about it was that in this day and age, with technological *and* magical healing techniques widely available, few people would choose to wear such a disfigurement. The fact that he did suggested he considered it a point of pride, not disgrace.

"If I'm going to be the subject of a fight that wakes me up, the least you could do is include me in it," I said icily as I looked from one to the other of them. "Who is this guy?" I added, in a query to Jack.

"His name is Gerald Montague," Jack replied quietly. "He works for Confed Military Intelligence."

I decided not to comment on the classic oxymoron. "What do you want, *Gerald?*" I asked him pointedly.

"*We,*" he began, his voice leaning over the border of disdainful into contemptuous, "need to know exactly who you are and where you came from."

"I thought Jack already covered that territory with the Adjuster's Office."

"We're not associated with the AO," he told me dismissively. "We work independently."

"Well, then, that's your problem right there. Go talk to Deryk Shea and leave Jack out of it."

Personally I considered this to be the most reasonable course of action. The Adjuster's Office had cleared me, gave me nominal Confed citizen status, and put me under Jack's temporary guardianship. The whole thing had been arranged by the Adjuster personally.

"I think you fail to understand what we're doing," he said with a dramatic sigh. "MI is revoking your AO credentials. Until *we* vet you and are assured that you pose no threat to the Confed, you have no legal status here whatsoever."

"Can they do that?" I asked Jack. "Just blow off the Adjuster's decision?"

"Apparently they *think* they can," he said in response. He leveled a sharp look at the MI agent. "I haven't yet bothered to disabuse *this* one of the notion."

He was only being partially humorous, I knew. At the core of his dry comment there lay hidden a sharp-edged stone of simple truth. He wouldn't back down from shielding any member of his chosen family, but he was particularly protective of me. As were the rest of the Lounge regulars.

Jack may have been the only normal human on Earth with the resources to back off the Confed military machine, at least temporarily. The Lounge was one of the largest independent consortiums of preternaturals and paranormals in the Confederation.

Even the mageships owed him, and us, and they knew it. Our sacrifices had prevented the Confed as a whole from learning that one of their number had gone rogue, and another had sacrificed itself to prevent any more fallout than what had already come out of it.

Deryk Shea knew what had happened, but we'd been asked not to tell the Confed Fleet or any of the Confed politicos anything beyond what was absolutely unavoidable.

So far, it had all been avoidable.

I had the feeling that this was an attempt to tighten the thumbscrews, to get us to reveal what had happened. How they knew *we* knew, we couldn't begin to guess. Most likely one of their clairvoyants had dredged up some of it, enough to realize we knew something that they wanted to know. And like any military intelligence outfit, they didn't like being kept in the dark. This was their way of driving the point home in such a way we couldn't avoid recognizing their intent. Basically telling us "play ball, or we'll screw you hard enough to make you bleed."

Have I shocked you, dear reader? I hardly sound like a twelve year old anymore, do I? Imagine the reaction I get when I say that sort of thing out loud. Normals don't get me at all. Let me make this perfectly clear—*I am not what I appear to be.* And I'm okay with that.

I'd had about as much of this bullying as I was going to tolerate. I stalked up to the MI agent and smiled as sweetly as I could manage. "What do you want from me?"

"Dammit, Anya," Jack growled, but I silenced him with a frosty glare. I didn't need him fighting my battles for me. I could deal with this joker myself.

I poked him in the chest with a forefinger. "As long as Shea says I'm a citizen, I'm a citizen. And I don't think you *really* want to start a fight between the AO and your outfit. Or am I wrong? You have anything to back up your claim of authority in this matter, or are we just supposed to buy it because you say so?"

I had the distinct impression I'd really thrown him a curve ball. He knew intellectually that I wasn't really twelve years old, but faced with me in the flesh, he was having problems making the connection between his expectations and the reality presented to him.

So, like most low-level government hacks, he compensated with pure bluster. "We're taking you into custody until we get this all sorted out."

"Bullshit. I'm not going anywhere. You'll need an army to pry me out of here and, y'know, I don't think you have one." My smile broadened into a grin. "But *I* do."

I was reminded of all the old cartoons I used to watch, back in the old days. When a cartoon character gets really pissed off, steam shoots out his ears. I could see that happening to this guy. I nearly burst out laughing at the sudden mental image of this guy blowing smoke out his ears.

Even Jack seemed a bit shocked at my response. I couldn't really blame him. This was the first time he'd really had the chance to see what I was made of.

When I first came out of the mirror I'd been disoriented and suffering from serious culture shock. I'd entered the Dimension of Mirrors in 2006, and spent over two hundred years observing other people's lives. Believe me, you'd be disoriented too.

But several months of tutelage from Kevin and Hades had brought me into the twenty-third century. Finally. Our little trip to 1987, and the resulting carnage, had made me take stock in who and what I am. I'm a bit of a miracle, someone who shouldn't even be here. A girl out of time.

I'd had enough screwed up stuff happen to me. From here on out, no one was going to bully me. I didn't care if they had the whole Confederation of Human Worlds backing their play. Not that this guy did. He just wanted us to *think* he did.

"Do you have a warrant?" I asked him. "A judicial authorization to take me into custody? No? Then, if I may, I'd like to suggest you go fuck yourself."

Oh, he didn't like that at all. If he wasn't a parahuman and pretty much immune to that sort of thing, he would've probably had a stroke on the spot. He reached out to grab me but I ducked away. Jack stepped between us, placing his hand on Montague's chest.

"You heard her, buddy. Hands off."

Montague shoved him. Hard. Jack stumbled back and managed to keep from falling by grabbing one of the bar stools. He pulled himself up and glared.

"Don't do that again." The voice sliced through the sudden silence. We all looked toward the door and saw the woman standing there. I was a bit surprised, but neither of the two men seemed to be.

"Captain Dylan Shepherd." Montague said with a cool smile. "It's *so* nice to see you again."

"So all of this was for *my* benefit, Montague? Quite unnecessary, I assure you."

"You resigned your commission and disappeared. How else was I supposed to find you?"

"Wait a minute," Jack growled. "You came here threatening *us* because you were looking for *her?*"

"Colonel Montague has a habit of being a tad...overzealous," Dylan said, as she strode up the ramp and approached. "Rules and regs have their place—but only when he says they do. Isn't that right, *Gerald?*" She didn't wait for an answer. She stopped about five feet away from him, her gaze nothing short of contemptuous as she dragged it over him. "What's it been...ten years?"

"Something like that."

"You don't need to worry. He doesn't have any authority over either of you. In fact, he's dangerously close to a court martial as it is. This little incident will probably push him over the edge. He's been running a rogue element within Military Intelligence for the last fifteen years—now I believe his chickens are coming home to roost."

"You don't have any evidence, Shepherd." He dismissed her claim with a casual wave of his hand.

"I wouldn't make any bets on that, Montague. You're done. And if you didn't already know that, you wouldn't be here."

His hand slid into his jacket and came out with a big gun, which he pointed at her. "Yeah...I got a call from General Wilson. You've managed to turn them all against me."

"*Turn* them against you? I didn't have to do anything. I just provided them with an unencrypted version of the code you injected into *Ranger*. There are some very important people who'd like very much to ask what the hell you thought you were doing."

"What good are fucking *pacifist* war machines?" he snarled, jabbing the gun at her. I quailed, seeing his finger whitening on the firing stud.

"Mageships aren't war machines, Gerald. They were never meant to be. They're protectors. *You* caused *Ranger* to go rogue, and the blood of all those innocents is on your hands."

She'd gone to Fleet after all. Once she had the evidence she needed against this man—the one she held responsible for what had happened.

"We have to take the fight to the enemy! We have to fight them out there so we don't have to fight them here again!"

"Yes, yes. We've heard all of that before. But the fact is, there are already people out there taking the fight to them. That's not our job.

"What you did *weakened* the Confederation. It cost us two mageships. Those ships were designed and commissioned to *defend* Earth Prime and the Confederation of Human Worlds. Not to "take the fight to the enemy". And you damn well *knew* it."

"You traitorous *bitch!*" He squeezed the firing stud.

The weapon whined and bucked in his hand, but did nothing else.

Dylan smiled sadly. "Add attempted murder to the list of charges," she said dispassionately. "You've lost your mind, Montague. And Fleet knows it. I've been recording this whole exchange."

"That," I said, unable to resist the urge to chime in, "counts as checkmate, asshole."

৪১৪১৫৪

We attended Montague's court martial in person. Ordinarily civilians weren't allowed to witness such proceedings, but we were there as witnesses for the prosecution. And not only us. When Stormchild and Rio, both legendary figures in their own right, took the stand, it was all over for Montague except for the crying.

Military strategies had changed a lot since the Cen War. Military *thinking* had changed a lot. The generals now understood that one could be both strong and peaceable at the same time, that diplomacy and negotiation *had* to be a part of any long-range military strategy. That unthinking aggressive action left you vulnerable, regardless of how the situation looked on the surface.

Montague had been a throwback—a type of militant left over from a bygone age who hadn't caught up with the new policies. He was fearful, and believed that the best defense was a good offense. Always.

These days, Fleet policy suggested the opposite. An effective and powerful defense was the best offense possible. Or, as Deryk Shea, the greatest hand-to-hand fighter in the history of the world, once put it—"attacking first leaves you vulnerable. Counter-punching allows you to take advantage of your enemy's vulnerabilities."

Reportedly, Napoleon had once said, "Never interrupt your enemy when he's making a mistake." And Montague had made a major mistake. He'd played fast and loose with the most powerful beings in this universe. And it had just come around to bite him in the ass.

Of course, as I was thinking this, he was implementing another plan entirely, and before Dylan could scoop him up, he vanished with a loud "pop"!

She stared at the spot he'd vacated. "Huh. That's not good."

Jack frowned. "Magic?"

"Psi. The fucker's a psi and we never knew it."

"Goes to show that even starships with the status of demigods don't know everything," Jack mused aloud. "Or djinn either, for that matter."

Dylan shot him a glance and snorted. "Yeah, well. Omniscience is over-rated."

"Speak for yourself," he shot back with a grin.

"What just happened?" I asked them both. I didn't fail to note how comfortable the two of them seemed to be together, and I wasn't sure quite what to make of it. Was Jack falling into a romance with this creature? Not that I could blame him, if you got right down to it. She was beautiful, after all, and intelligent, and powerful.

But she wasn't human anymore. She didn't really wear flesh, though she cloaked herself in the semblance of it. She was less *alive* than the vampires that hung out in the Lounge. I could see her true form in magesight, a kind of perception Jack was, fortunately or unfortunately, completely unable to attain.

In magesight she appeared ghost-like, spectral, the core of her a hard knot of interwoven silver mana strands, a weaving so complex I couldn't have begun to count all the threads that had gone into forming the heart of her. Her outer form, the spectral one, was made up of more strands, these ones bent and manipulated into particular guises.

All in all, I estimated her inner and outer bodies were composed of as many as fifteen hundred mana strands.

Unlike a mage, she could not see and manipulate *other* strands, but, then again, she hardly needed to. The spell at her core could generate limited numbers of its own threads, and she could manipulate not only those, but any currently being used to form her outer shell in much the same way as any mage.

Truth be told, she was probably even more powerful than Sirius had been. The mageship *Radiance* had divested itself of all its magical power at the moment of its destruction, and invested every strand of it into Dylan's resurrected form.

I turned and looked straight at Jack. "Now that we've got *that* bit of nonsense out of the way," I told him, "I want to move."

His brow furrowed and he frowned at me. "Move? You don't like living above the bar anymore? I suppose we could go somewhere else, but—"

"I want to move *out*," I told him simply. "I want my own place. I want to get on with my life, to make up for all the years I missed."

I knew it would hit him hard, this admission, and I felt a brief stab of sympathy for his stricken expression. He'd enjoyed his little stint as my surrogate parent, and, I must admit, it was nice to actually experience what a real father may have been like.

But though I was still trapped in the body of a child, I wasn't one. And, though it gave me a sense of security to be guarded and treated as if I were what I appeared to be, I knew that time was coming to a close. Jack didn't know it, but another woman had him in her sights and far be it from me to stand in the way of what could be a romance of epic proportions.

Or tragic proportions.

"I don't understand. Have I done something to offend you, Anya?" It about killed me to see that hurt puppy-dog look in his eyes.

"It's not about you, Jack. It's about me. It's about the fact that I've spent long enough as a child, under someone else's wing. It's time for me to see if I can fly on my own. And believe me, I can."

"I believe you," he told me. "So when do you want to do this?" I could almost see the wheels turning in his head as he considered potential places for me to live, safely ensconced within a few blocks of one of the Lounge patrons.

I considered avoiding anywhere near the others, but decided that might be carrying it too far. There was no reason to completely dodge the people who'd become my friends in order to assert my independence. That would be the actions of a child, not the adult I desperately wanted—*needed*—to become.

"If you don't mind, Jack, I'd like to speak with her for a moment," said Dylan, and I froze. What could she say?

Had I been being entirely honest with myself at the time, I would've acknowledged, at least privately, that part of my decision to become more independent was in reaction to the apparent affection growing between the two of them. I was jealous.

I'm not sure why I should have been, considering I didn't see Jack as anything more than a father figure. If anyone, my romantic interest, subtle as it was, had fallen on Kevin. To him, however, I was a child, regardless of how precocious I may have been.

In some ways he was right. My ability to deal with the social requirements of an adult, and my sense of emotional balance were seriously undeveloped, but the growing awareness of my lack had also made me realize that I needed to be on my own. As long as I was treated like a little girl, it would be that much harder for me to present myself as a grown-up.

Let's just say the whole thing tied my thinking up in knots. I think I was doing the right thing, for the right reasons, but I doubt I'll ever be a hundred percent sure of that. I kept stumbling over my emotions. All that which I experienced inside the Dimension of Mirrors may have given me some perspective, but I was still physically just entering puberty. Which meant that my hormones were raging, my brain wasn't completely routed properly, and my concept of adulthood was still as much a personal theory as any kind of living reality.

I looked beseechingly at Jack, who of course had no real say in the matter. She'd asked as a point of courtesy, not because she required or requested his permission.

He nodded abruptly. "I'll be upstairs."

We both watched him leave and, once we'd heard the upstairs door close, I turned to inspect her. She was truly beautiful, I noted, with a distinct pang of something approaching envy. She was everything I was not: a fully formed woman with curves in all the right places and a perfect, heart-shaped face that no man could see as anything but breathtaking.

Even if she was no longer human, she was still gorgeous. I sighed. "What?" I didn't feel like being diplomatic or polite. Not at the moment. Yes, it was juvenile, but what difference did *that* make in the scheme of things?

"This decision of yours...it has nothing to do with me, does it?"

"Shouldn't you be out chasing Montague?" I asked her. Hardly a subtle change of subject, I know, but it was the best I could come up with on short notice.

"He can't get far," she replied, raising one eyebrow.

I wondered if she could do that *before* she became a djinn or if that was a useless but interesting side effect of the transition.

"I like Jack a lot," she continued, "and I'm pretty sure he feels the same way about me. I'm not trying to horn in on your life here—"

"You're not," I interrupted. "I need to make my own life and this provides me a good opportunity."

She wasn't buying it. Not entirely. Her calm gaze turned sympathetic and it made me want to scream at her. I didn't need her sympathy. I didn't need anything from her.

"You are legally an adult," she stated, unnecessarily, "but I'm not sure this is the best thing for you right now. A few months of tutelage with a couple of mages doesn't take the place of real schooling. If I were you, I'd consider enrolling in one of the retro high schools here in the city. There are a lot of skills you'll need if you really plan to make it on your own out there. Magic will only get you so far."

Don't you just love unsolicited advice? I wanted to tell her to go screw herself, but didn't see how that would help matters any. "I'll keep that in mind," I said dryly. "Is there anything else?"

"What do you have against me?" she asked, surprising me a little. I guess it was a little silly of me to expect her not to notice.

"You're not human," I told her. "You're immortal now and Jack's falling for you. I don't see how that can end any way but badly."

She let out a short laugh. It sounded a little bitter to me. "For *me*, perhaps. Jack's an ordinary mortal, not even parahuman or a mage. His lifespan *may* reach a hundred years and I've lived nearly half of that already. I'm the one who's going to have to watch him slowly descend into decrepitude and sit by him on his deathbed." Her lips quirked into a sad smile. "And what's really bad about it is that I could easily grant him eternal life. But I know he won't take it. He *likes* being a normal. It's who he is—the one ordinary man surrounded by freaks. A part of them but apart from them.

"He knows what I am, Anya. And it doesn't bother *him*. Why does it bother you so much?"

I really didn't want to answer that question. Primarily because I didn't *have* an answer. Not even for myself. So I shrugged.

Her gaze took on a piercing aspect, as if she were trying to penetrate a veil that didn't exist, to read something in me I couldn't identify myself. "Dammit, stop it!" I snapped. "I don't *know!* I'm surrounded by freaks all the time and don't care one way or another *who* they become involved with, but for some reason it bothers me that you're becoming involved with Jack!"

She nodded as if this was nothing more or less than she'd anticipated. I hated how smug she seemed at that moment. She might not have been all-knowing, but she played the part entirely too well for my taste.

"I don't know the whole story of how you became trapped in the Dimension of Mirrors, Anya, but I have a feeling it has to do with a very serious betrayal. Something with which you've never had the opportunity to come to terms. So you're dragging around a large piece of baggage and you refuse to let anyone else try to lighten the load for you."

I wanted to snarl at her, but she was right. As far as it went. My trust for adults—for most other people—went only so far. I trusted Jack, but I guess now that someone else, someone I didn't know very well at all, was entering his life, I expected *him* to turn away from me too. It was an all-too familiar pattern in my life.

My mother had done that. She'd put the wants and needs of the men in her life before my own. Every time. And I'd finally paid a very high price for her neglect. The way I saw it, the only higher price I could have paid was with my life, and even that was debatable.

On some level I might have been grateful, because the bastard had given me the gift of magic—though he had no idea that was what he was doing at the time. How could he have known? He must've been one of the first few infected by the arcane virus. And since he was half blotto most of the time on alcohol or other drugs, he probably never recognized or even noticed the change in perceptions it inevitably brought.

*I looked outward once again and saw Dylan shaking her head.* "You don't need parents, Anya. You've grown beyond that need, mentally, if not emotionally and biologically. What you need most now are friends, adult friends who can teach you what it means to be a grown-up in this brave new world. And I know you harbor some resentments against me, but I'd like nothing more than the chance to be your friend. In fact, I'd consider it an honor."

Her words and the sincere tone carried with them seemed to paralyze my tongue. I tried to make it work, to send words forth, but it was as if she'd glued the organ to the roof of my mouth.

She didn't appear to notice. "Most humans in this time, freak or no, grow up surrounded by a loving family, raised by parents who work very hard to teach them the ins and outs of a strange, strange society where monsters are only rarely monsters in the truest sense of the word and the most innocuous can be the most dangerous. But, in the end, Anya, you're nobody's child but your own. We can guide you, we can protect you when you most need it, but the only one who can really teach you about this world and your place in it is you yourself.

"And that's the one thing you can't ever forget. What you do and choose to be is on you. No one else."

I stared at her. She was right, of course. I think all of us had tried to think of me as a kid who needed parents, someone in particular to gradually introduce me to this world and its strange inhabitants and customs, all so different from the one into which I'd been born. But I wasn't a child. None of them were, or could be, my parents. In an odd way, it was as if I had been born fully formed, able to speak, to learn, and to work magic in a world that made no real sense to me.

And it *was* my task to figure out where I belonged within it. No one else could determine that for me. No parents could guide me in their footsteps. There was no family business or legacy to which I could be attached. I was alone and yet I wasn't.

I had all of them, my freakish brethren. None able to act in loco parentis, but as strange siblings to prop me up when I faltered. Not blazing a trail for me to follow, but traveling alongside me wherever it may lead.

I understood what she meant now, and suddenly I realized that I'd been about to make a terrible mistake. I *wasn't* ready to leave the nest completely. I needed to ease myself out of it, not abandon my strange family, but expand my horizons.

"Tell me more about these retro high schools," I said to her, offering up a tiny, slightly apologetic smile. It was really the best I could do. But at least I meant it.

# Episode II:
# The Dream of the Djinn

Most people mistake me for a human being. This is good because I don't want to have to explain what I am to anyone I should happen to meet on the street. Mages can see what I am if they look, but few of them are rude enough to question me.

I'm a djinn. Possibly the only djinn on Earth Prime or in the whole Confederation of Human Worlds. That makes me more unique than anything that walks or flies in this universe.

And I'm in love. With a mortal man.

I look at him sometimes and it makes me ache to know that his short life will be over in what amounts to the blink of an eye. He will be gone and I will remain.

I understand why many immortals forswore love and even passion for thousands of years. They could not tolerate watching those they loved wither and die in front of them, powerless to do anything about it.

I can't imagine how many times they had the lesson driven home before they were able to grasp this reality, though. Our emotions are not so easily bent to our will. Agony must be piled on top of anguish for us to learn how dangerous love can be.

My name is Dylan Shepherd. I was once a mageship pilot, a member of one of the most elite units in all of the Confed Fleet.

But my ship destroyed itself in an act of desperation, trying to save what has become an alternate Earth from the depredations of another of her kind—a rogue mageship whose base programming had been altered by a human intelligence operative. The way I see it, that agent himself is responsible for *Radiance's* death and my own.

Yes. I died. But in her last breath, so to speak, my ship used every erg of her magical power and skill to bring me back from beyond the grave. She grabbed my spirit and forced it into the artificial construct of an extremely complex spell weave. I was dead and then I wasn't. I personally buried my own body, along with the others who'd died in that short battle, some half mile beneath the place where we had fallen.

When I returned to Earth Prime, the world at the center of the immortals' sphere of influence, I resigned my commission from Fleet. I didn't belong there anymore. My ship was gone, my memory of her sacrifice too bitter in my mouth for me to pretend to respect my superiors.

I had changed in more ways than immediately apparent.

I sought out the Magitech Lounge and the man who ran it. The one who had been brought into the past by *Radiance* and had witnessed both my death and rebirth. An ordinary man with an extraordinary heart.

I was already falling in love with him, though I didn't really know it yet. I knew I wanted to see him again, to look into his eyes and see myself reflected there.

When I arrived he had company, a Military Intelligence agent of my acquaintance, one who'd been involved during the design phase of the second run of mageships—the run that had produced *Ranger*, the ship who'd gone rogue.

I'd spent the last couple of days putting things together, using my new power to dig in places no one would ever have expected and coming up with answers I didn't like at all. Military Intelligence, the armed forces version of the civilian Adjuster's Office—the agency that monitored all preternatural and parahuman elements serving in the Confed military—had implanted an illegal code during *Ranger's* initial programming.

Don't ask me how I discovered this. Suffice to say that some of the things I did were not quite legal, even by today's rather libertine standards.

Ask me if I care. If you dare.

The man in charge of their little operation was named Gerald Montague and he was a throwback to the old, super-paranoid types that pretty much ruled the roost in the days before the Cen War. How he rose to any position of prominence within MI, I have no idea. Most of the time his kind are shunted into career paths in which they can do very little damage. Certainly to some low-level perfunctory office where no one takes them seriously.

Unfortunately, unbeknownst to anyone including myself, Montague was a psi. A rather powerful psi, as things turned out. Maybe even a meta. He was powerful enough to hide his talents from the rest of the world and from the military's own psi corps.

My guess is that he used this talent to further his own ambitions and managed to infect a whole section of the intelligence community with his own paranoia.

Something tells me we need better screening procedures.

I returned to the Magitech Lounge to see Jack again and found Montague there. How he knew to seek answers among Jack and his friends, I don't know. I can hazard a few guesses, but that's all they'd be.

He didn't recognize me for what I am when I appeared on the scene. He leveled a hand blaster at me and I, of course, handily rendered it inoperable. When he tried to shoot me with it, nothing happened.

Now, I'm pretty certain it wouldn't have done anything to me, since I'm only nominally physical and only when I want to be, but there was no reason to reveal that to him. Plus the particle beam weapon would've done damage to the bar, and that wasn't any more desirable to me at the moment than revealing to him the fact that I was no longer human.

Also on scene was Jack's adopted daughter, a girl who'd been rescued from the Dimension of Mirrors by the immortal, Hades, after being trapped there beyond time for over two hundred years. She looked at me with undisguised suspicion and I can't say I blamed her much. She'd been through hell, quite literally, tossed into the midst of a war even *I* couldn't understand very well at the time. And this atop centuries of imprisonment in a world so alien I can't begin to describe it to someone who'd never been there.

I have. Once. I'd prefer never to go again. It's very easy to get lost, even if one does know a way out. Nothing is ever quite what it seems there.

The girl's origins are even darker than one might suppose. She was a child of the earliest days of the Arcane bug, the nano-virus that returned magic to humanity. Loki, the immortal bioengineer who'd crafted the viruses, had programmed them initially to transmit through sexual contact alone. He'd wanted only adults infected at first, thinking that they would be more adept at handling what he was giving them.

He wasn't entirely correct about this, but that sort of mistake was forgivable for a being twenty-five thousand years old and not socially savvy in the first place.

Loki's a scientist, and a truly decent human being. It never occurred to him that some of those infected would be the kind of pervert and piece of shit that Anya's stepfather was. He infected her with the arcane virus and she became a mage. Not knowing what she was doing, she opened a doorway into the Dimension of Mirrors and fled there in an attempt to escape his filthy attentions.

She succeeded beyond her wildest dreams.

I did not know all these details at the time, but I knew she had reason to distrust adults. Her mother had betrayed her by looking the other way, pretending not to see what was being done to her, and her stepfather...well, let's just say death would be too gracious a fate for him. If I believed in such things, I'd wish for him an eternity swimming in a lake of fire.

I don't, of course. Belief in the old philosophies of heaven and hell isn't all that common on Earth Prime anymore. For that sort of religious path, one had to seek out specific colonies spread throughout the interstellar neighborhood of the Confederation of Human Worlds.

For all I know, the bastard could still be alive. A two hundred plus lifespan isn't entirely unknown for magi. Though, by the sounds of it, he wasn't the type of guy who'd bother to learn the skills necessary to rejuvenate himself. Even with magic, one had to pursue the knowledge that went with it. It wasn't like wishing things into existence, after all.

I found myself speaking with the girl, trying to reach through that hard shell of suspicion. I wasn't sure why. She'd announced her intention to move out and get her own place, a decision that had left Jack a bit emotionally bruised. I'd had the immediate impression that I was at least partially the cause of this decision on her part.

I think on some level she was jealous of me. Not that she harbored the kind of feelings for Jack that I did, but she obviously loved him. In a way, I was taking something from her and she didn't like it. She was reacting emotionally and not aware of herself enough to recognize what she was doing.

So I showed her.

She grasped it quickly. Her brain may be wired as a young teen's, but she has many, many years to draw upon, and there's some wisdom knocking around in there too.

She decided to stay. And to go back to school.

I didn't plan on sticking around to play the mother figure. Okay, I'll admit it, I'm not sure what I expected. All I had in mind was spending some time with Jack while I used my free time—like when he was sleeping—to chase down that bastard Montague.

I offered to be Anya's friend. I meant it sincerely. She seemed to take it in the spirit in which I'd meant it, but the last thing I expected was her to embrace the idea as if it were a lifeline.

Silly me. She was a thirteen-year-old girl in desperate need of a female friend she could claim for herself. And I *did* volunteer.

It was about a week after our little talk when I found myself standing with her at the base of a wide set of concrete stairs leading up to the double doors marking the entrance to Golden Gate High. Or so the huge sign over the doors proclaimed in golden-hued block letters.

"So this is it, huh?" she asked in a small voice.

I nodded. "I checked it out. Golden Gate currently serves about a thousand students—eighth through twelfth grade."

She blinked up at me. "I thought the old system had been abandoned. Y'know, the ancient grade system and all."

"For the most part, they have been. One of the greatest flaws of the old system was the lack of attention to individual abilities and learning styles. They tended to teach to the lowest common denominator, or at best, the average. Those who required accelerated programs and those who needed a little extra help were often marginalized one way or the other. And the social structure made learning even more difficult for some.

"The downside to the distance learning techniques that were adopted after the Cen War was that they neglected the socialization end of things. There were some students who had very little organized interaction with their peers *until* they left school to enter the job market. That didn't work too well either.

"So places like Golden Gate are trying to capture the best of both worlds—they employ roughly three times as many educators as did comparable schools of your time and also make great use of the super databases that have become available over the past couple centuries as well.

"Grades are divided into modules, aimed at teaching the students the skill sets necessary for the career paths in which they're most interested. You can choose between business, legal, technology, medical, education, or civil engineering. You're allowed to intermix certain introductory courses to help you choose a solid path, but once you've figured out the direction you want to go, you're fast-tracked toward a college level module once you're ready to continue."

"Sounds...interesting."

Poor girl was terrified. Not that I blamed her. In her shoes, I would've been terrified too. I wish I could have told her what she could expect, but I was one of those who'd been focused from an early age in a certain direction. The schools that taught mage students exclusively, particularly for future government and military careers, were an entirely different breed from this one. This one would be at once very similar to the schools she remembered and quite divergent at the same time.

I knew she could handle it though. Anyone who could deal with being stuck in the Dimension of Mirrors for two centuries without going completely bonkers could handle high school. "We hedged a little on your background," I told her. "We said you were fourteen. It's the minimum age for enrollment at Golden Gate."

"But can't they just check?"

"Check where? The only place any records for you exist are in the Adjuster's Office databanks, and they're not available to just anyone. They seemed perfectly willing to take our word for it. The preliminary tests you did last week revealed that you're at a comparable level with your fellow students here, so we thought we'd leave it at that."

"Thanks, Dylan." She peered up the stairs and heaved a sigh. "You don't have to come with me. I can handle it from here."

I pulled her into a hug, which she resisted at first, then grinned over her head as she relaxed into it. "You'll do fine. You'll be out at 2:30 and Jack, Bone, or maybe Hades will be here to pick you up then."

"Hades?" By the sound of her voice, I decided she was caught between amusement and trepidation. Hades wasn't exactly an unknown figure. Having him arrive on the scene to transport her home would either serve to make her extremely popular or a pariah for the rest of the year.

We would see which way it broke if and when Hades showed up. "I've got some stuff to take care of, so I might not be around when you get home. I'll catch up with you when I get there later, though."

She headed up the steps. I waited until the door had swung shut behind her and transported out, making the leap between San Francisco and Tacoma in one easy step. I accessed the mage road this time, though unlike most mages, I could've done it on my own without having to make use of the magical transportation infrastructure. I might have not been able to see or touch ambient mana anymore, but considering that my very form was made up of far more mana than any mage could hope to touch or command, I figured the trade-off was well worth it.

There's been considerable speculation in certain circles as to my comparative power. Let's just put it this way. The average mage can grab two strands at once and produce two separate mana effects or weave them into either a simple spell or the beginnings of a more complex spell. A very skilled mage may create a spell using up to fifty mana strands, though, in my estimation, this requires an immortal mage. The spell at my core that holds my soul on this plane is made up of three hundred interwoven threads. The rest of me—the physical illusion I wear around my core—is twelve hundred more threads that I can manipulate in any way I choose. They are a part of me and cannot dissipate, and as far as I know, cannot be destroyed. Each one is worth a single effect at a time and I can manipulate as many as I choose at the same time.

No mage, even an immortal mage, is anywhere near my equal. Though I must admit, the immortal Hades and the vampire Rio are closer than any other beings I can name. Magically speaking, of course.

I transported myself into Deryk Shea's office, interrupting the squat little man in the midst of a golf putt. The ball went awry and slammed into the corner of a bookshelf before scuttling under it. He looked up at me with a pained expression and grunted a greeting.

Ever since I resigned my commission with Fleet, I'd been negotiating with Shea to take me on as an Adjuster's Office agent. So far he hadn't taken the bait. I couldn't imagine why not and, frankly, I was getting a little annoyed by the whole damned thing.

"You again," he muttered, shaking his head and tossing the golf club in the corner. "Still want an answer, do you?"

"Nah. Thought I'd take a walk and happened to show up here by accident," I replied with a casual smile. Falsely casual, of course. I wanted to be a part of something bigger than myself. If I could no longer serve the Confed as a mageship pilot, I thought working for Deryk Shea and the Adjuster's Office might be a decent alternative.

I couldn't quite understand his reluctance to bring me on, though. I doubt it was because I wasn't human anymore. He didn't have a reputation as a bigot. And it wasn't because of any lingering doubts about my loyalty to the Confed either. I'd made the greatest sacrifice possible for the Confed. The way I saw it, the Confed owed me.

Many people describe Shea as an ugly little man, but I guess I've never seen him that way. He's short, squat, and his facial features aren't exactly proportionate. The effect is startling, but not in the least bit hideous.

What's really amazing is that immortals can re-arrange their bone structure to alter their appearance at will. He wears that face because he *wants* to. Damn strange, if you ask me. But then again, no one ever accused Shea of being a normal sort of guy, even when compared to his fellow immortals.

"Have a seat," he told me. "You want something to drink?"

I considered both the suggestion and the question. I extended a thread, dragged his guest chair over, and dropped my butt into it. I threw my feet onto the edge of his desk, crossing my ankles and summoning one of the cigars from the ornate box on the other corner into my hand. "What do you have to drink?"

I lit the cigar with the tip of a finger and puffed contentedly while he affixed me with a baleful expression. A tiny gleam in his eye, barely visible, revealed that he was more amused than irritated by my audacity. This fit in with what I'd heard about him over the years. He respected nerve more than just about anything else.

I could work with that.

"Something tells me you can rustle up whatever poison you have a taste for," he grunted. "But, if you insist on drinking my booze, I've got cognac, single-malt, bourbon, vodka, and rum. All premium, of course. Take your pick. But you can damn well get it yourself."

"Maybe I'll just have a beer." I shot out a strand and liberated a bottle of something exotic from nowhere in particular.

His brow shot up. "That's theft, you know," he remarked casually.

"How do you know?" I asked pointedly, grinning at him. "Maybe I got it from my own cooler."

"And maybe I'm a fucking Martian," he snorted dismissively. "What do you want, Dylan?"

I popped the cap and took a long swig. As I swallowed, I lowered the bottle and glanced at the label. I'd have to remember this brand. It was pretty damned good. "You know what I want, Shea. I want a job."

"No, Dylan, what you want is my official sanction of your personal vendetta in pursuit of Gerald Montague."

I blinked at him. I wouldn't have put it that way myself, exactly, but he had a point. "And this is a problem?"

He shrugged. "Not particularly. I just didn't like the fact that you weren't being completely honest about it—to yourself,

257

or to me. I've never had an issue with operatives being personally involved in their cases. I know that classic police wisdom says it's bad juju, that it leads to mistakes and endangers not only the investigation, but the agent as well. I say that's only true if one doesn't truly know the stature of the investigator in the first place.

"This is why I vet all my agents personally and interact with them on a regular basis. I like knowing who I have working for me, what makes them tick and where their trigger points are."

"Oh? So what are *my* trigger points?" This also fit into his reputation, I mused. He backed his people all the way. He'd gone on record as saying that Adjuster's Office agents were incorruptible, the twenty-third century's version of the 'Untouchables.'

He settled into his chair behind the desk and regarded me silently for a long, pregnant moment. "You believe in duty. You believe that you owe something to the community and believe that your talents should be used for the greater good.

"In short, you're an ideal AO officer."

I disappeared the cigar, which was frankly starting to smell pretty foul. "I hear a 'but' in there somewhere."

"Perceptive of you," he remarked dryly. "As much as I think you'd be an asset to the AO, I also have to say I don't think you're quite ready yet. You're too detached...no longer mortal or anything remotely resembling a real human being anymore. And the transition was so swift I don't believe you've come to terms with it. Not so far, anyway.

"You need to rebuild a life outside the agency to anchor yourself to the real world again. Without it, you'll lose perspective and become caught up in your own power."

"Oh?" I lifted a brow and regarded him with undisguised skepticism. "And you know this how?"

His thick lips curved into a gentle smile. "I've had a lot of time to study people, human, superhuman, and *other.* I was good at reading people even before I became immortal. Now I'm probably as good at it as any psi who's ever lived. Not because I have some preternatural gift for it, but because I *care.*

"Becoming a djinn did not make you any less human than you were, Dylan. I know deep down you worry about that. Because you've absorbed the unconscious meme out there that your biological self is what makes you human. But these days that meme is simply bullshit. We are *all* human. The definition has grown from what it once was. I am human, you are human, vampires are human, lycanthropes are human. 'Human,' in this day and age, simply means 'born of the race of humanity.'"

I stared at him, literally astounded by what he was saying. I'd never heard it put quite this way before. He made it sound so simple.

"At one time there was a strong movement here on Earth Prime to marginalize preternaturals and paranormals, to legislate them into second-class citizens, to actually force them to register themselves with the government so their movements and activities could be tracked.

"I threw my not-inconsiderable resources into opposing this, at least here in what used to be the United States as well as in Europe. There were places where I had very little influence, and for a while, those places were hellholes for anyone who wasn't 'normal.'

"Some regimes were afraid of them because they couldn't control them the way they could ordinary humans. Others saw them as inherently evil, a direct result of ancient Cen social engineering, as it turns out. People back then didn't know how much of your religious doctrine had been crafted by the Cen to keep you weak and fractured. Hell, *we* didn't even know it.

"Of course," he admitted with a shrug, "most of us were too damn self-involved to pay attention to anything beyond our own personal diversions. I have to tell you, I was quite disappointed in my kind when I called upon them to help us oppose the Cen's invasion plans and the vast majority of them couldn't be bothered. That's one of the reasons I backed Loki's play. Crazy as it was, it might well have been the only thing that could have saved us from the Cen."

"So basically you're not saying 'no,' you're saying 'not right now.'"

He nodded somberly. "Precisely. Go out and find yourself an anchor, Dylan, and come back to see me when you think you're ready."

I finished off the beer in a single gulp, vanished the bottle, and stood. "I'll think about it, sir."

"Sir? A little late to be kissing my ass, don't you think?" He grinned up at me.

"It's never too late," I told him and transported myself back to San Francisco.


I didn't go straight to the Lounge, instead finding a relatively secluded spot in Golden Gate Park and sprawling out on the forest floor. I didn't need to sleep anymore, but I found moments of deep meditation to be quite useful for sorting through the myriad of life's little details.

I needed an anchor, Shea had said. I needed something to tie me to the mortal world. Something to remind me I was once human, and reason to believe part of me still was.

I laughed aloud when I realized what should have been obvious from the beginning. I already had something that fit the bill, though I hadn't really thought of it at the time. I was falling in love with Jack. And I was growing damn fond of Anya too, in a maternal sort of way.

Now *that* was a weird thing to realize. I'd never thought of myself as the maternal type. But there was something about that kid that got under my skin.

Of course, she wasn't really a kid, was she?

I leaned back, folded my arms behind my head, and stared up at the blue sky through the shifting emerald canopy of the eucalyptus trees towering above me.

Maybe I should have revealed all of this to Deryk Shea, and maybe, if I had, I would have walked out of his office a shiny new Adjuster's Office agent. But, then again, I was still uncertain myself what it all meant. *Was* I entering a relationship with Jack, or was I just fooling myself? It wasn't as though we'd even kissed yet.

What *did* he feel for me? I experienced a brief moment of longing for empathic abilities to go along with my magical ones, but, thankfully it passed quickly enough. I didn't really want to be empathic, though I wouldn't mind being enough of a psi to be able to track down Montague and stop the bastard from 'porting out again.

I stood, threw out a transit tube, and stepped through to the Lounge.

I knew something was wrong even before I exited the other side. I can't even say why. They say transition is instantaneous, but I think it's just slightly slower than that. There was time for something to impinge on my awareness in that split second before I stepped out onto the dance floor.

Something large and furry barreled past me, venting a roar of rage and pain. A crimson blossom of flame spread across its back as it thundered down the ramp and through the front door. I spun away from it to see Montague and several other ordinary-looking humans standing by the stage, armed with hand blasters and nearly identical expressions of icy disdain.

Jack lay unmoving at their feet and Anya struggled in another's grasp, her face twisted into an expression of shock, fear, and pain. Her eyes were clenched shut and I detected the bitter fragrance of mace in the air.

A mage's greatest weakness is his or her eyes. If they'd come upon her by surprise and sprayed her in the face, effectively blinding her, she would've been easy prey. Most mages would have been. I felt anger rise in me like a radiant tide as I stepped forward.

Montague took a long step sideways and laid the barrel of the blaster against the side of her head. She stopped fighting and took a long, shuddering breath.

He smiled. It wasn't a pleasant expression, even had his face been whole and unscarred. The scar simply made it uglier. "The question here is whether you can act fast enough to stop me from pulling the trigger," he said. "I'm betting you can't."

I spoke through clenched teeth. "What the hell do you want, Jerry?"

"Your cooperation," was all he said in reply.

My gaze flicked down to Jack and I wondered whether he was dead or simply unconscious. I couldn't tell from here without sending out a probe. And if there was a mage among them, that might be perceived as a prelude to an attack. "My cooperation with *what?*"

"We want another mageship. And you're going to help us get one."

"You're out of your fucking mind. Even if I was willing, there is no way I could pull that off."

He reached into a breast pocket of his suit and tossed something to me with his free hand. I caught it and glanced down. It was a sliver of crystal, about as large as my pinky, octagonal in shape. A data sleeve. "This carries the same virus with which we infected *Ranger*. I want you to get aboard a mageship and place it in its primary receiving port." He paused at my look of disbelief. "Or maybe you'd rather I kill the girl."

"I don't think you're that crazy, Montague. If you did that, there isn't a force in this universe or any other that could protect you from me."

"We'd have to see about that, wouldn't we?" None of his madness showed in his gaze, I noticed. We might as well have been discussing the weather for all that it showed in his eyes. Not even the slightest glimmer of fear revealed itself in him. And he should have been afraid. There was no way he could guess what I could do to him.

Possible scenarios were flying through my brain even at that very moment. I could make him very, very sorry.

They were all staring at me and missed the slow, deliberate movements of the man at their feet. Jack twitched, then edged himself farther onto his side. "Lady of Blades!" he cried suddenly and the men jerked as one.

Montague shifted the weapon in his hand from Anya's head to point it at Jack. "You're tougher than I expected," he muttered, shaking his head. "I'll have to shoot you again." He chuckled, shaking his head. "You don't *really* believe an urban legend is going to save you, do you?"

Behind them, at the back of the stage, there stood a full-length mirror. The surface seemed to ripple and two women stepped out of it, one after the other. The first one through was tall and almost too beautiful for words, with a cascade of raven hair tumbling around her broad shoulders. She held a gentle curving katana in one hand, the length of its amethyst blade glittering like spun glass. She was clad in what looked to be a green karate gi.

The second woman was smaller, but no less striking. She looked Hispanic and she wore a black body-suit marked with a distinct pattern of what looked like spider webs. On her hips hung two short, sharply curved swords and the butt of a pistol hung in a holster under her arm.

Their arrival had been completely silent.

I felt a chill. The taller woman's pale green eyes flicked down to take in the scene and narrowed when they caught sight of Anya in the minion's grasp. She shook her head almost imperceptibly and moved forward, that shimmering blade describing a tight horizontal arc.

The minion's eyes widened and his arms flew away from Anya, who stumbled forward. His hands came up as if reaching for his face and his weapon tumbled to the floor. Then slowly, his head slid from his neck and fell into his reaching hands.

The Hispanic woman leaped high into the air, tucking into a double somersault, and came down on another one of the men's shoulders. In one of her hands was one of the curved swords, its broad surface black as pitch. She drove the blade downward, through the top of the man's skull.

Blood poured from his mouth as he slumped to his knees.

I was abruptly reminded of an old expression—like a fox in a hen-house. Though they were outnumbered five to one, the two women moved among the men like veritable whirlwinds of carnage.

Jack rolled away, pushing himself to his feet and snatching the stumbling Anya along with him as they retreated to where I stood. I surrounded them both with a web of mana and watched in growing horror while the women performed an almost obscene rite of devastation on Montague's men.

It was like watching a ballet with blood and swords. They didn't have a chance against the two women, and within ten or fifteen seconds, only Montague still stood. He'd been disarmed, the blaster thrown across the room by a single sweep of the taller woman's katana, torn from his grasp and sliced in two.

She leveled the point of the weapon at him and spoke in a husky contralto. "Anyone who enters this place with murder on their mind will face the same fate as these," she said, gesturing toward the corpses littering the floor with her free hand. "I am *not* an urban legend."

I took a moment to scan Jack. He'd taken a blaster bolt to the shoulder, leaving a scorched, ragged hole through which I could see blackened muscle and tendons. It oozed fluid, but the bolt had cauterized the wound and prevented him from bleeding out.

It had to hurt like hell.

Montague looked around at his minions, his face ghostly white. "I...I had no idea."

"Now you do," the woman replied humorlessly. She stepped back and to the side so she could look over at us without losing sight of Montague. "Is the girl all right?"

Once I'd done a quick inspection of Jack, I'd moved to Anya. Her eyes were still screwed shut, but other than the damage inflicted by the mace, she seemed mostly unharmed. I nodded.

"Good. What do you want to do with this guy?" she asked me. Not Jack. Me.

Before I could formulate an answer, the other woman gestured and the bodies disappeared, taking along any trace they were ever here, blood and other bodily fluids included. The room still held the stench of sudden, violent death, but I knew that could be fixed easily enough.

All the things I'd thought about doing to Montague flashed through my mind once again, but I rejected them all. I wanted him rendered harmless, but I no longer thought flaying the skin from his bones would be all that satisfying. In fact, after what I'd just witnessed, the thought of inflicting anything like that kind of damage sat in my stomach like a lump of molten ice.

Okay, so I'm more squeamish than I'd realized. Blood and gore just isn't my thing. "I just want him neutralized," I told her finally. "I thought I wanted revenge, but what good will that do?"

"Personal satisfaction," said the smaller woman with a wry grin. Her voice was even deeper than her taller companion's. I hid an amused smile at Jack's seemingly involuntary shiver. He was in serious pain yet something about those tones had a libidinous effect on him.

Men are weird.

I simply shrugged. "Do what you will with him. Just get him out of our hair."

"We'll give him to Deryk," said the taller of the two, with an evil grin. "He'll know what to do with him."

The other woman snickered.

I frowned. "You know Deryk Shea?"

She laughed at that. "I used to work for him, a long time ago." She cocked her head and peered at me curiously. "I'll be damned. You're not human." She strode forward and reached out the hand not still holding the katana. "I'm Jasmine Tashae."

Now I realized who she was. She was a legend. More than one legend, apparently, if she was indeed the Lady of Blades. "Dylan Shepherd."

"Well," she said, in an odd tone, her emerald eyes scraping across me in a most disconcerting manner, "aren't *you* interesting?"

"He's a psi," I told her with a glance toward Montague, trying desperately to send her unsettling gaze elsewhere.

"We know. Nyx has already taken care of that. She paralyzed the psychic centers of his brain. It should last long enough. Believe me, he's not going anywhere unless we take him. Unless he wants to try to run." She flashed a brief, feral smile. "That's actually the scenario I like the best. I've been on vacation and my other swords are clamoring for a good work-out. They've been terribly bored."

This woman was truly scary, I decided. She and her friend had just slaughtered nine men and neither of them seemed to think it anything out of the ordinary. I suppressed a shudder. She might misinterpret it. Or, rather, interpret it all too correctly.

She scared me. Hell, they both did.

"I've been trying to get Deryk Shea to hire me," I told her. "I just recently resigned my commission in Fleet, and would love a position at the Adjuster's Office."

She frowned. "So what's the problem?"

"Ask him," I told her.

"Okay. I will. Nyx? You ready?"

The other woman nodded and shoved Montague toward her friend. "Time to pay the piper," she told him.

They all winked out at once, leaving us behind to pick up the pieces. I began by healing Jack's injury, then took Anya into the restroom to rinse the nasty stuff off her face and out of her eyes.

By the time I'd finished with her, Jack had apparently gotten in touch with all the Lounge regulars who were able to move around in the daylight. Nearly all of those who'd accompanied him on his trip into the past were present. Much to my surprise. But that wasn't near as much as a surprise as what he was saying.

"I'd like to talk to you all about something," he said. "I'm going to invite Dylan to live with us," he said slowly, lifting his gaze to mine as I stood outside the restroom door with my arm thrown around Anya. She was wiping at her face with a towel and stopped abruptly when she heard these words. "I think I've fallen for her," he continued. "I know some of you have had problems with her since what happened, but I'm asking you to put all that aside now."

"Have you talked to *her* about this?" asked Hades, leaning against one of the support columns and grinning broadly. "She looks as though you hit her with a club."

Jack shrugged. "Yeah, maybe I'm doing this all backwards. I was just shot with a blaster—give me a break."

This prompted a round of laughter, which faded as he raised his gaze to me. "I want you in my life, Dylan. I want you in *our* lives."

"Well," I said, raising my voice to be heard throughout the Lounge, "when you put it *that* way, how can I resist?"

This was met with an embarrassing round of cheers. I looked down into Anya's face and saw her grinning. "I was wondering when you two would stop dancing around and actually get around to doing something about your feelings."

Great. Save me from ancient children and their wisdom. I sighed mentally. "Keep in mind," I told them as I weaved my way through the crowd, "that I'm trying to get a job with the Adjuster's Office. That means if any of you step out of line, it'll probably be *me* who's sent out to get you back on the straight and narrow."

"I don't care *how* powerful you are, Dylan," said Hydra in his booming voice. "There are some of us who've never even *seen* the straight and narrow."

This pronouncement engendered another round of laughter and some hoots of derision as well.

"Be that as it may," I told them, reaching Jack's side and looping one arm around his waist, "I plan on keeping you guys in line. Anyone have any problems with that, take it up with Anya here."

I couldn't wipe the grin off my face. Even if I didn't manage to get hired on at the AO, I thought my new life looked like it been worth all the sacrifices. Maybe I was right and maybe I was wrong.

I was just happy to have the opportunity to find out.

# Epilogue:
# The Lady of Blades

We leaped into Deryk's office and tossed the man at his feet.

Sighing, he set his golf club aside. "I'm not going to get *any* practice today, am I?" he asked rhetorically.

"I think you're looking for this fuck," I said, planting a boot in the guy's ass by way of illustration.

He grimaced. "Well, it's nice to see you too, Jaz. And you, Nyx."

"Same here, Deryk," Nyx answered back, not much sounding as if she meant it. She didn't have anything against Deryk, of course, but she was feeling a bit out of sorts at the moment. That summons had interrupted at exactly the wrong moment and she was feeling a bit cranky. The real object of her ire was sprawled on the floor in front of her, but she'd turn it on anyone in a heartbeat if given an excuse.

I grinned at him. "Was I misinformed?"

Deryk shook his head. "Nope. I was looking for him, but I actually expected someone else to deliver him."

"Yeah. She's busy. She asked us to do it for her."

He shot a suspicious look in my direction. "Uh-huh. And you're doing it out of the goodness of your heart?"

I chuckled a little at that. "Hell, Deryk...you more than anyone should know I don't *have* any goodness in my heart."

He shrugged, dialing a lopsided grin. "So what's the story?"

"She wants to work for you, but it sounds like you have something against her."

"I don't. In fact, she reminds me a lot of someone else I once took under my wing—a youngster with a lot more power than she knew what to do with. Dylan has less of a fondness for violence, thankfully, but still..."

I knew exactly who he meant. I really didn't want to hear any more of this. It was bound to get sappy at some point. "That's nice, Deryk. You still aren't answering my question."

"Oh, I'll hire her eventually. But she needs mortal roots before I can consider her application seriously. The last thing the AO needs is a rogue djinn dispensing her own brand of justice under my authority with no mortal interests to keep her in check."

"She *has* mortal interests," I told him with a sigh. "She's involved with Jack at the Magitech Lounge."

He looked a bit surprised at that. "Oh, really? I had no idea. How seriously?"

"Looked pretty serious to me. I take it you know something about Jack?"

"You might say that. I've had an agent on him for a long, long time."

Now that caught my interest. "Why is that?"

He shook his head with a wry grin, his way of telling me he wasn't going to discuss it with me. I've always hated when he did that.

I sighed again. "So you're going to hire her?"

"Yep. If she's building a mortal life, she's exactly the type of person we need right now. We're starting to pick up some rather disconcerting murmurs from the clan vampires. They're starting to amass some political power here on Prime, and, to tell you the truth, I'm a little worried about what they plan on doing with it."

I frowned at that. "I'm not sure how much use she'd be, since most vampires are pretty resistant to magic."

He shrugged. "Depends on how you use it. I'm no mage, as you well know, but I can think of a couple ways she could use it to devastating effect while negating their immunities at the same time."

As you can imagine, this piqued my interest. Deryk didn't often weigh in on magical matters because he *wasn't* a mage, but he was a smart son of a bitch regardless and I generally consider it wise to pay close attention to anything he had to say.

"I've gotta hear this," Nyx said, planting her shapely ass on the corner of Deryk's desk. As Montague tried to push himself to his knees, she swung out a foot and caught him in the ribs. He collapsed back onto the grass-like carpet with a hoarse wheeze.

Sometimes she can be even harder than I am, and that's saying something.

Deryk had one of his telltale grins in place, the kind that says "I'm so smart I scare myself". "Imagine having hundreds of mana threads at your disposal. What would happen if you used them to channel sunlight from one side of the globe to the other?"

"Will that work?" Nyx asked me as if I'd know. I'd never tried *that* particular trick. The best I could do was to string together fifty or so threads. The idea of being able to manipulate hundreds, or even over a thousand, left me a little dazzled. But I had the feeling that the djinn—Dylan—could do just that.

"How good a mage *was* she?" I asked. As a djinn, she could no longer see or touch free-floating mana, but she had an awful lot to work with anyway. Her core was a spell, but the energy that formed her physical shell was made up of a myriad of strands that were hers to command.

If anyone could do what Deryk was describing, it would be that woman.

"She was a mageship pilot," he said, which told me everything I needed to know. Only the best of the best were chosen for that position. If she beat out the literally hundreds of other candidates for the post, she was among the best the Confed had to offer.

"Sounds like a perfect AO agent," I said.

Nyx nodded, then turned a baleful eye on the guy on the floor. "You try to get up again, I'm going to kick a field goal with your head," she told him.

He sagged back down and lay there, huffing comically.

"What are you going to do with this bozo?" I asked him.

"Hell, I don't know. I don't want him. I'd just have to transport him to some penal colony, and arrange for him to be psychically deadened every so often so he didn't affect an escape. Fucking pain in the ass."

"We could just kill him," Nyx said blandly. "Less trouble all around."

For some reason, Deryk has never received suggestions like this one very gracefully. He shot her an icy glare and shook his head. "Uh-uh. That's not the way we do things here and you both know it."

Nyx waved a hand as if brushing away a fly. "Some people are just a waste of oxygen," she said.

Many folks find it hard to believe, but Nyx actually has less regard for human life than I do. Particularly the lives of people like Montague. Those who preyed on innocents were my particular pet peeve and I usually had no qualms about sending them skipping merrily off this mortal coil. But Nyx despises people who abuse their authority. If given free reign, she'd leave a bloody trail of tyrant corpses through all the universes and not feel a minute's guilt over it.

I love her, but sometimes she scares the shit out of me. There are times I find myself wondering if she's waiting for me to step over some invisible line. Let me tell you, that line of thinking gives me the creeps. I like to think she'd warn me first, but sometimes I can't help remembering that this is a woman who has slain two different versions of herself, doppelgangers who in her opinion had taken the wrong path.

Admittedly, they were some screwed up individuals. But the notion of killing another version of myself makes my head spin. I don't know if I could do it. So far I haven't had to. Thank God.

"Well," I suggested to Deryk, "what if we take him with us to Starhaven and let the Immortal High Court decide what to do with him?"

He cocked an eyebrow. "You could do that?"

"Sure. Why not? When the mageship he meddled with jumped universes, it took the whole ball of wax into the Court's court, so to speak. He can be tried under its authority."

Deryk clapped his hands together. "Good! Let *them* decide what to do with him. I like that solution best of all."

I considered pointing out that he was dumping the whole matter in his son's lap, but thought better of it. Deryk still hadn't really come to terms with his son's death and resurrection and I thought it would be pretty cruel of me to bring it up now.

Nyx chuckled evilly. "You hear that, Montague? We're taking you somewhere where you have a chance of experiencing *real* justice. Not like the mamby-pamby justice they have around here. Get up."

He shakily rose to his feet, keeping his gaze pointed at his shoes. He wasn't about to do anything else to rouse her ire. He was smarter than he'd seemed at first, I decided.

"If you want to take him to Starhaven now," I told her, "I'll follow in a few minutes. I've got a couple more things to discuss with Deryk."

She hit me with one of her piercing stares and then nodded. "Okay. Don't take too long. Remember, we're supposed to be meeting Gimp for lunch."

Trust her to remember something that had completely slipped my mind. "I'll only be a few more minutes," I repeated.

"Love you," she said.

"Love you too," I answered back. And, damn me, I did. Am I crazy or what?

Once she'd gone, Deryk fired off a sympathetic look, which I deflected with a glower. Yes, I know she's a handful, but she's *my* handful. I don't need anyone's pity, least of all Deryk Shea's.

"So what did you want to talk about?" he asked.

"Who do you think's behind this whole clan business?" I asked.

"I don't know," he replied.

Seeing my skepticism, he shook his head. "I'm serious. It may be that Jason Keening's back in the picture, but I don't think so. Several months back a powerful female vamp showed up, but she got thoroughly spanked at the Lounge."

I nodded. "Yeah, I know."

"That's right. You were involved in that, weren't you?"

I shrugged. "The Lounge is my territory," I said simply. "I know what goes on there."

"I imagine you do. No, I think Keening is too chickenshit to come here personally. He'd rather send others to do his dirty work."

"Like killing his mother?"

"Yeah...like killing his mother. What a bastard. I liked Gina, though I didn't know her very well."

"She created the Conclave," I said. "That speaks well of her in itself."

"Indeed." He sighed heavily and walked around his desk to throw himself into his chair. "No, I think Keening has sent another powerful minion in to cause trouble. We're going to have to find out who it is and deal with him—or her—before things get out of hand."

"If you need any backup, let me know, will you?"

"I will, Jaz. I appreciate that, even though I've never taken you up on it. My agents do pretty well for themselves."

"You've always picked the best, Deryk." I grabbed a spell sigil and used it to activate a worldgate to Starhaven. "Take care of yourself."

"You too, Jaz." He told me.

I threw him an irreverent sketch of a salute and stepped into infinity.

# About the Author

Saje has been a Northwest native for most of his life, and currently resides in Tacoma, WA, with his wife and an assortment of furry kids. He's also the proud father of two bipedal children as well, but they currently live elsewhere.

When not writing, he's either working, thinking about writing, or doing both at the same time. This tends to cause a bit of confusion when he's standing at a sixth-floor window gauging the distance between the building in which he works and the adjacent parking garage and wondering whether a vampire could easily make the leap.

He happens to believe a vampire could make that leap, but he's reluctant to discuss the matter with his co-workers.

Saje is currently awaiting the publication of the next two novels in his genre-bending paranormal science-fantasy series, the Infinity: Earth Saga. He's also a recipient of the Loveromances Rising Star award.

His website address is www.sajewilliams.com His yahoo group is groups.yahoo.com/group/Infinitycollective_.

Look for these titles by
*Saje Williams*

*Now Available*

Sword and Shadow

*Coming Soon:*

Death of Heroes

*On the run from an intergalactic mob boss, she kidnaps the
earthling security expert who helped her. Her plan?
Make him forget about tomorrow.*

# Forget About Tomorrow
## © 2007 Liz Kreger

Larissalyia Ashanti, is hiding out on Earth, a barbarian
planet unsanctified by the FOW—Federation of Worlds—and on
the run from an intergalactic mob boss who plans to use her as
leverage to force her magistrate father to clear his criminal
record.

Mac, an earthman, witnesses the evidence of aliens when
the mob catches up with Lacey. After he helps her fight them
off, she does the only thing she can think of—she kidnaps him
and takes him with her as she flees Earth. Mac learns the
answer to that age old question of whether there's life out
there...in spades. But not only does he have to convince Lacey
that his numerous skills are indispensable, he has to find a way
into her heart.

The chase is just beginning...and so are the romance,
adventure and danger as they cross the universe in search of
safety and answers.

*Available now in ebook and print from Samhain Publishing.*

*Enjoy the following excerpt from Forget About Tomorrow...*

"So, now what?"

Her attention snapped back to Mac. He hadn't turned from his contemplation of the stars outside the ship, yet something in his manner told her he was aware of everything she did.

"Now we go to Cyber Five where we regroup and make plans."

"We?"

"You are along for the ride, Victor."

The use of his name gained her a look of irritation. For a moment she thought he was going to protest her use of his name, but then he shrugged.

"Do you plan to wipe my memory there?" he asked.

Larissalyia hesitated. It would be a good place to do it. She had everything she needed for the procedure. There was really no reason to wait. Other than the fact that she couldn't return Mac to Earth yet. Not while it was likely that one of the Kyrions might be lying in wait. It didn't make sense to wipe his memory quite yet.

Finally she shook her head. "No, as I said, I cannot return you to your world until the danger is past," she replied as she justified her decision in her own mind. "I have no doubt my father will succeed within another one of Earth's moon's cycles. I'd only have to wipe it again after that time."

"That's reassuring."

She pretended not to notice his dry tone. "Cyber Five is just a stop off for supplies and somewhere I can figure out where to go to create a new identity for you."

"Is that necessary?"

"Very. I am not quite sure what the F.O.W. would do with you if it is discovered you are from an unsanctioned planet, but I do know I would be in big trouble."

"So it's in your best interest that I keep my mouth shut."

She slid him a quick glance. This conversation was entering dangerous space. "It is in *both* of our best interest."

"I'd say you're the one who's ass deep in alligators, honey. After all, you kidnapped me. It isn't like I had much of a choice."

Larissalyia twisted in her seat to focus on the look of satisfaction in his face. *He thought he had a hold over her.* Her anger threatened to erupt.

"Look, barbarian. It would be just as easy for me to jettison you from this ship."

"I doubt you'd do that." There was no mistaking the smugness in his tone. He too swiveled his chair until he faced her. "Seems to me you went through a lot of trouble on Earth to make sure I took no harm from that *Sinion* blade thing. You could have just as easily let me die from that wound. You're not the type to commit cold-blooded murder."

"And how would you know that? I am an alien to you. You have no idea what I may be capable of."

"Let's just say I'm a great judge of character."

Larissalyia could think of nothing to counter his self-assurance. He was right. She could not ruthlessly dispose of him in such a manner. Damn, he did have the upper hand.

She'd be a fool to let him know that. Giving him a cool glance, she said nothing and turned back to the console. Checking their coordinates, she made a few more unnecessary adjustments.

Once again she was aware of his gaze on her. It slid over her like a warm hand gliding down her body. She could almost feel the brush of it and a response sprang to life deep within her. It uncurled deep in the pit of her stomach and spread outward in ever-widening circles. It was not an uncomfortable feeling, just unfamiliar.

Frowning, she glanced over at him once more. He hadn't moved. He merely continued to watch her with that fathomless expression. A slight smile quirked his lips and drew her gaze to that portion of his face. He had a beautiful mouth. Firm, the lower lip slightly fuller than the upper. It was a mouth made for kissing. Made for pleasure.

"Look, I'll make you a deal." He waited until her gaze returned to his. There was a gleam of satisfaction in his eyes. "I promise to cooperate with you in keeping this F.O.W. ignorant of my presence in the hallowed halls of the known universe, and..."

"And?"

"And in return, you don't wipe my memory of all of this."

Larissalyia stared at him, stupefied. "Impossible!"

"Why?"

She blinked. Why, indeed? Standard procedure dictated alien species not sanctioned by the F.O.W. be kept ignorant of the existence of the federation. Harsh penalties ensured this rule was followed. To her knowledge, no one had ever violated the dictum of the Council. Who would know?

But if she agreed with the Earthman, who would know? And was it a gamble she was willing to take?

Although she'd known him a short time, something about Victor MacNaught told her she could believe him. She sensed an honorableness about him that instinctively made her trust him from the moment he held out his hand to her in that bar.

In her business she had honed a highly refined instinct when it came to sizing up people. She had never entertained any doubt he was trustworthy.

Still, to take such a chance...?

"This is an adventure of a lifetime, Lacey," he went on when she didn't answer. "I want to experience everything I can. Savor it. I don't want to have all of this wiped from my memory. I don't want to forget what it looks like to stare out that screen." He nodded toward the panoramic view, for a moment recapturing the awe of the experience. When he brought his attention back to her, there was something different in his expression. His gaze slowly slid over her face, lingering on her lips with an intensity that made her breath catch and brought a responsive rush of heat. "I don't want to forget you, Lacey."

He reached out and took one of her hands, holding it between both of his. He smoothed her fingers open before he slowly raised her hand to his lips to press a tender kiss to the very center of her palm. Larissalyia felt that gentle caress all the way down to her toes. He looked up at her.

"Do we have a partnership?"

"Partnership?" she repeated in a faint voice, completely undone. He was manipulating her. She knew he was, but was powerless to stop him. Didn't want to stop him.

"I will do whatever you say, behave in any manner you deem appropriate. In return, you don't remove any of this. I give you my word of honor I will never repeat anything I've ever seen or done while I'm with you. Even after I return to Earth."

"Are you willing to take a blood oath on that?" Larissalyia felt rather than saw Tutsi stir in protest, yet the *Mandujano* warrior said nothing. Her cheeks heated as she realized she had forgotten all about the presence of the third person on the bridge. Somehow with a few words and a tender gesture, Mac had completely scattered her wits.

"Yes."

For a moment longer she stared into his eyes, searching for some sign of subterfuge. He gazed back at her, his steadiness convincing her of his sincerity.

Well, she was the gambler here. How could she blame him? In his place, she would do anything possible to hold onto this experience.

*Vampires are immune to many things. Apparently love isn't one of them.*

# Sword and Shadow
## © 2007 Saje Williams

Assigned to monitor a backwater version of Earth, Raven enjoys his job immensely. Play at being a native, watch for operatives of the voracious Cen Empire, and keep an eye out for evil mages. Not too difficult for the undead hero of the Cen War. It's almost like a vacation.

Unfortunately, when he stumbles upon a cache of advanced weapons, he is forced to report that fact back to headquarters, who in turn send him an agent trained in such matters—the vibrant, vivacious, and utterly aggravating Valerie Winn—to deal with the problem.

On her first solo assignment for the Technological Activities Unit (TAU), Val can't help but take her job seriously. But dealing with the legendary Raven's maddening disrespect for any rules but his own pushes her patience to the breaking point.

Even though they strike sparks from one another, they have to learn to work together. The seemingly simple assignment turns out to be much more important than anyone realized. The fate of a thousand versions of Earth might well hang in the balance.

*Available now in ebook and print from Samhain Publishing.*

Val woke suddenly, clawing her way out of the chair and facing the shadow standing across the room.

Raven doffed his coat and hat and turned his eyes to her. Something fluttered in the pit of her stomach. Just hunger, she told herself, not really sure if she was being completely honest or not. The guy irritated the hell out of her. There was no reason for her to be having this sort of reaction to him.

Then he shocked her by stripping out of his black shirt and tossing it across the back of another chair. His slim, muscular torso gleamed like polished ivory in the dim light from the gas lantern in the corner. His chest was hairless, and completely unscarred, she noted. He drifted from the room without a word. A moment later the shirt vanished from the chair. She stared at the spot it had vacated.

What the hell was that? she wondered. Why wouldn't he change his shirt in privacy? Why peel it off right in front of her?

Unless, of course, he hadn't even noticed she was there. Maybe he was that distracted.

He walked back through the doorway about ten minutes later, chest sheathed in a tight blue linen shirt. His hair looked wet. "That was a quick bath," she observed.

He ran fingers through his hair and shrugged. "Guess so."

"Sounds like a good idea to me. Where's your tub? How do you get hot water to it? You don't have a staff here, do you? Do you use magic? Isn't that risky, considering the Deacons might spot you working mana?"

He just stared at her for a long moment. "I have a shower. With a water heater."

Her jaw dropped. "Hidden, I suppose."

"Buried about a hundred feet below the house. I plumbed this place myself—believe me, magic makes the job a lot easier.

But I'm sure you'd rather use a water closet than a chamber pot. Am I wrong?"

"Water closet?"

"Old Earth term. Means a toilet."

"We're trained to handle—"

"—handle has a different definition than appreciate. Sure you're trained to handle primitive conditions. Doesn't mean you have to do it when an alternative is available."

She frowned. "Okay, sure. So why would you include toilets in your plumbing plan if you don't need to use one?"

"Sheer perversity. Seriously? Because this is a dimensional station—and if I get company from anyone not a TAU fanatic, they'd appreciate being able to use decent facilities."

"And what makes you think I won't?"

"You getting your panties in a bunch about my shooting that 'thrope, for one thing. I gotta say, TAU's brainwashing techniques are pretty damn impressive. Nearly every TAU agent I've run across is a damn freak for technological purity. I'm not sure why. The worst thing that might happen is that some fifty years in the future, after I've been reassigned and the house has fallen into disrepair, someone might come along and accidentally unearth the water heater. The wizards will debate its purpose for a few weeks and forget all about it. It won't contaminate shit."

She opened her mouth to object and snapped it shut again. "You have a point."

Printed in the United States
105861LV00002B/151/A

9 781599 987491